ARCLIGHT

art and colors
Marian Churchland

story
Brandon Graham

letters
Ariana Maher

IMAGE COMICS, INC.
Robert Kirkman—Chief Operating Officer
Erik Larsen—Chief Financial Officer
Todd McFarlane—President
Marc Silvestri—Chief Executive Officer
Jim Valentino—Vice-President

Eric Stephenson—Publisher
Corey Murphy—Director of Sales
Jeff Boison—Director of Publishing Planning & Book Trade Sales
Chris Ross—Director of Digital Sales
Kat Salazar—Director of PR & Marketing
Branwyn Bigglestone—Controller
Susan Korpela—Accounts Manager
Drew Gill—Art Director
Brett Warnock—Production Manager
Meredith Wallace—Print Manager
Briah Skelly—Publicist
Aly Hoffman—Conventions & Events Coordinator
Sasha Head—Sales & Marketing Production Designer
David Brothers—Branding Manager
Melissa Gifford—Content Manager
Erika Schnatz—Production Artist
Ryan Brewer—Production Artist
Shanna Matuszak—Production Artist
Tricia Ramos—Production Artist
Vincent Kukua—Production Artist
Jeff Stang—Direct Market Sales Representative
Emilio Bautista—Digital Sales Associate
Leanna Caunter—Accounting Assistant
Chloe Ramos-Peterson—Library Market Sales Representative
IMAGECOMICS.COM

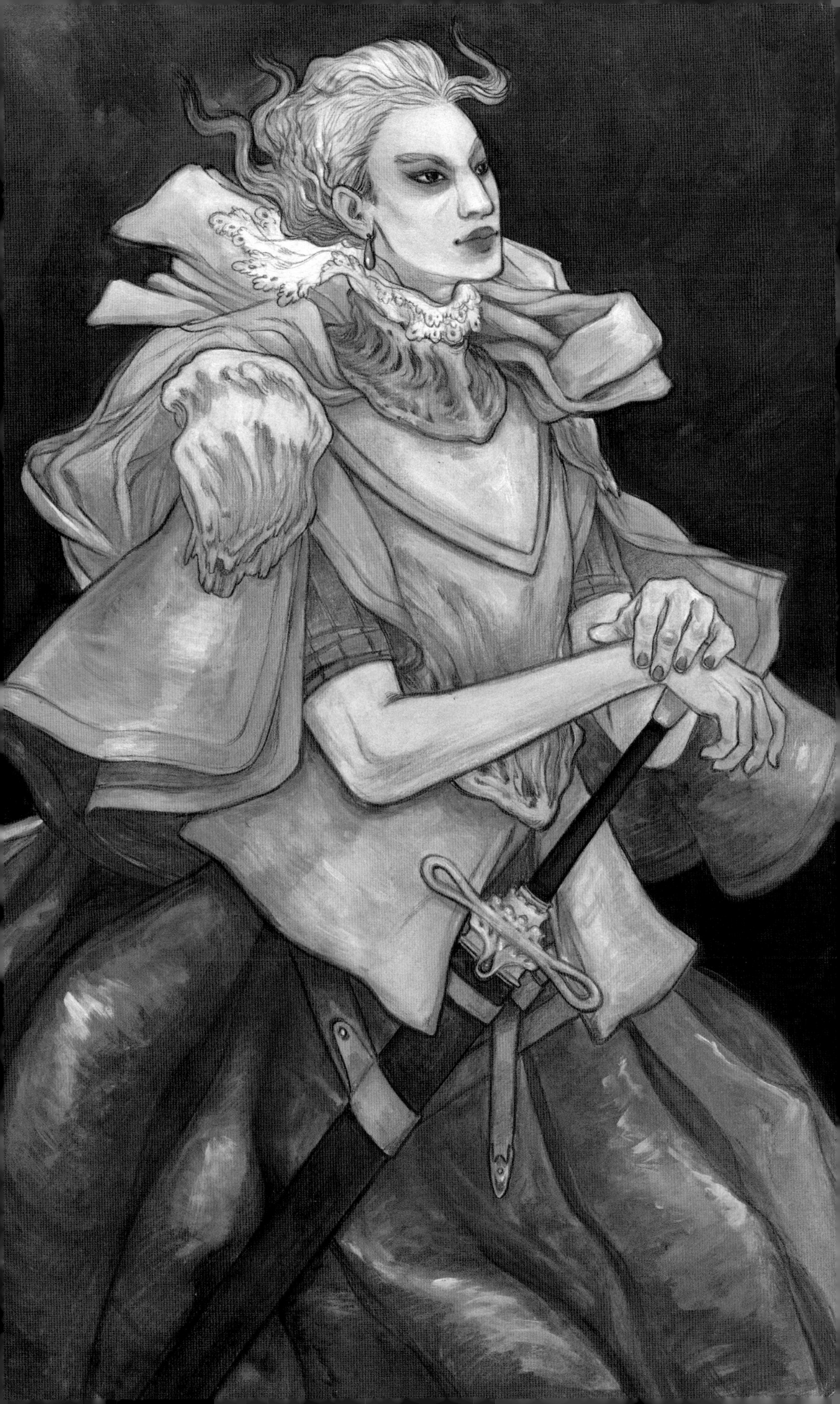

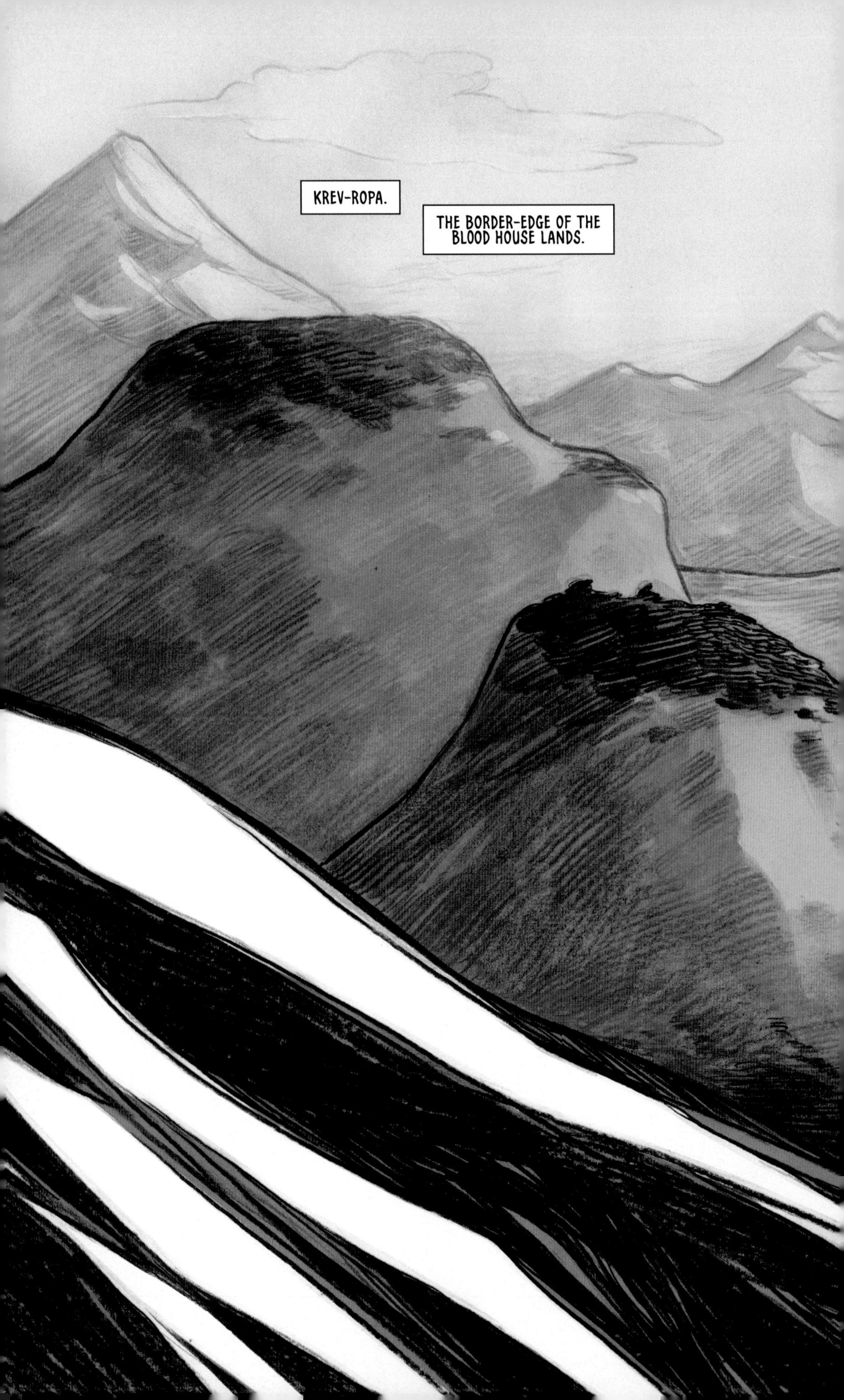
KREV-ROPA.
THE BORDER-EDGE OF THE BLOOD HOUSE LANDS.

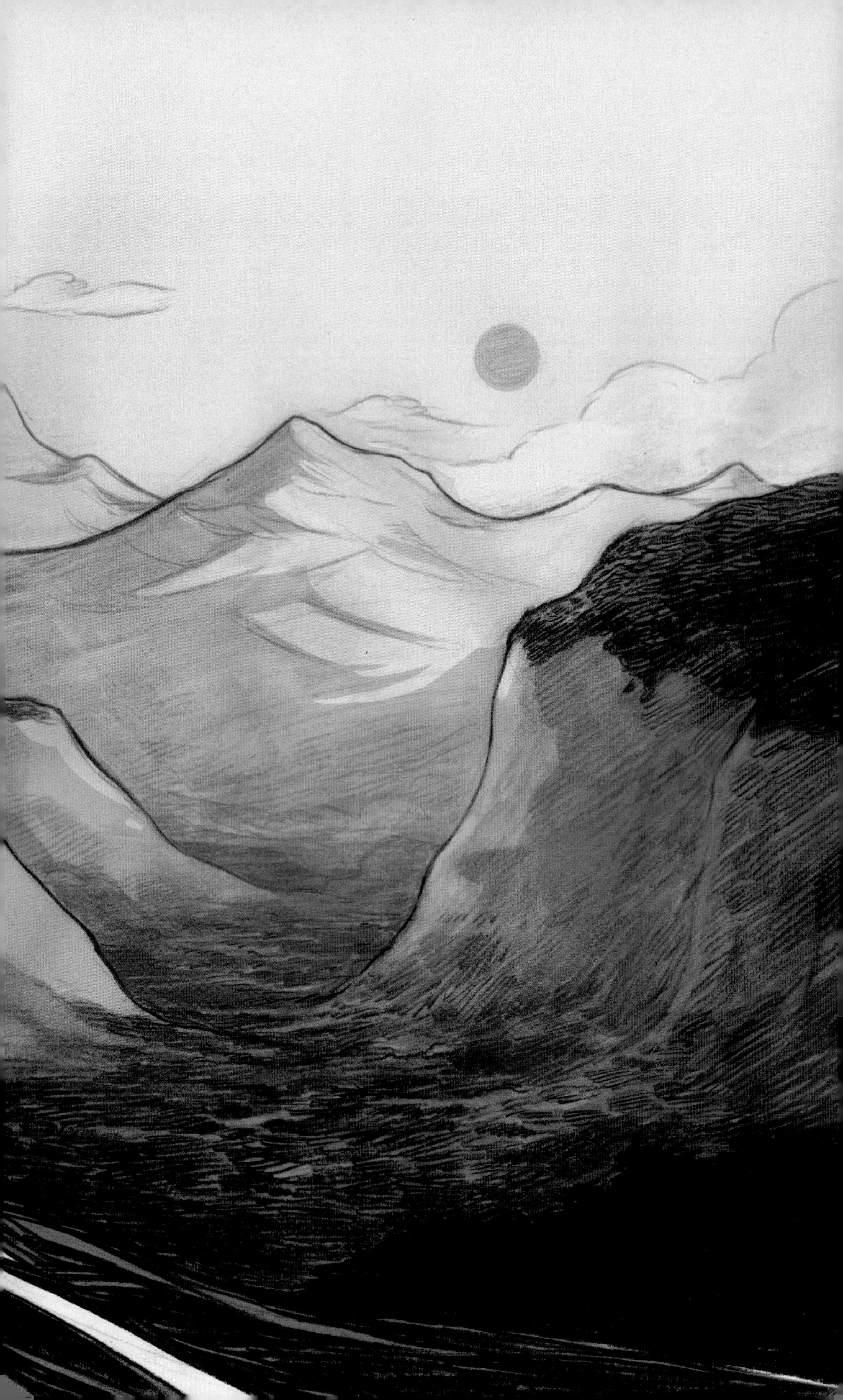

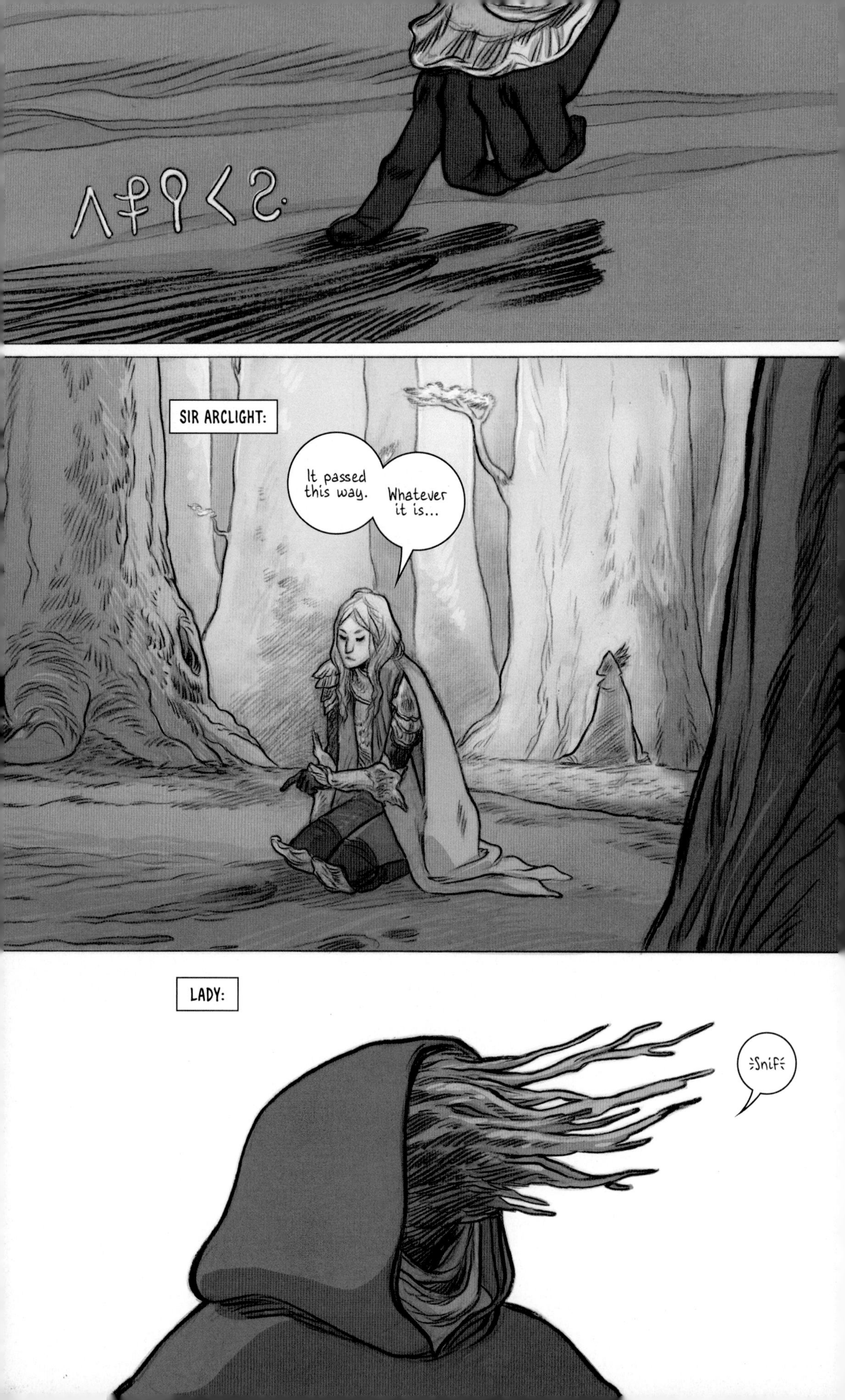

SIR ARCLIGHT:
It passed this way.
Whatever it is...
LADY:
Snif

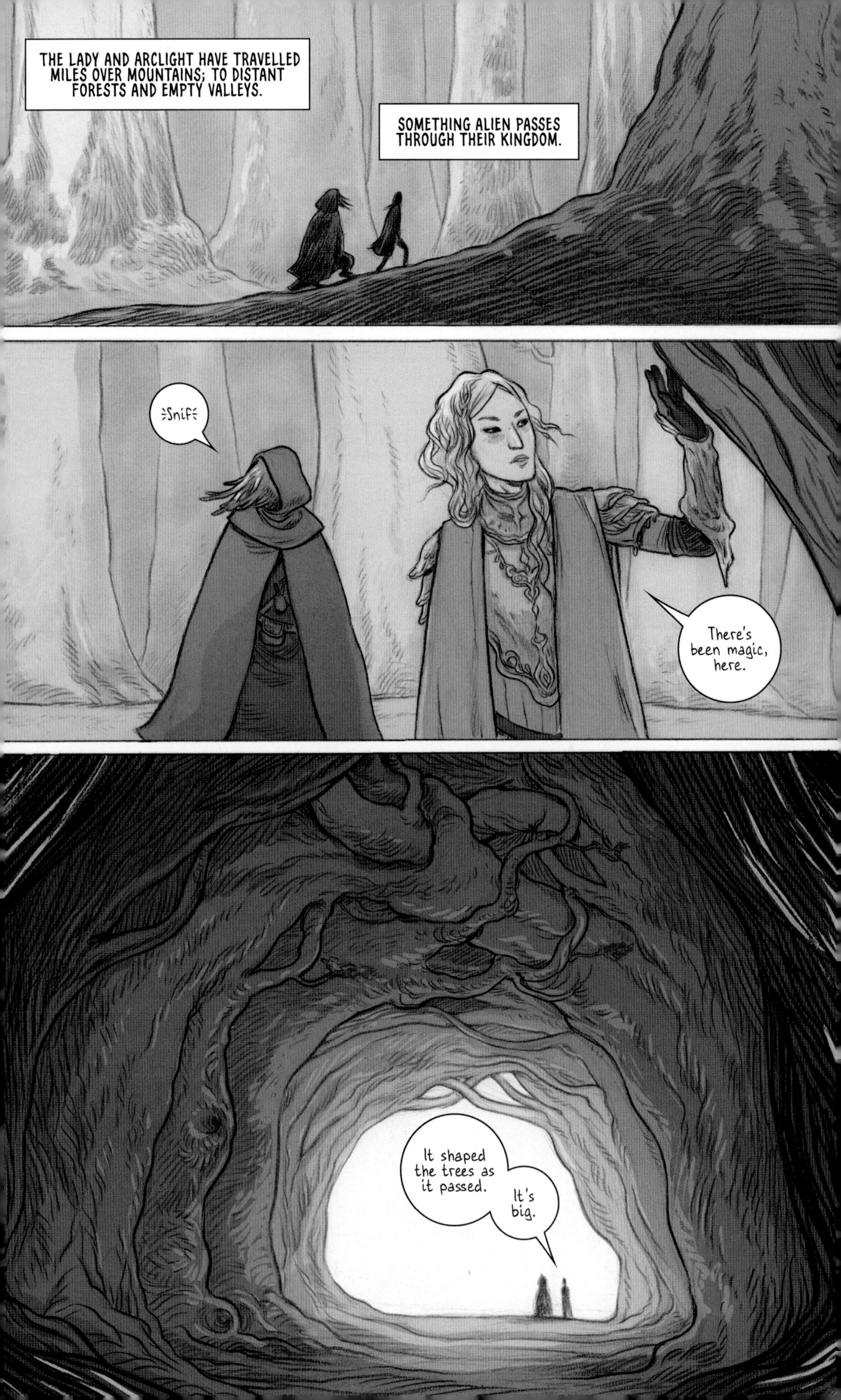
THE LADY AND ARCLIGHT HAVE TRAVELLED MILES OVER MOUNTAINS; TO DISTANT FORESTS AND EMPTY VALLEYS.
SOMETHING ALIEN PASSES THROUGH THEIR KINGDOM.
Snif
There's been magic, here.
It shaped the trees as it passed.
It's big.

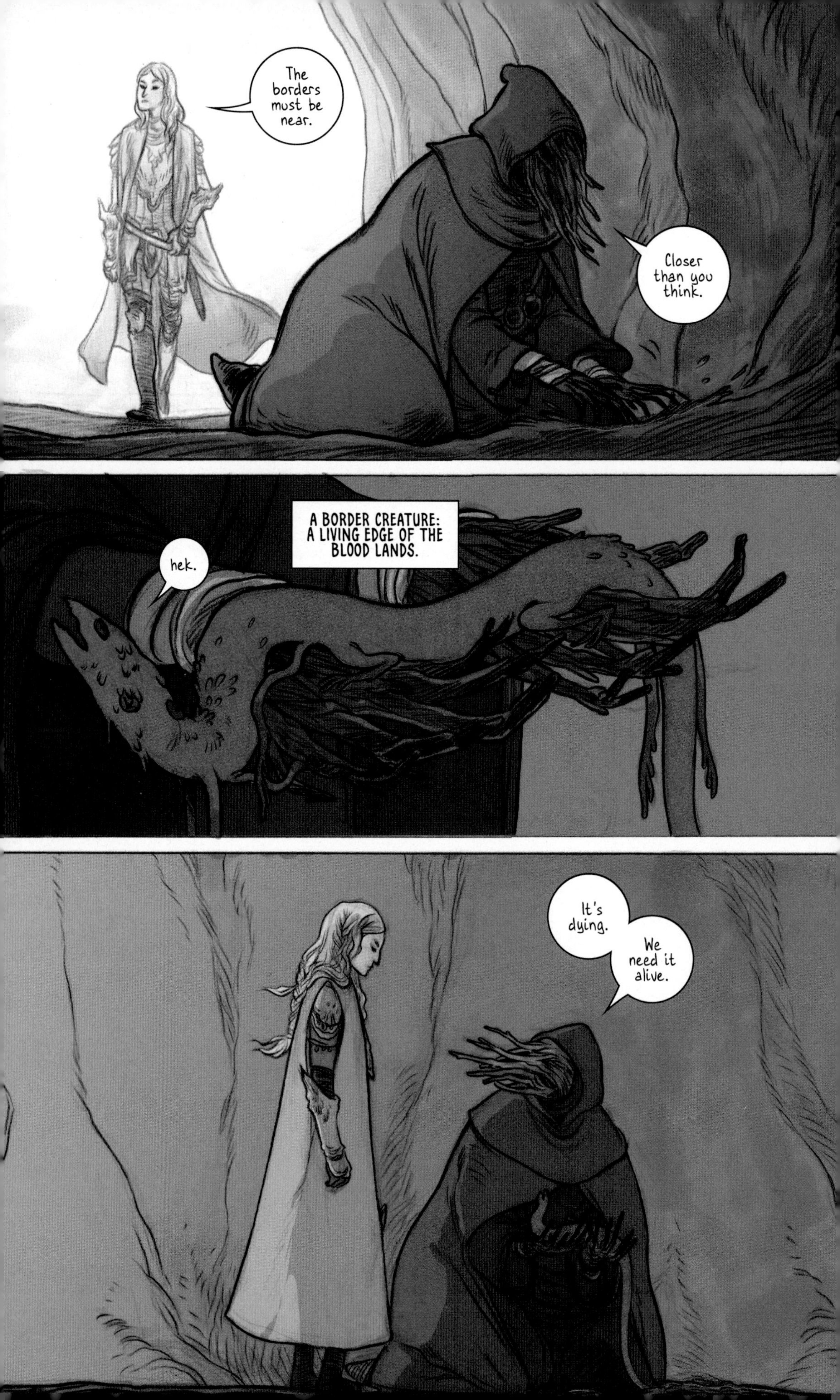
The borders must be near.
Closer than you think.
A BORDER CREATURE: A LIVING EDGE OF THE BLOOD LANDS.
hek.
It's dying.
We need it alive.

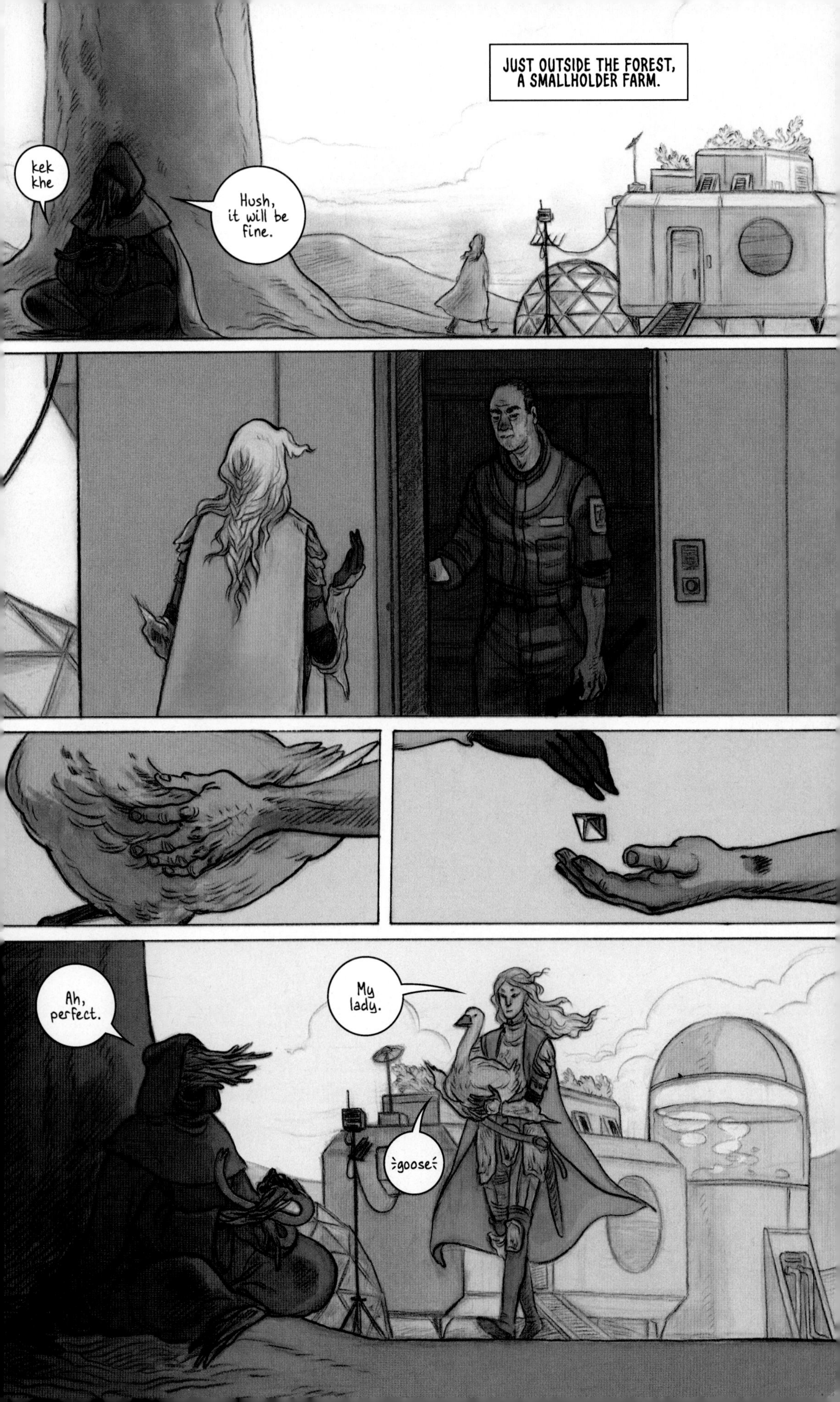
JUST OUTSIDE THE FOREST, A SMALLHOLDER FARM.
kek khe
Hush, it will be fine.
Ah, perfect.
My lady.
goose

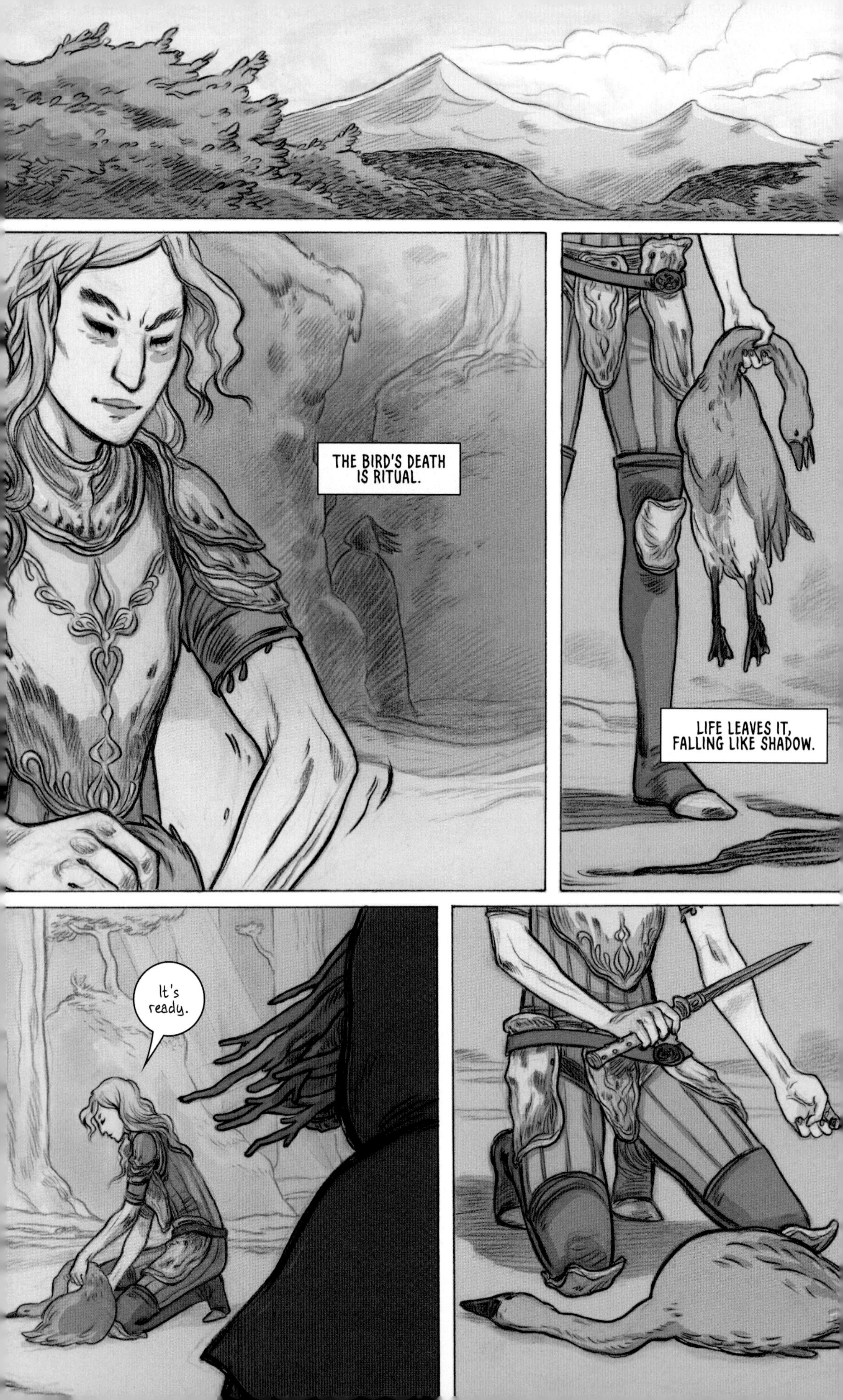
THE BIRD'S DEATH IS RITUAL.
LIFE LEAVES IT, FALLING LIKE SHADOW.
It's ready.

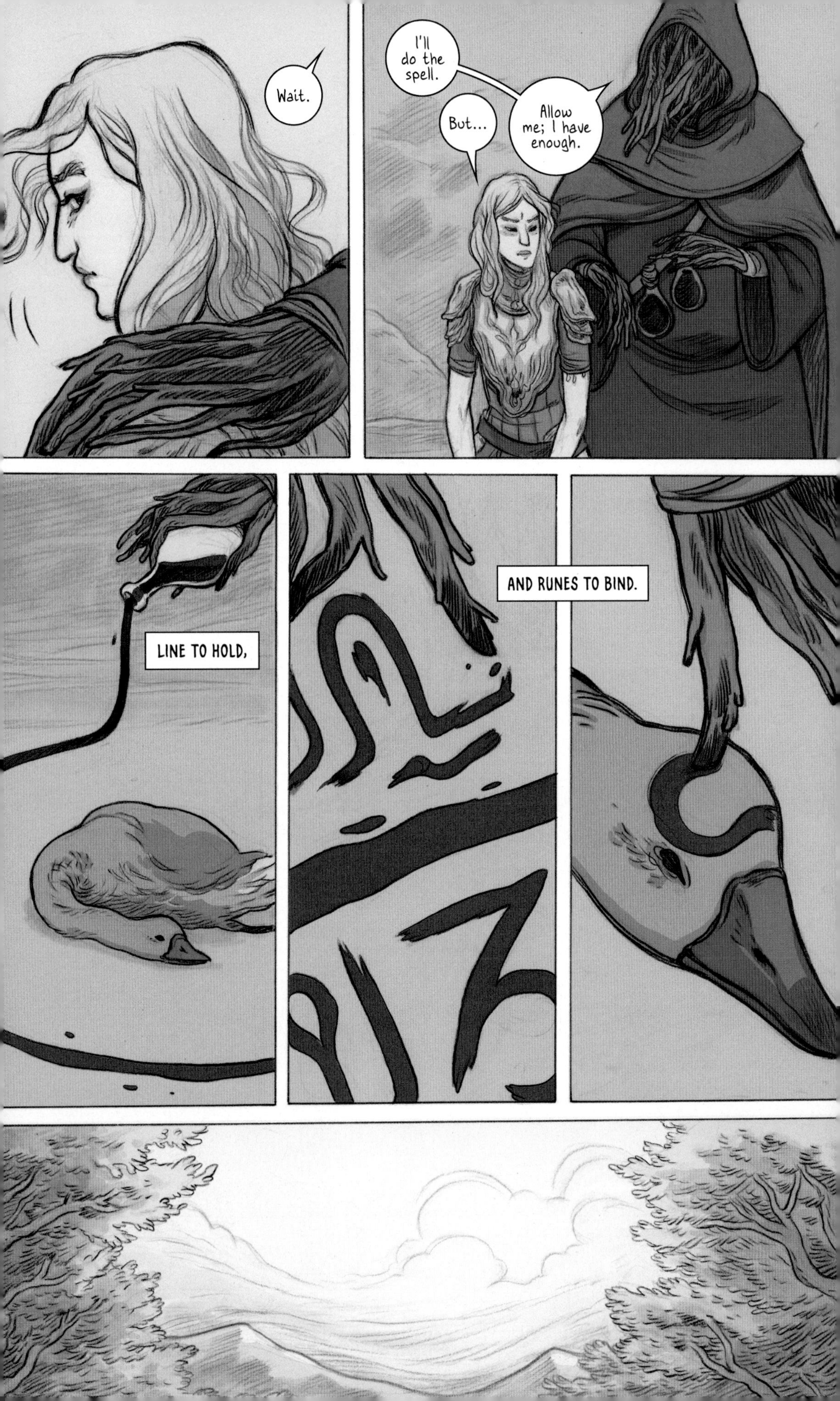
Wait.
I'll do the spell.
Allow me; I have enough.
But...
LINE TO HOLD,
AND RUNES TO BIND.

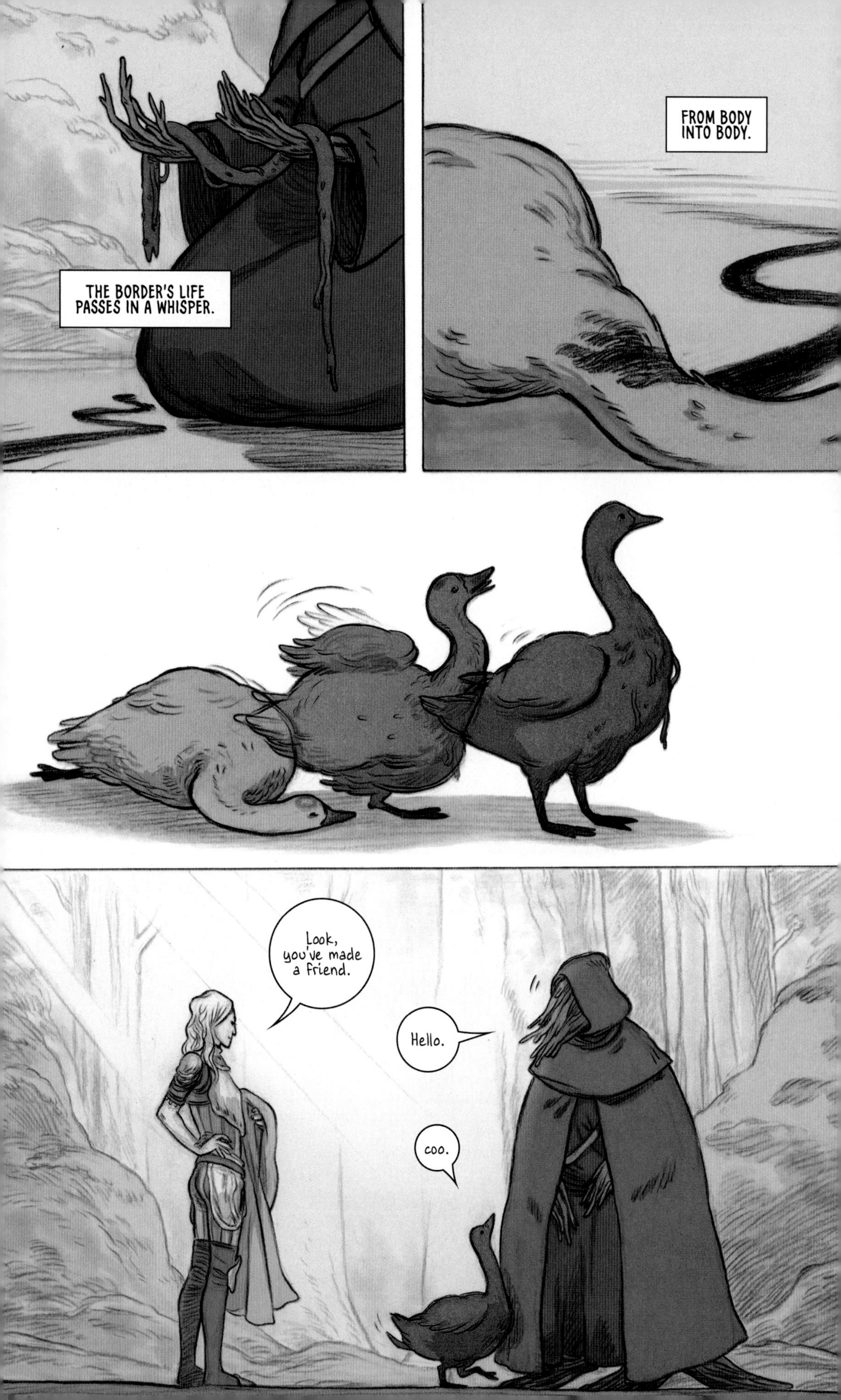
THE BORDER'S LIFE PASSES IN A WHISPER.
FROM BODY INTO BODY.
Look, you've made a friend.
Hello.
coo.

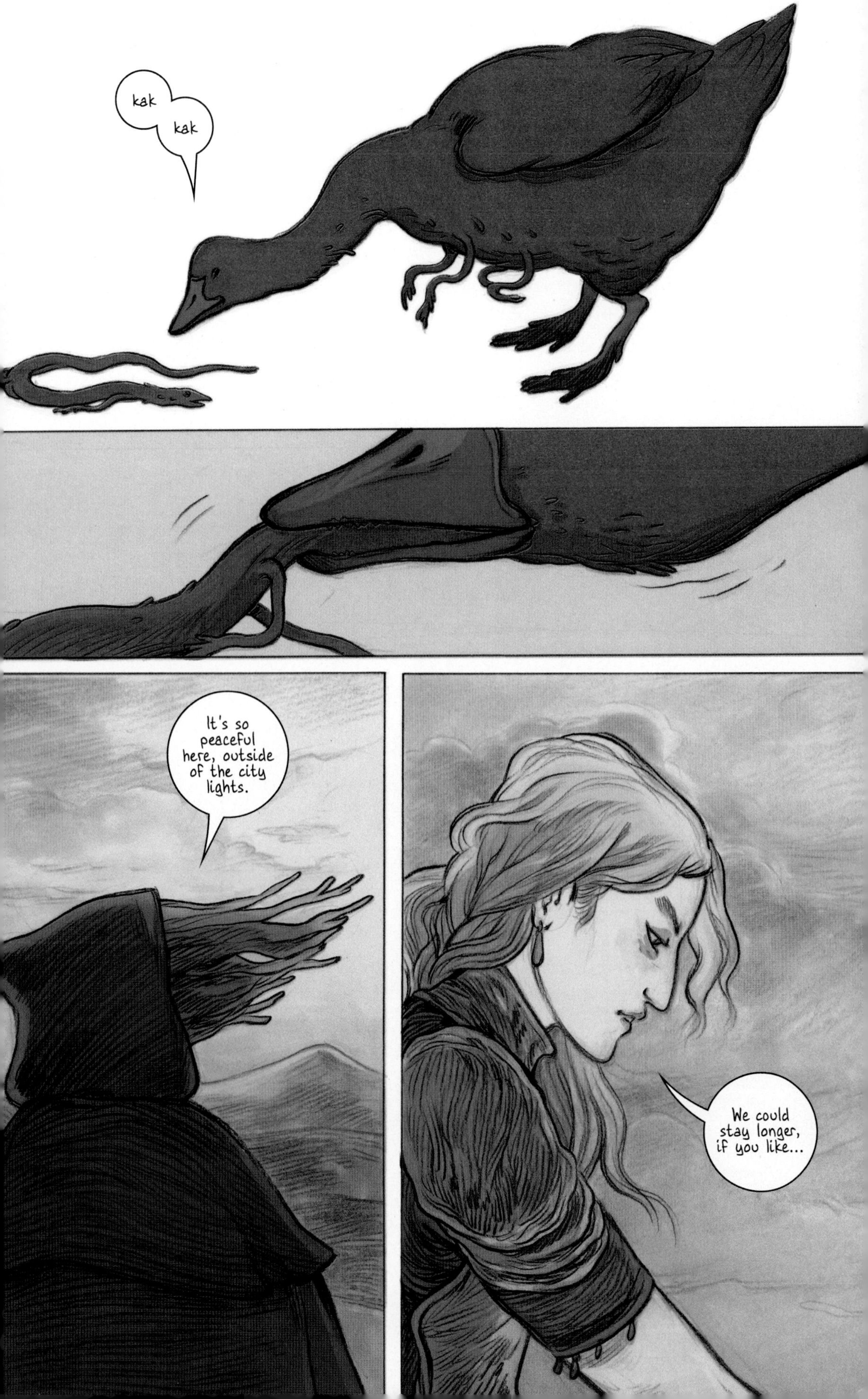
kak
kak
It's so peaceful here, outside of the city lights.
We could stay longer, if you like...

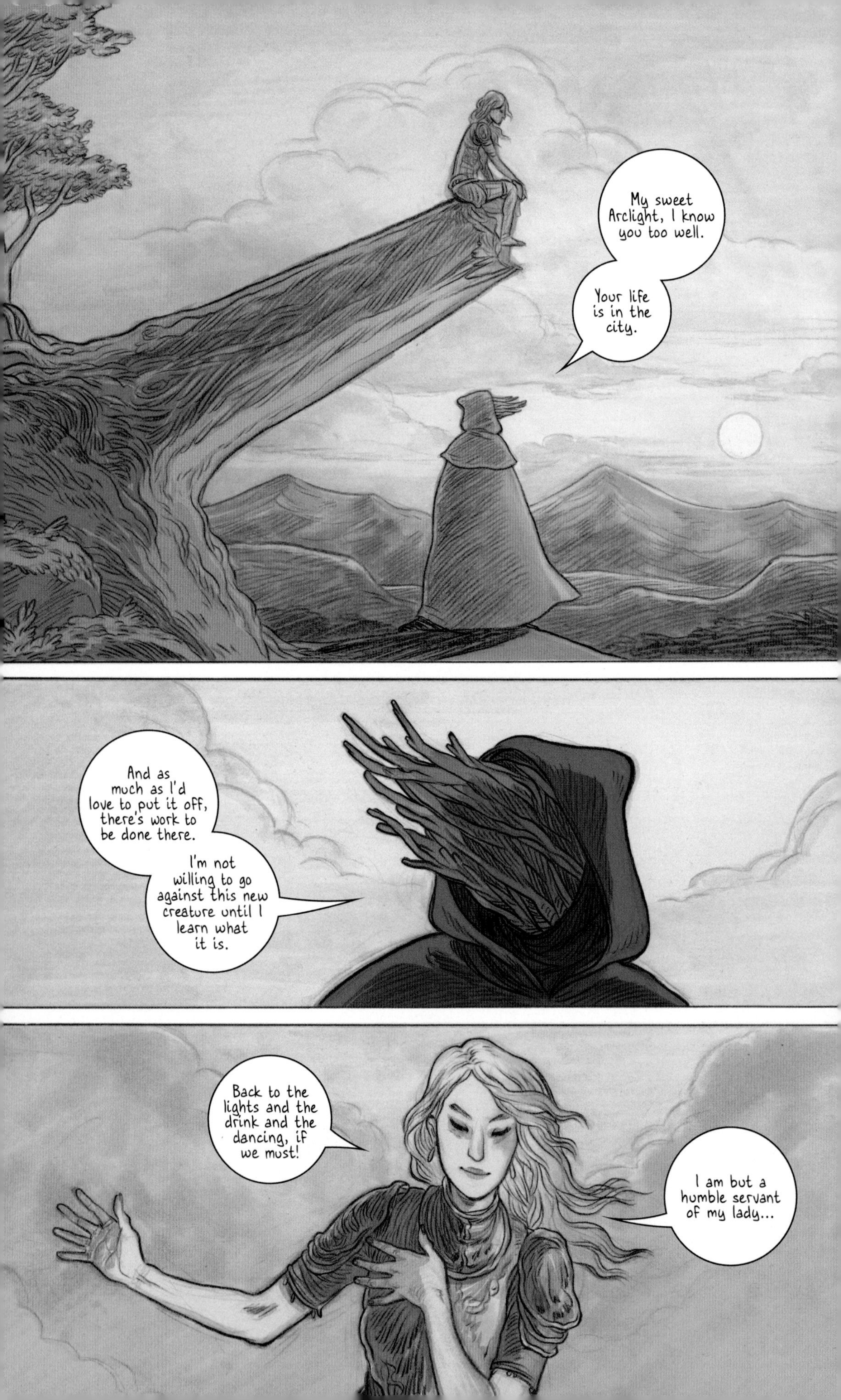
My sweet Arclight, I know you too well.
Your life is in the city.
And as much as I'd love to put it off, there's work to be done there.
I'm not willing to go against this new creature until I learn what it is.
Back to the lights and the drink and the dancing, if we must!
I am but a humble servant of my lady...

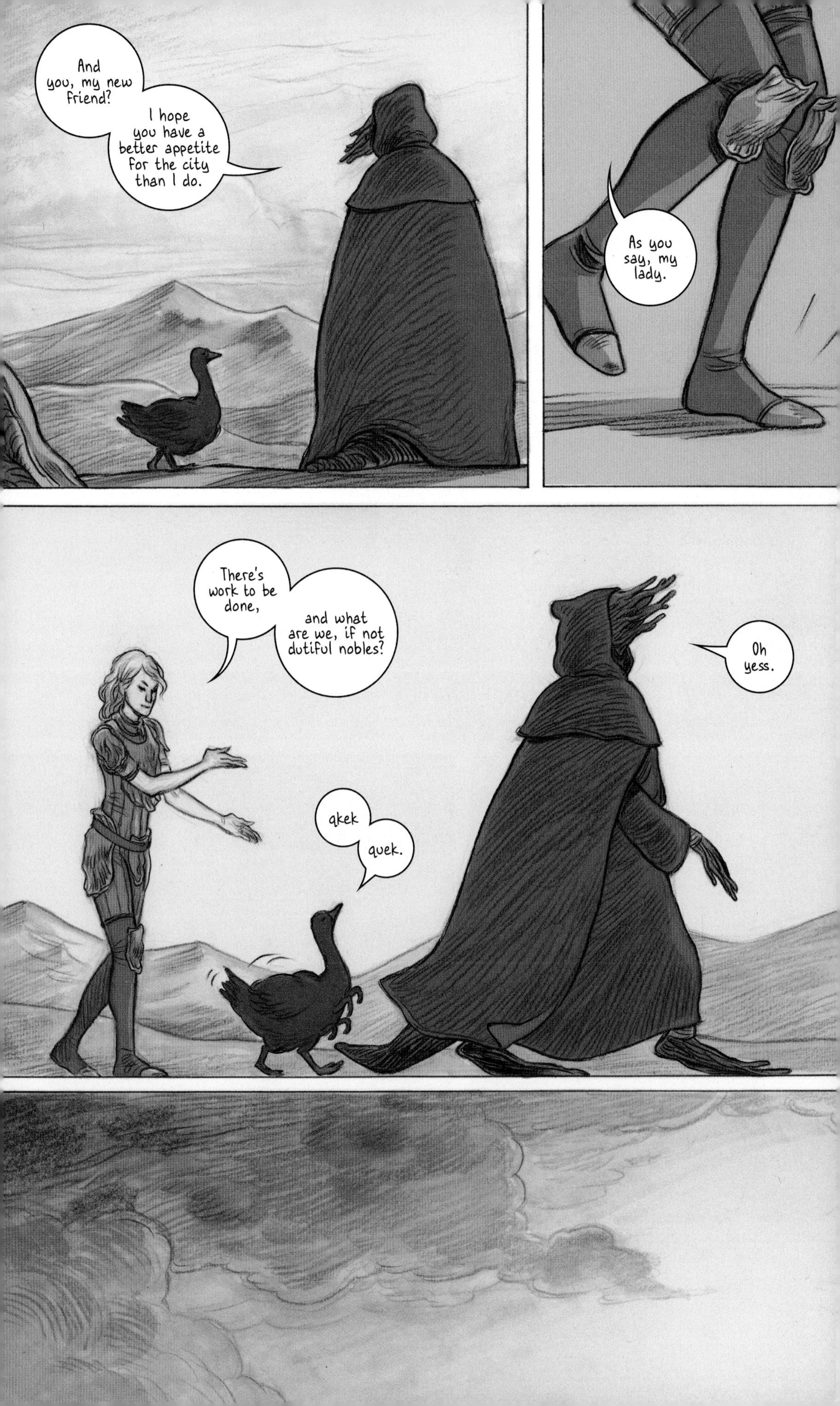
And you, my new friend?
I hope you have a better appetite for the city than I do.
As you say, my lady.
There's work to be done,
and what are we, if not dutiful nobles?
Oh yess.
qkek
quek.

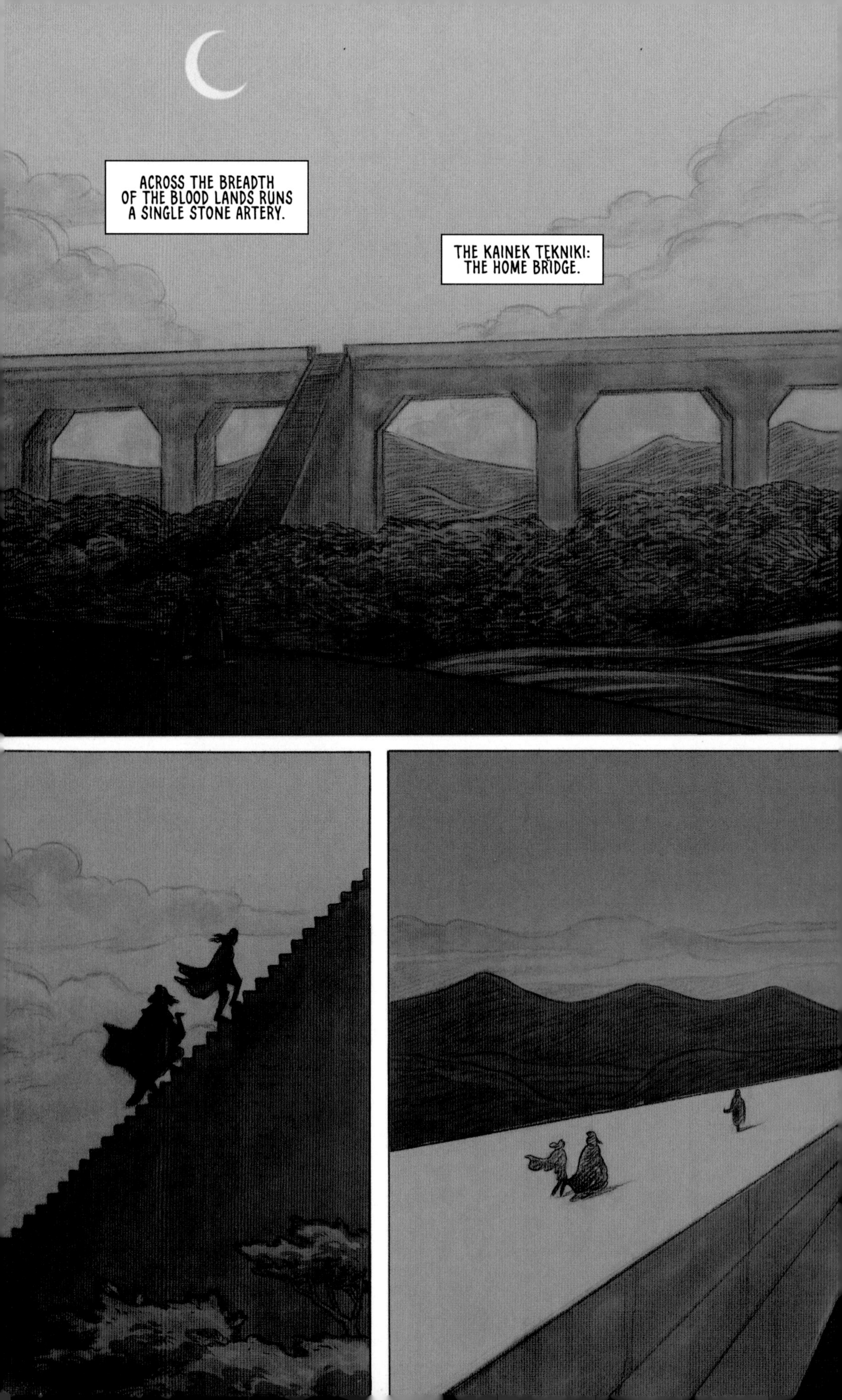
ACROSS THE BREADTH OF THE BLOOD LANDS RUNS A SINGLE STONE ARTERY.
THE KAINEK TEKNIKI: THE HOME BRIDGE.

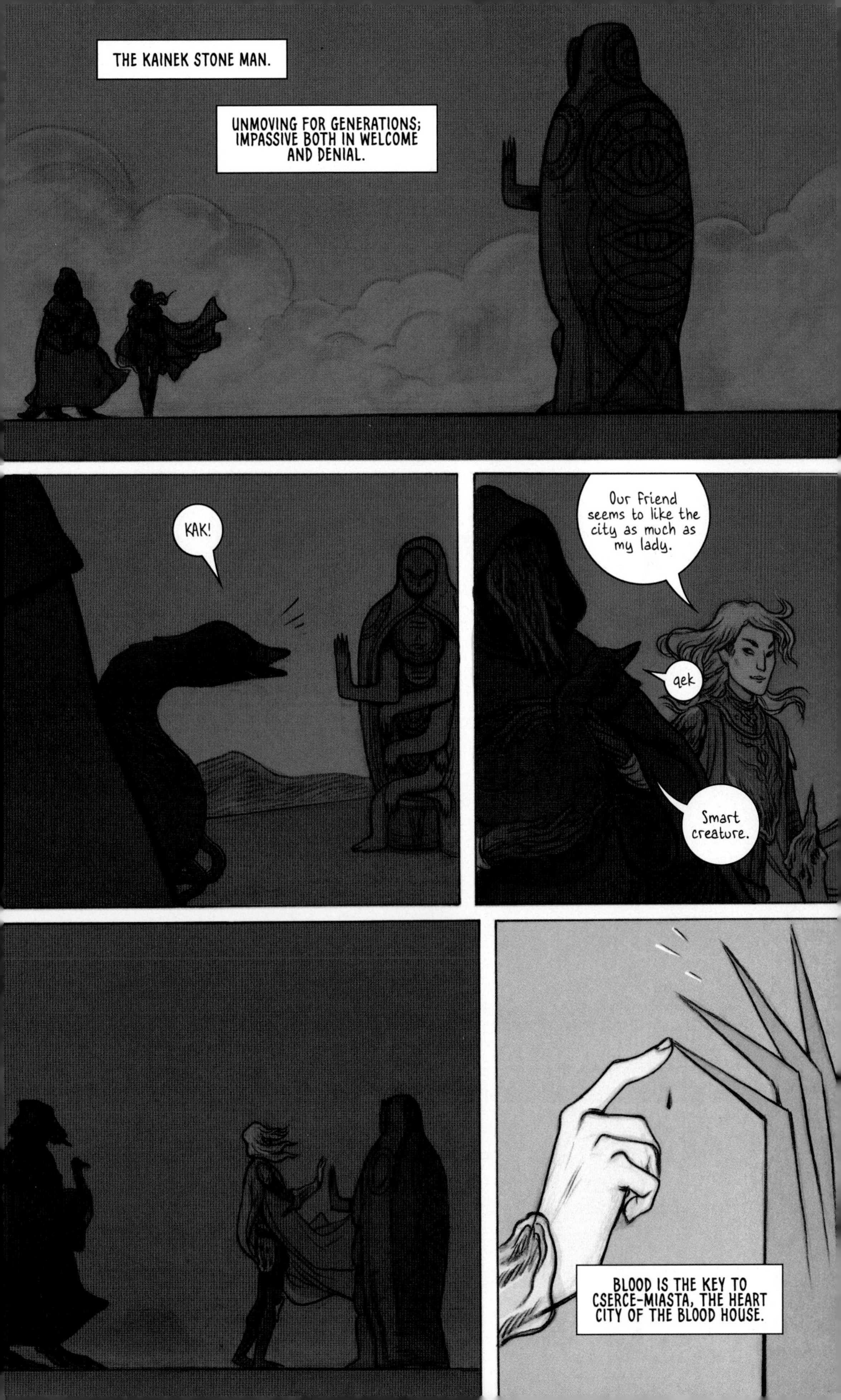
THE KAINEK STONE MAN.
UNMOVING FOR GENERATIONS; IMPASSIVE BOTH IN WELCOME AND DENIAL.
KAK!
Our friend seems to like the city as much as my lady.
qek
Smart creature.
BLOOD IS THE KEY TO CSERCE-MIASTA, THE HEART CITY OF THE BLOOD HOUSE.

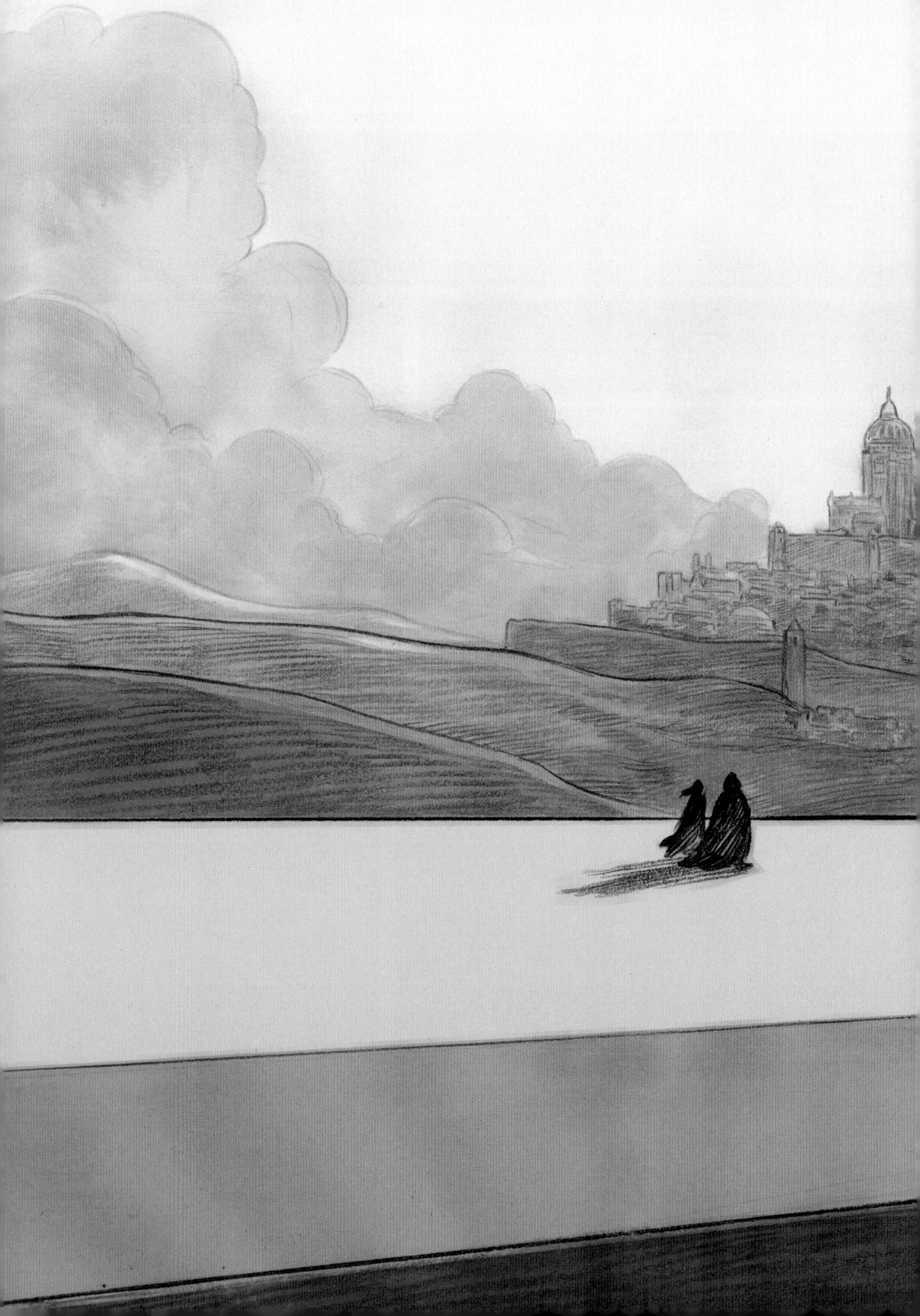

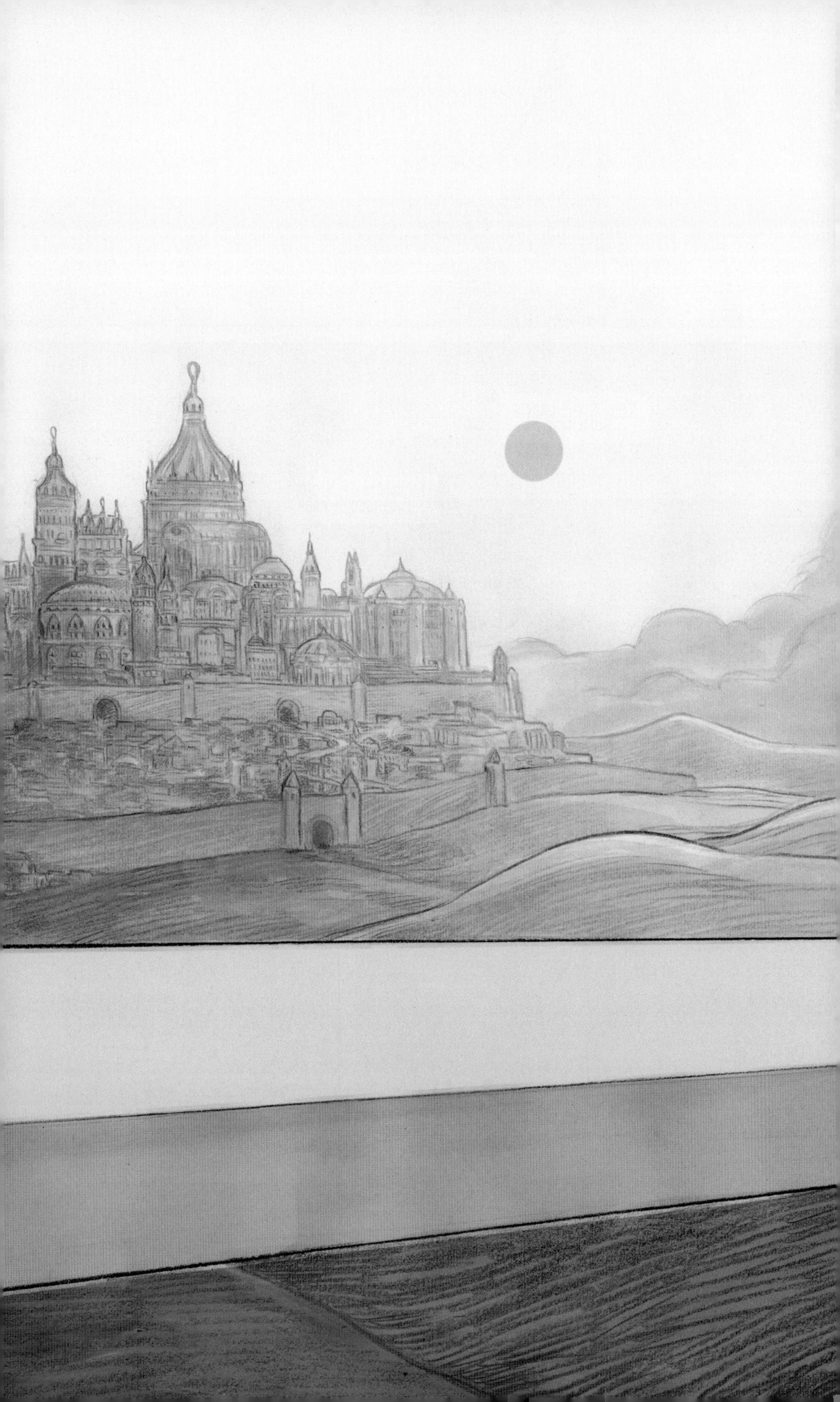

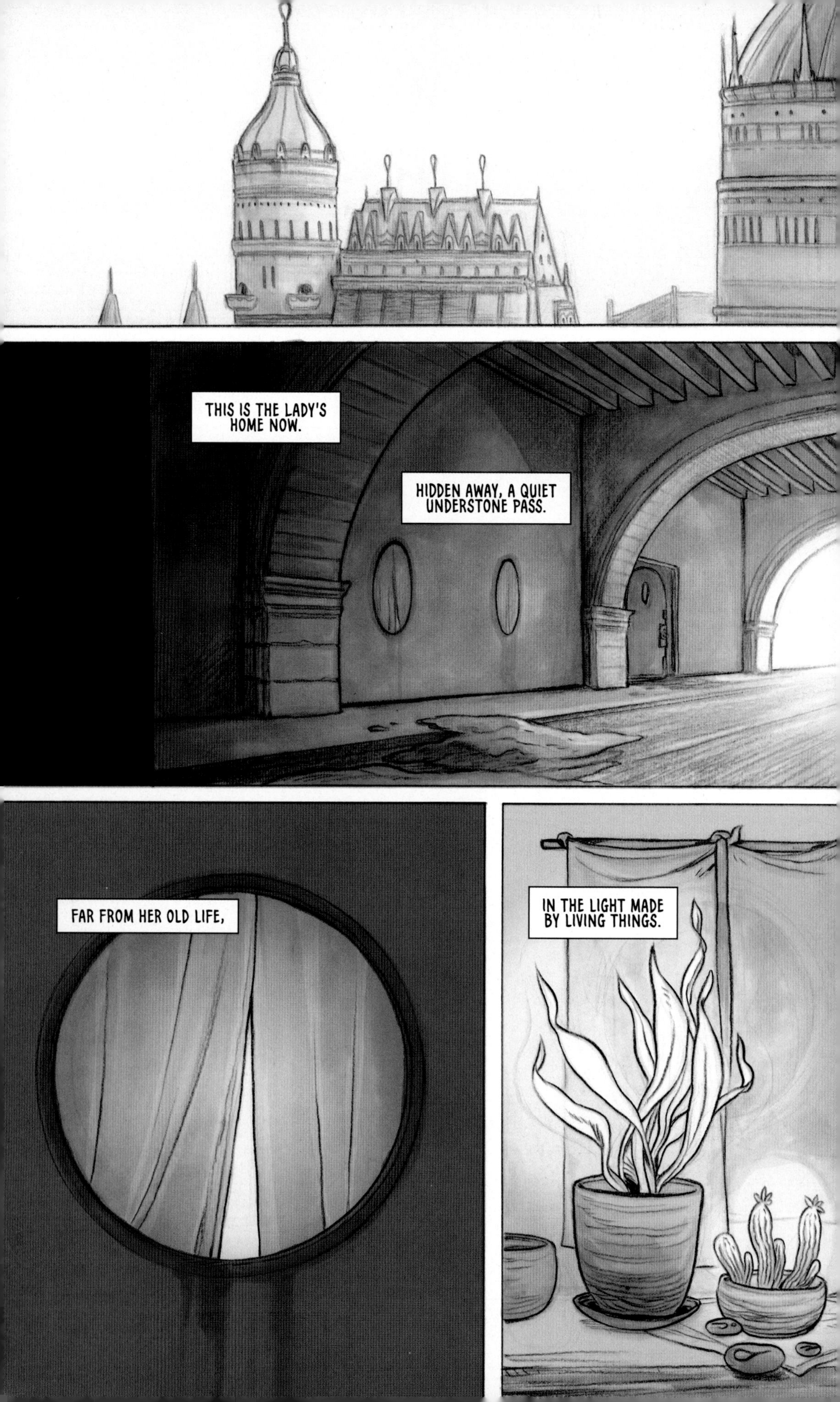
THIS IS THE LADY'S HOME NOW.
HIDDEN AWAY, A QUIET UNDERSTONE PASS.
FAR FROM HER OLD LIFE,
IN THE LIGHT MADE BY LIVING THINGS.

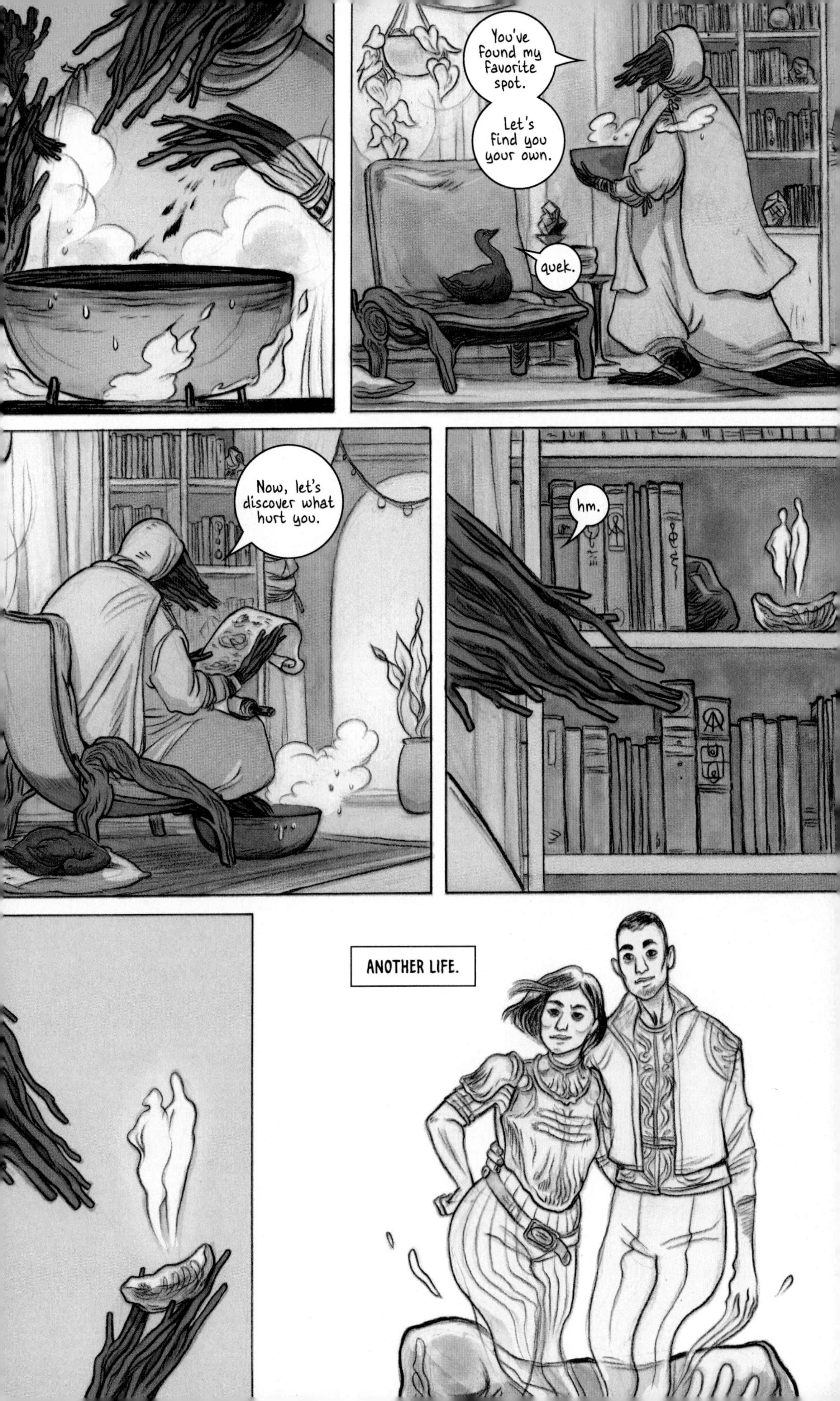
You've found my favorite spot.
Let's find you your own.
quek.
Now, let's discover what hurt you.
hm.
ANOTHER LIFE.

NO POINT IN
DWELLING.

SHE TRIES TO STAY
IN THE NOW.

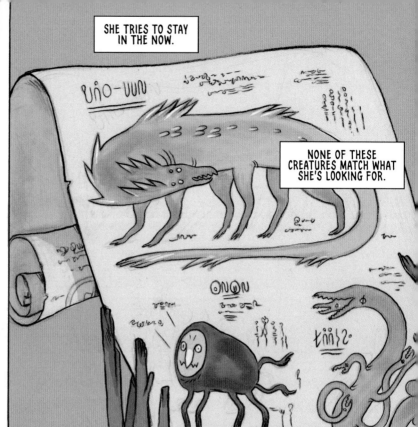

NONE OF THESE
CREATURES MATCH WHAT
SHE'S LOOKING FOR.

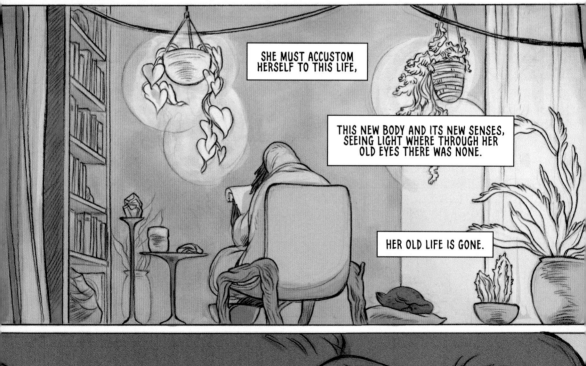

SHE MUST ACCUSTOM
HERSELF TO THIS LIFE,

THIS NEW BODY AND ITS NEW SENSES,
SEEING LIGHT WHERE THROUGH HER
OLD EYES THERE WAS NONE.

HER OLD LIFE IS GONE.

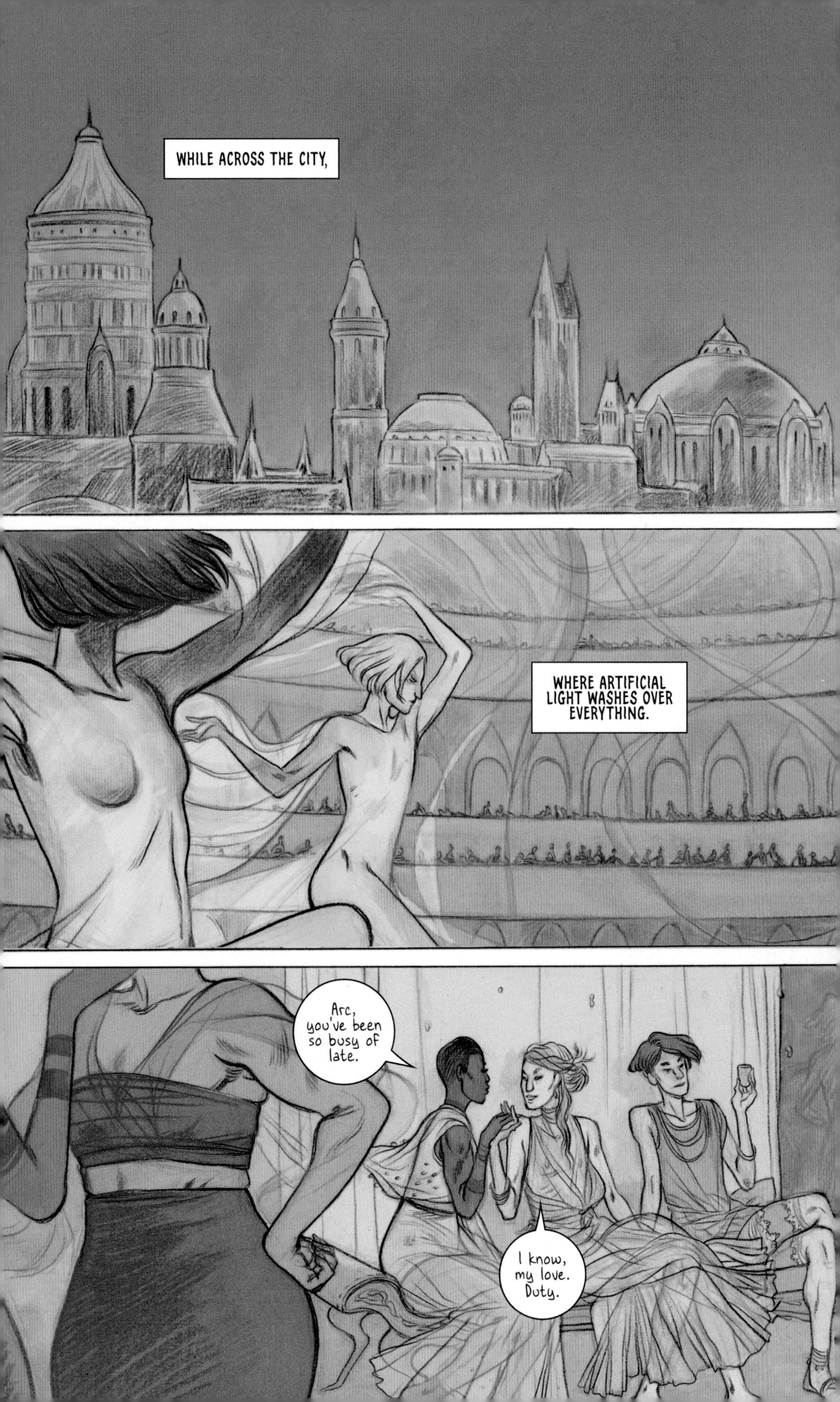
WHILE ACROSS THE CITY,
WHERE ARTIFICIAL LIGHT WASHES OVER EVERYTHING.
Arc, you've been so busy of late.
I know, my love. Duty.

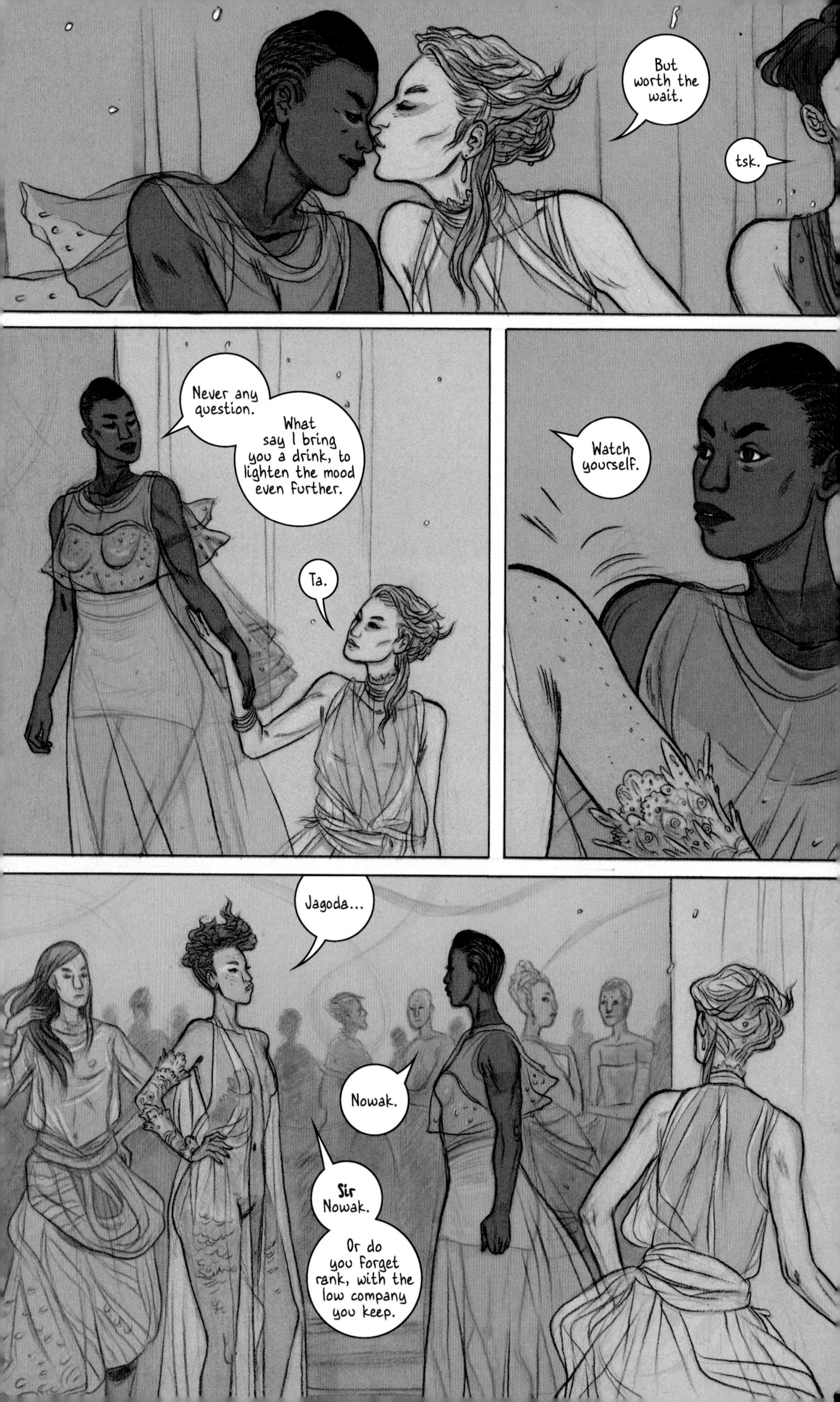

But worth the wait.
tsk.
Never any question.
What say I bring you a drink, to lighten the mood even further.
Ta.
Watch yourself.
Jagoda...
Nowak.
Sir Nowak.
Or do you forget rank, with the low company you keep.

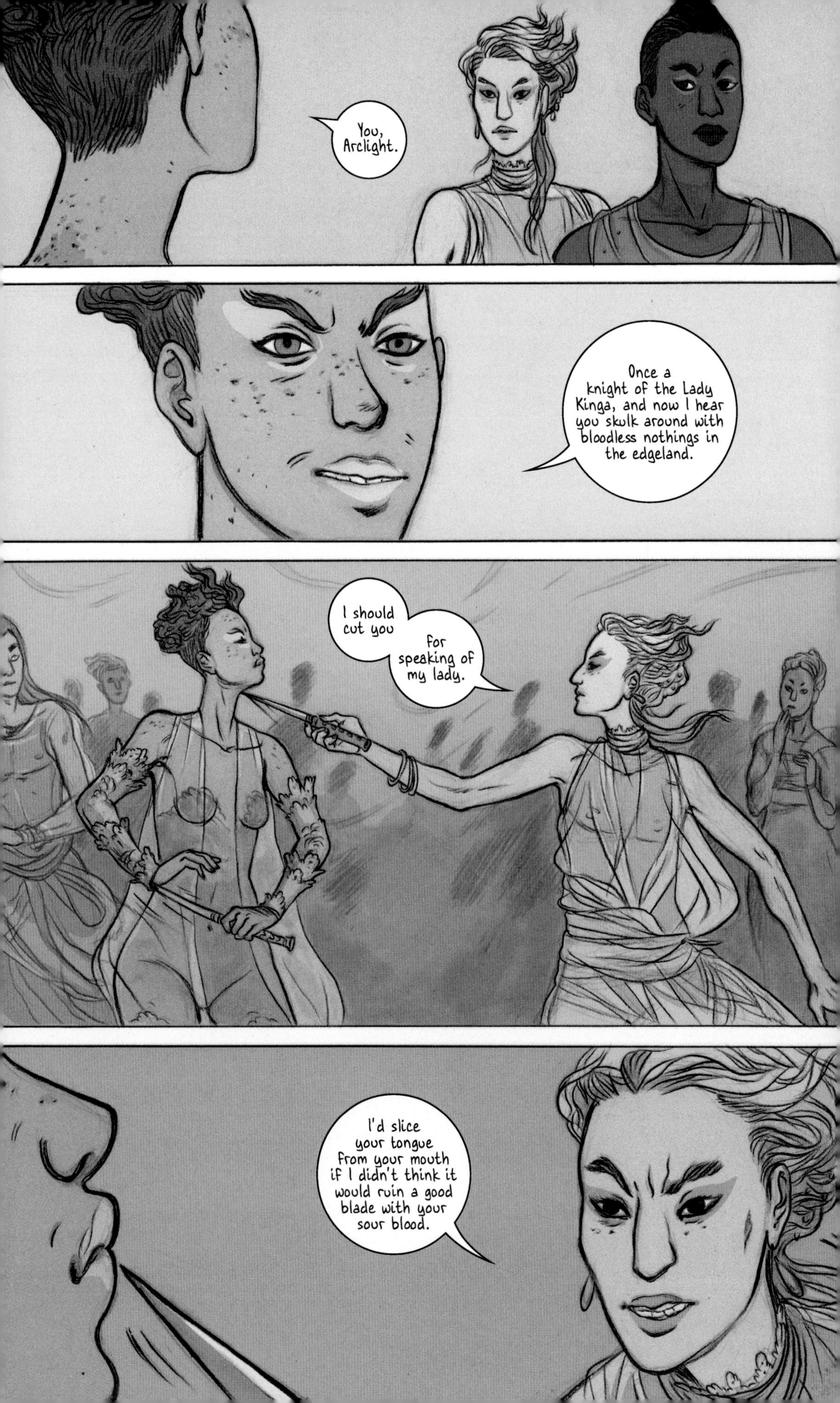
You, Arclight.
Once a knight of the Lady Kinga, and now I hear you skulk around with bloodless nothings in the edgeland.
I should cut you
for speaking of my lady.
I'd slice your tongue from your mouth if I didn't think it would ruin a good blade with your sour blood.

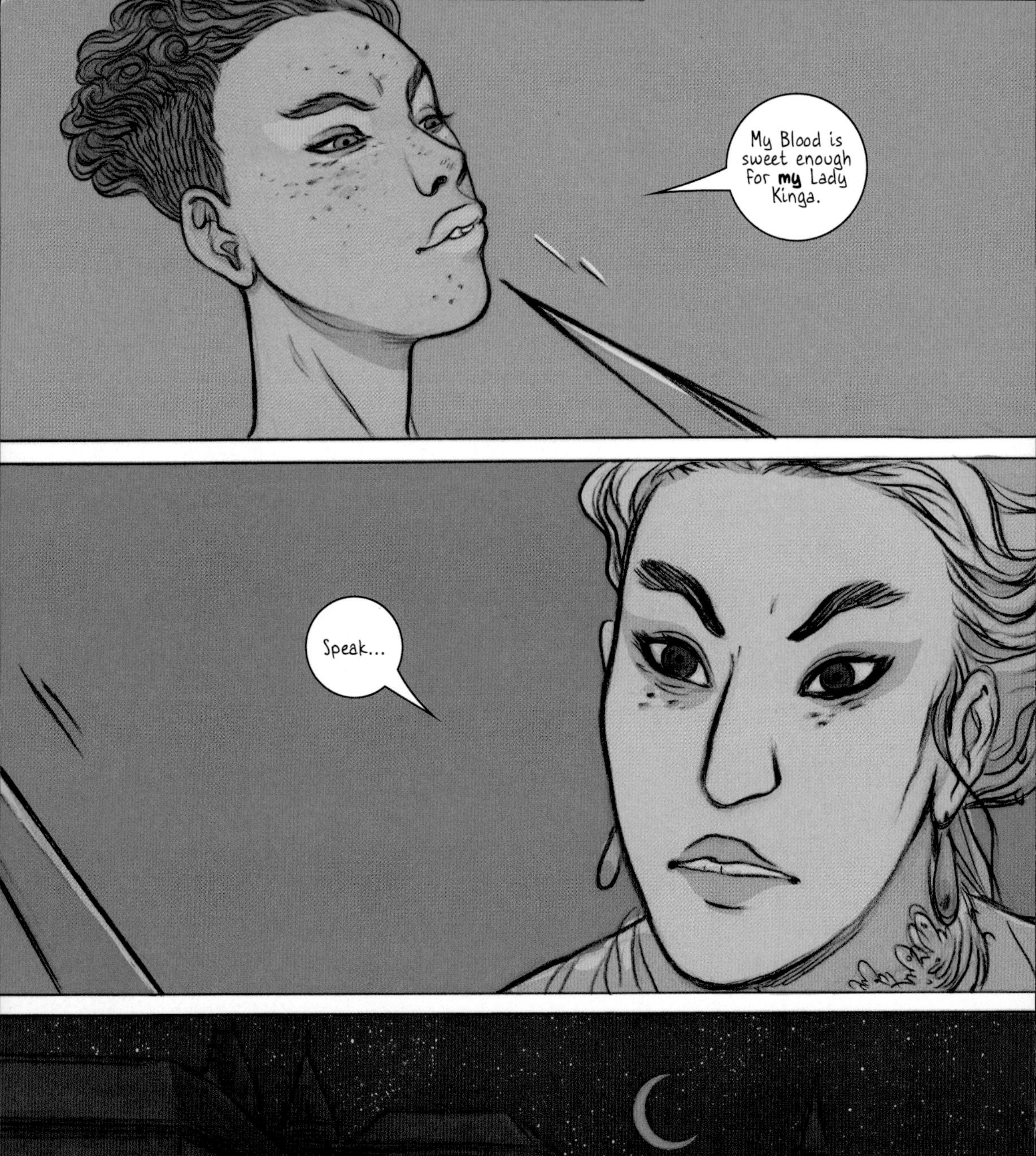
My Blood is sweet enough for **my** Lady Kinga.
Speak...

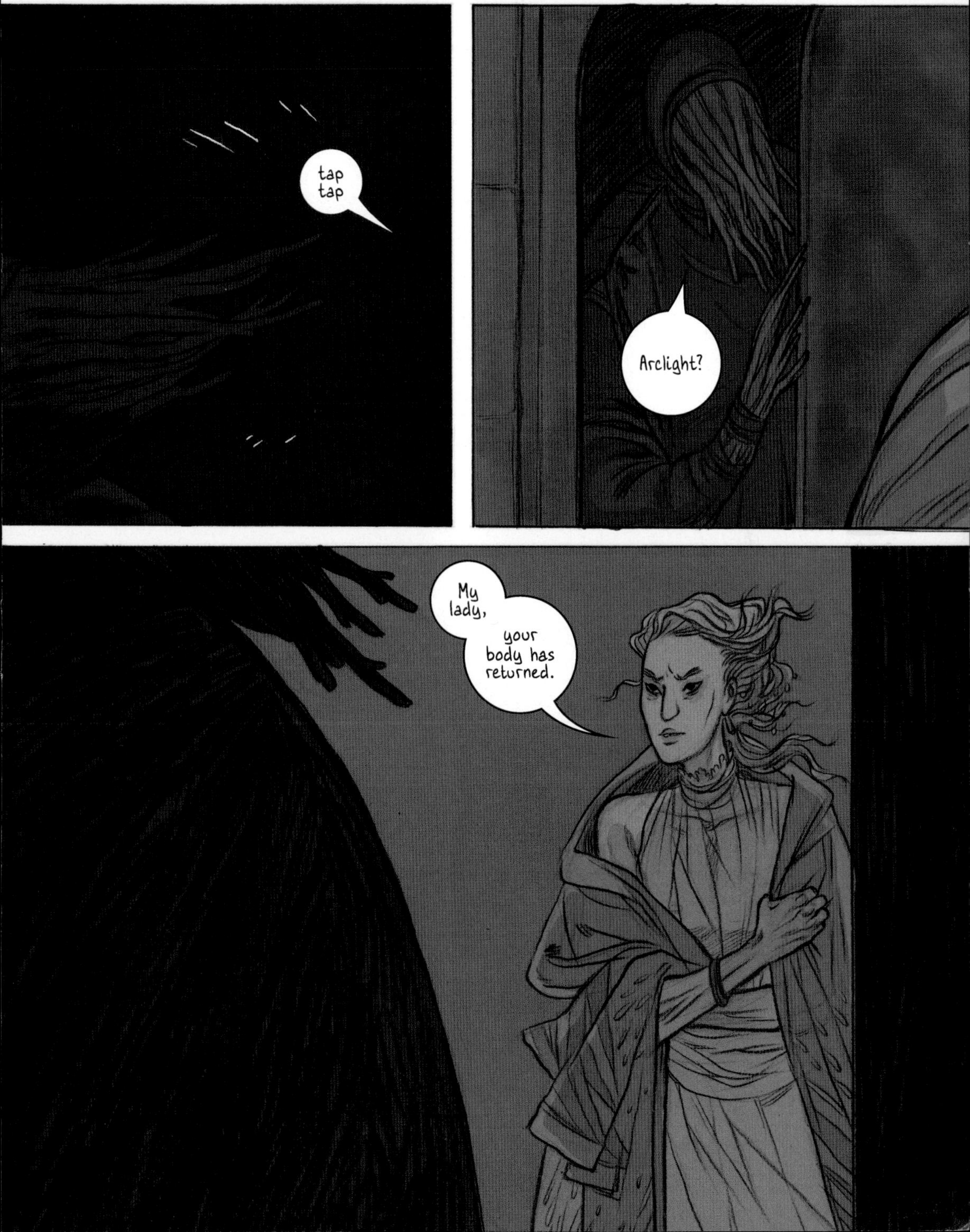
tap tap
Arclight?
My lady,
your body has returned.

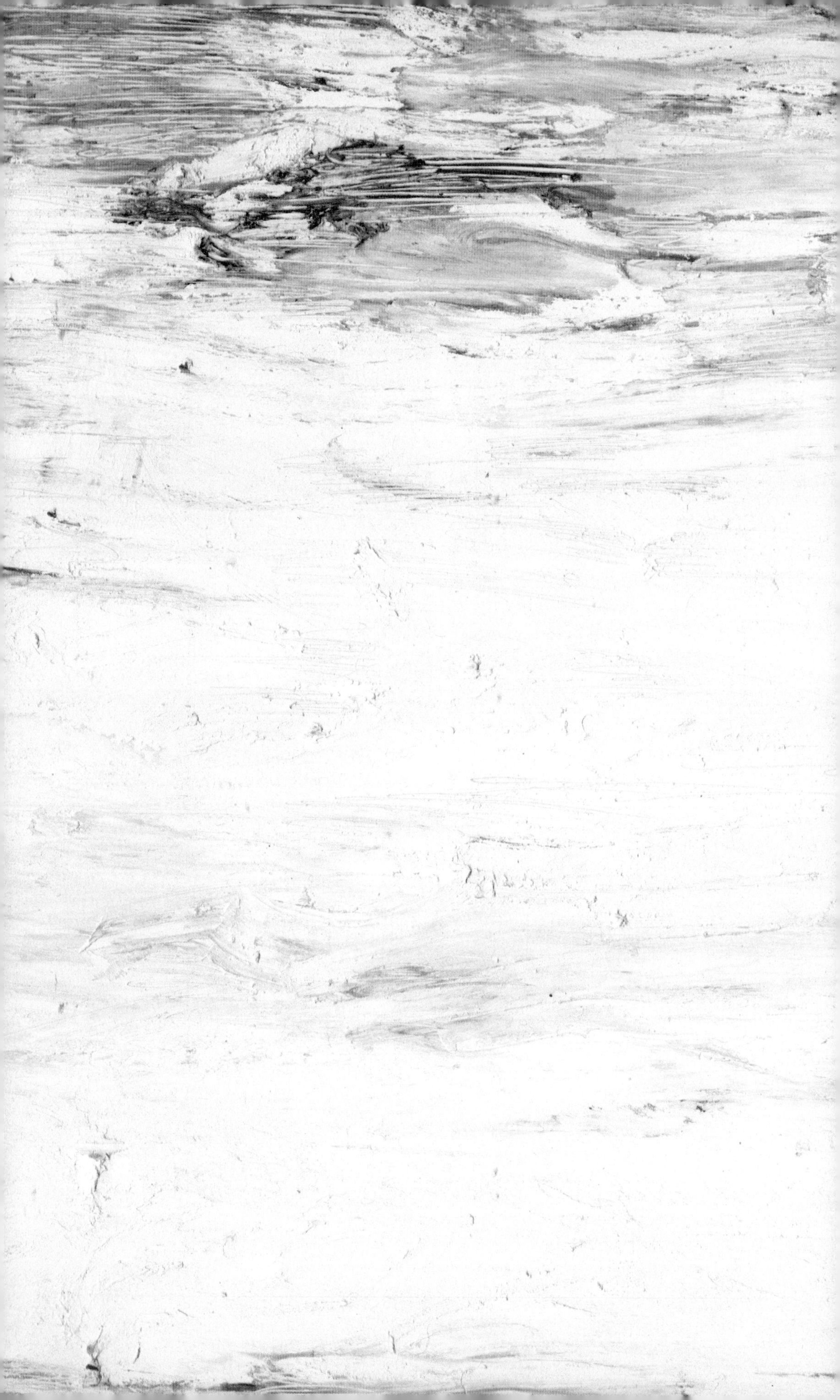

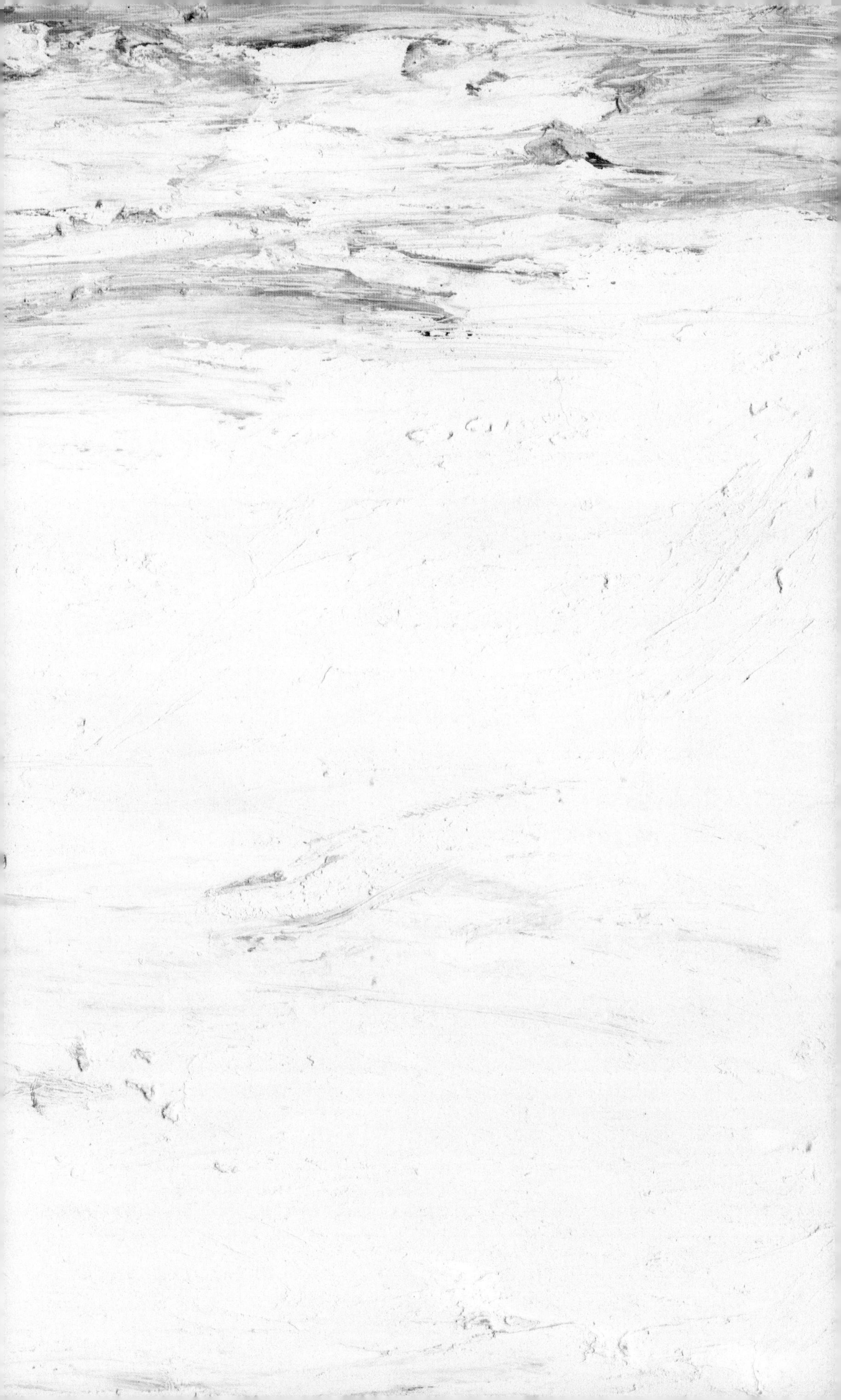

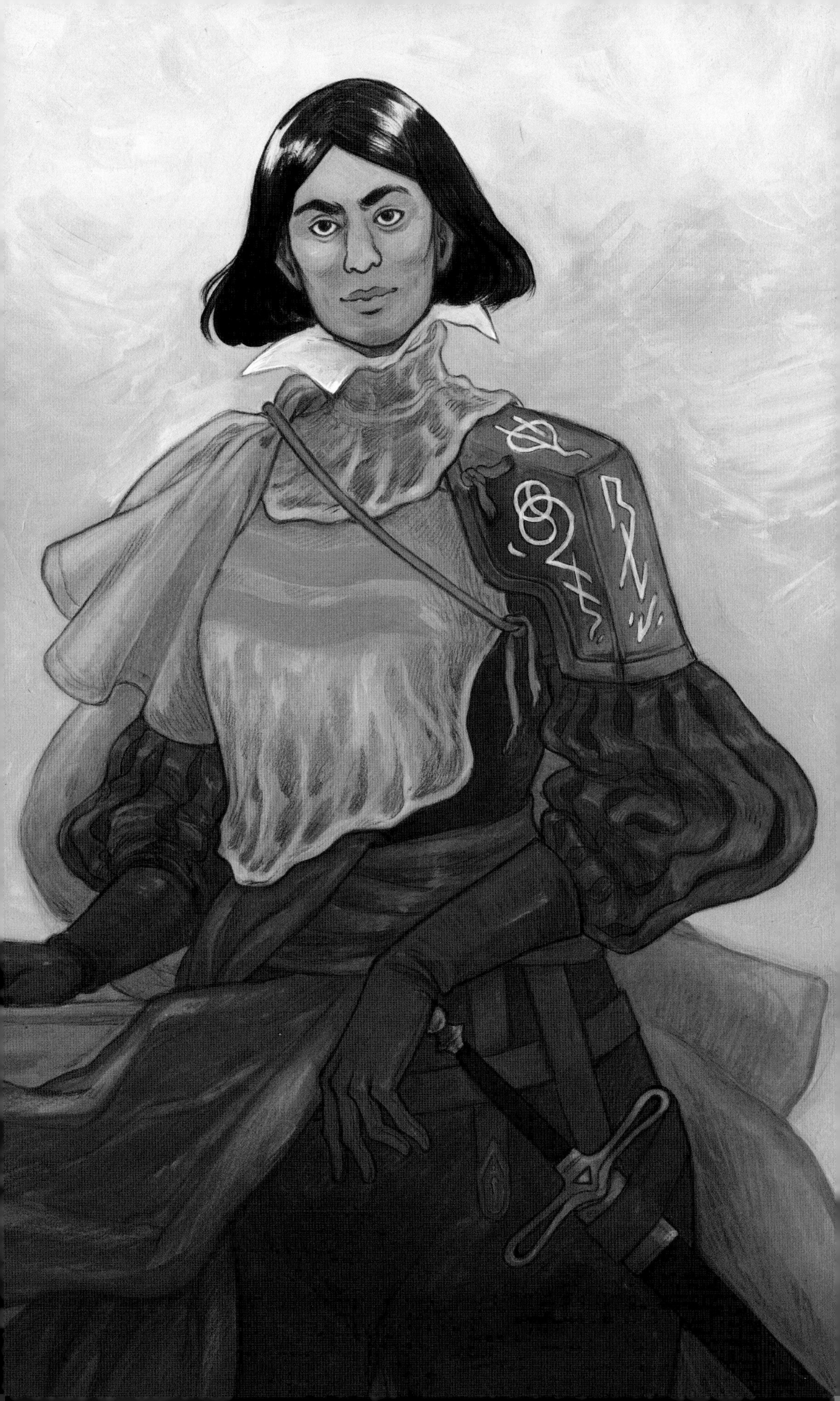

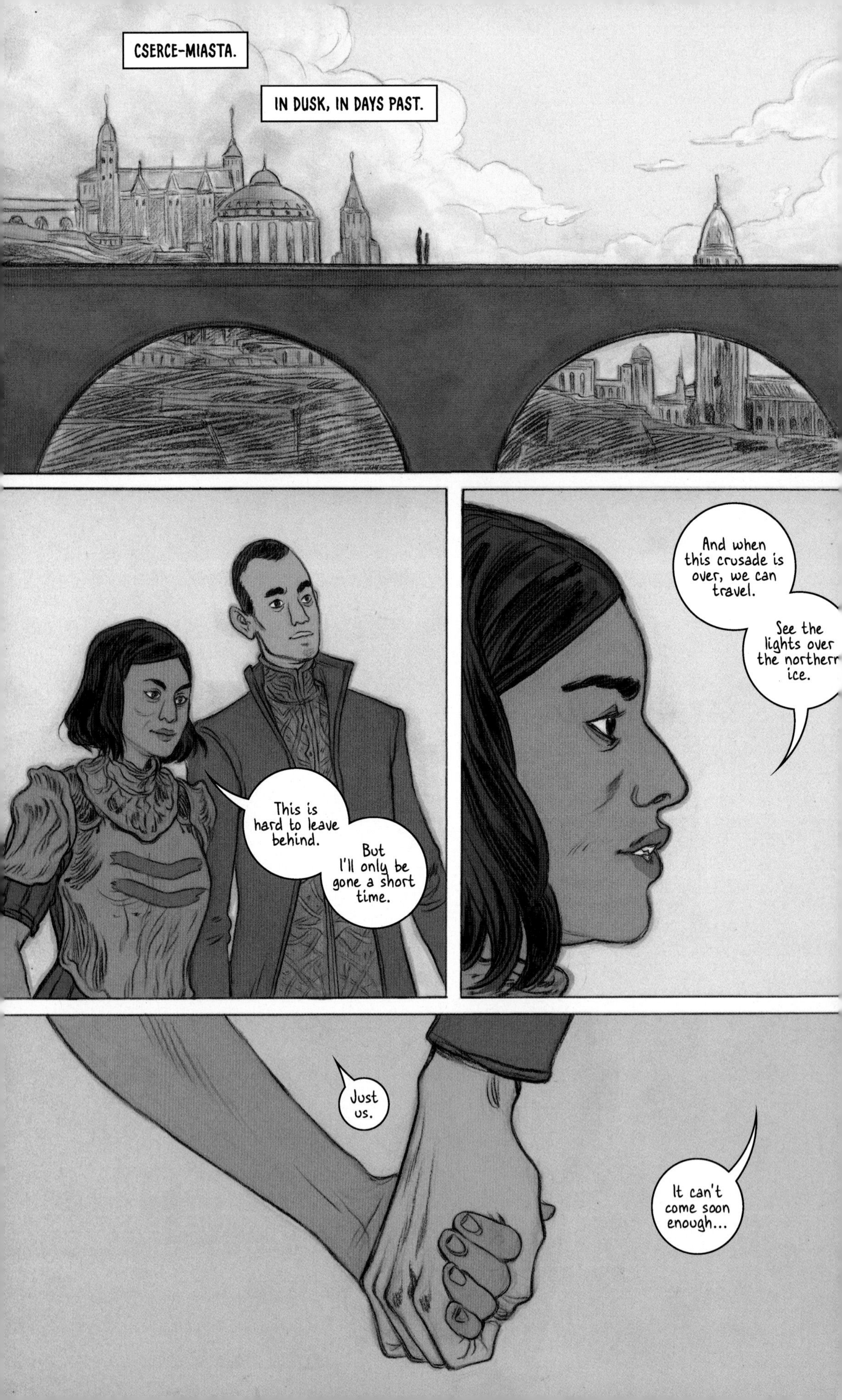
CSERCE-MIASTA.
IN DUSK, IN DAYS PAST.
This is hard to leave behind.
But I'll only be gone a short time.
And when this crusade is over, we can travel.
See the lights over the northern ice.
Just us.
It can't come soon enough...

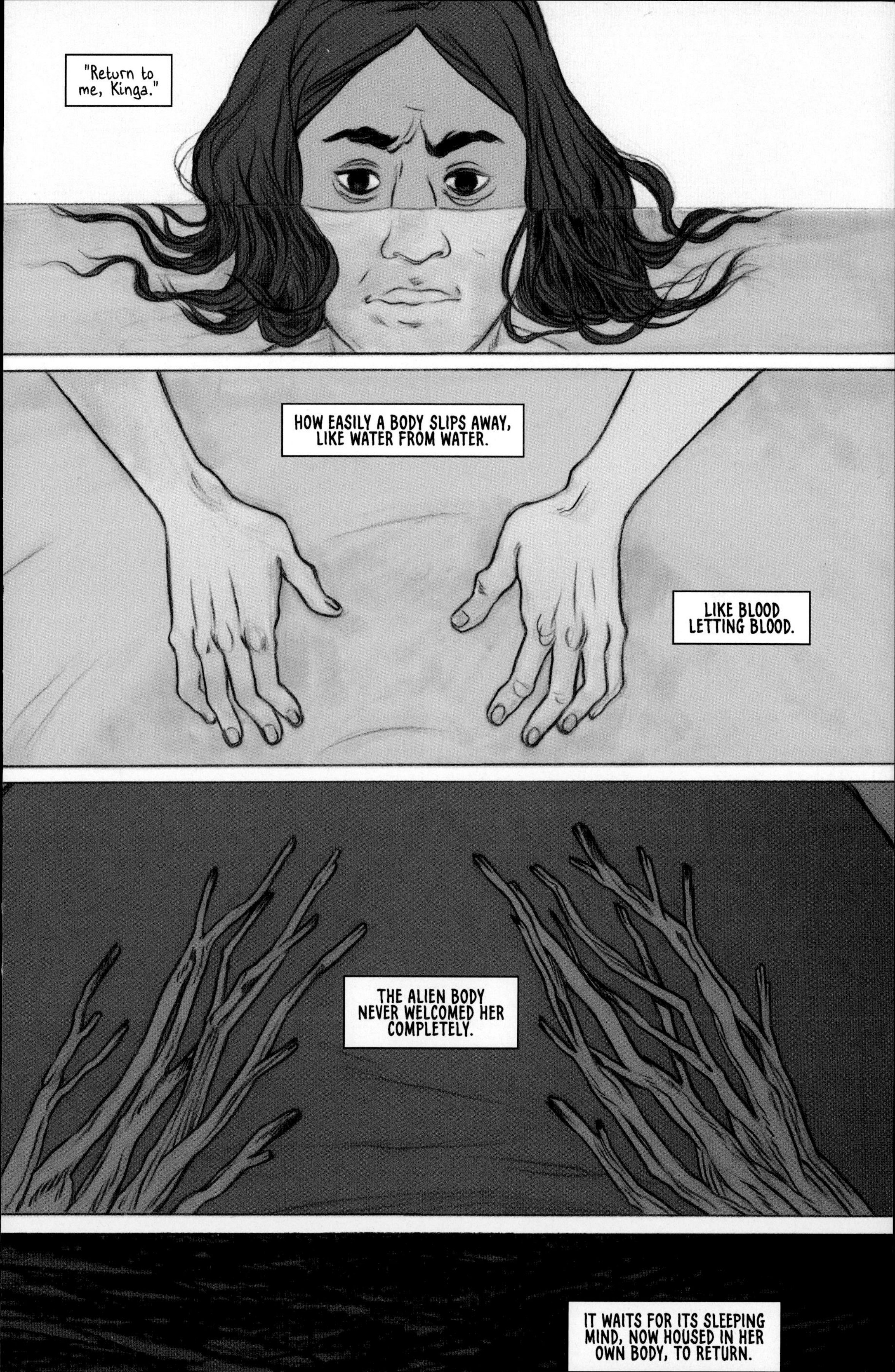
"Return to me, Kinga."
HOW EASILY A BODY SLIPS AWAY, LIKE WATER FROM WATER.
LIKE BLOOD LETTING BLOOD.
THE ALIEN BODY NEVER WELCOMED HER COMPLETELY.
IT WAITS FOR ITS SLEEPING MIND, NOW HOUSED IN HER OWN BODY, TO RETURN.

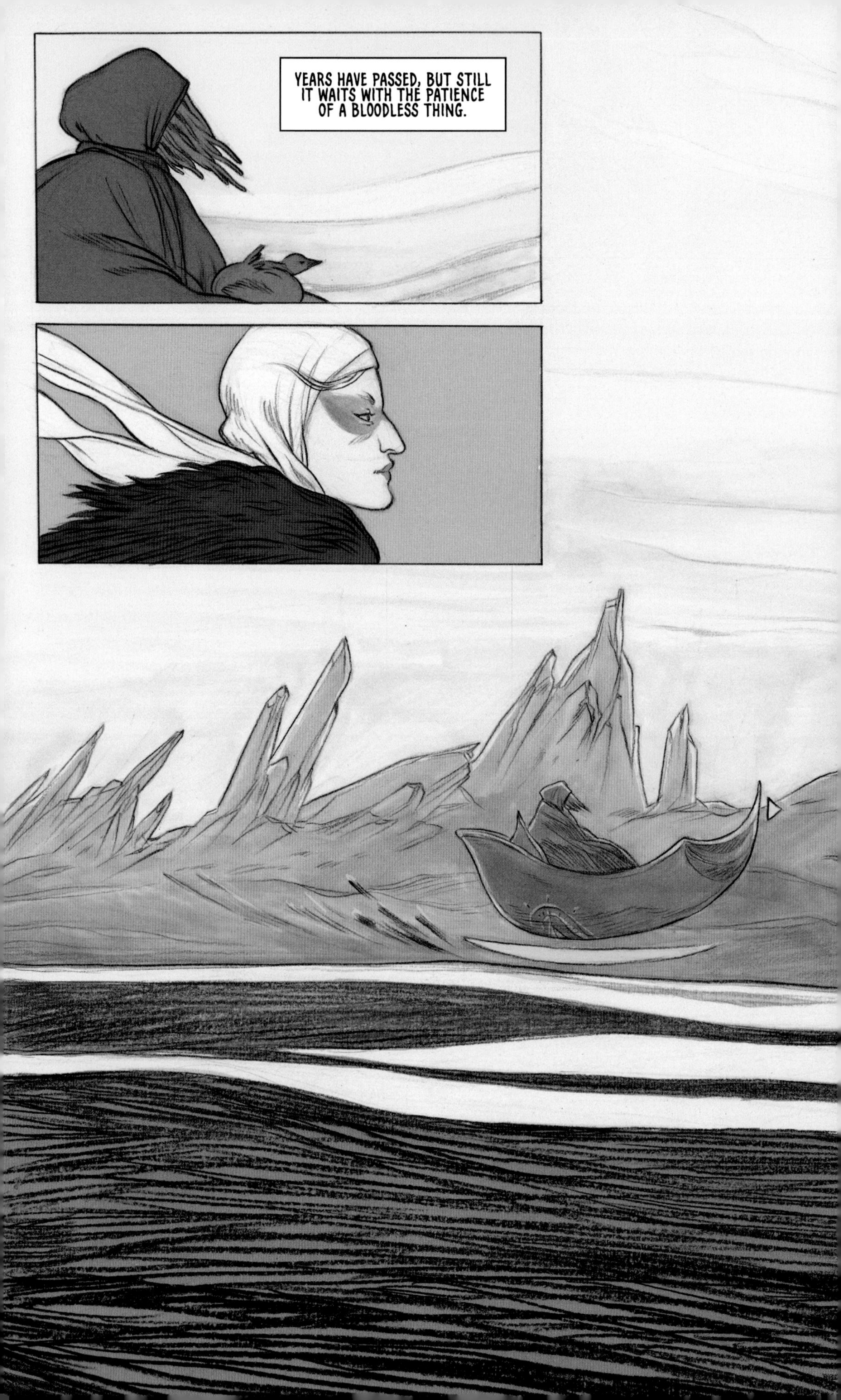
YEARS HAVE PASSED, BUT STILL IT WAITS WITH THE PATIENCE OF A BLOODLESS THING.

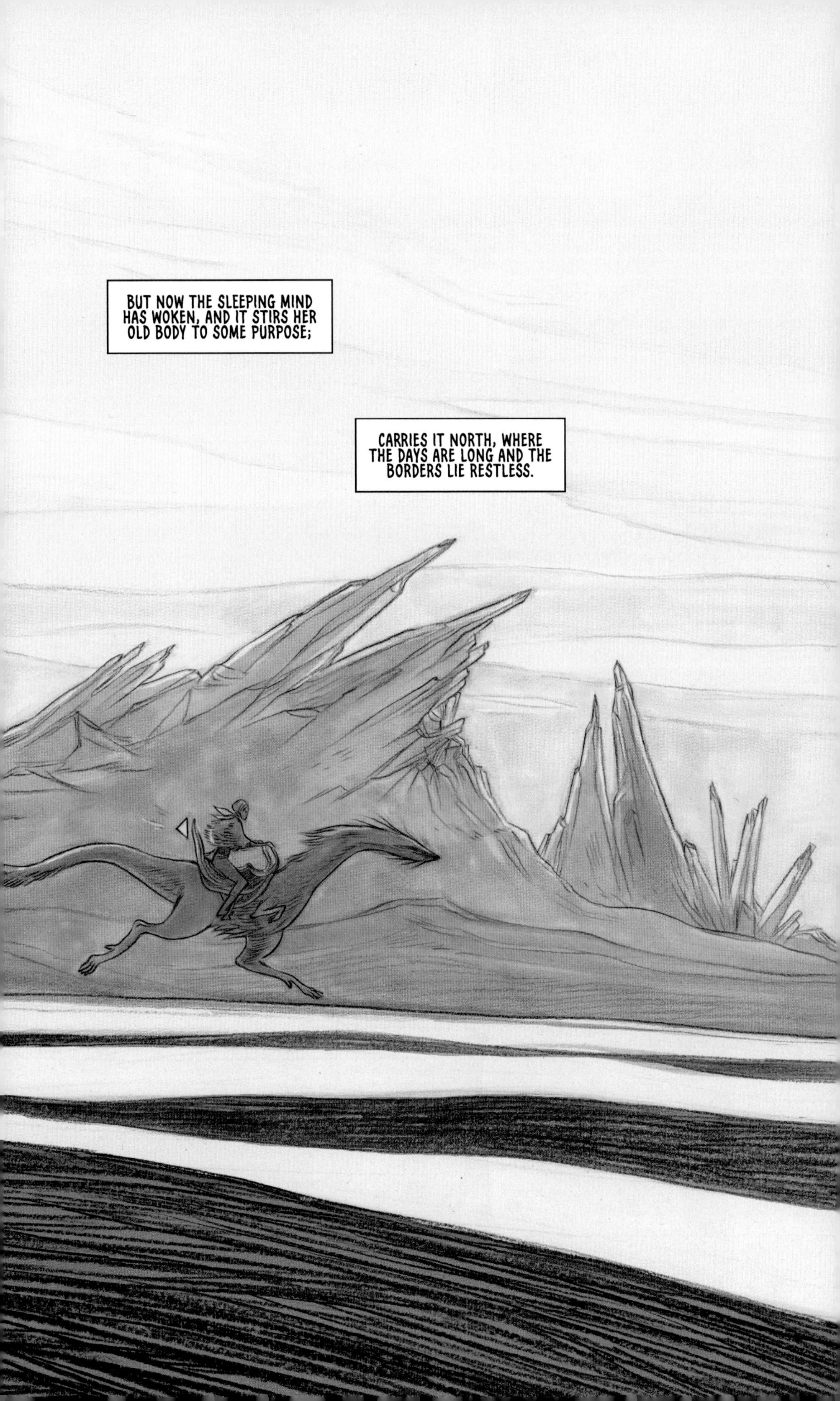
BUT NOW THE SLEEPING MIND HAS WOKEN, AND IT STIRS HER OLD BODY TO SOME PURPOSE;
CARRIES IT NORTH, WHERE THE DAYS ARE LONG AND THE BORDERS LIE RESTLESS.

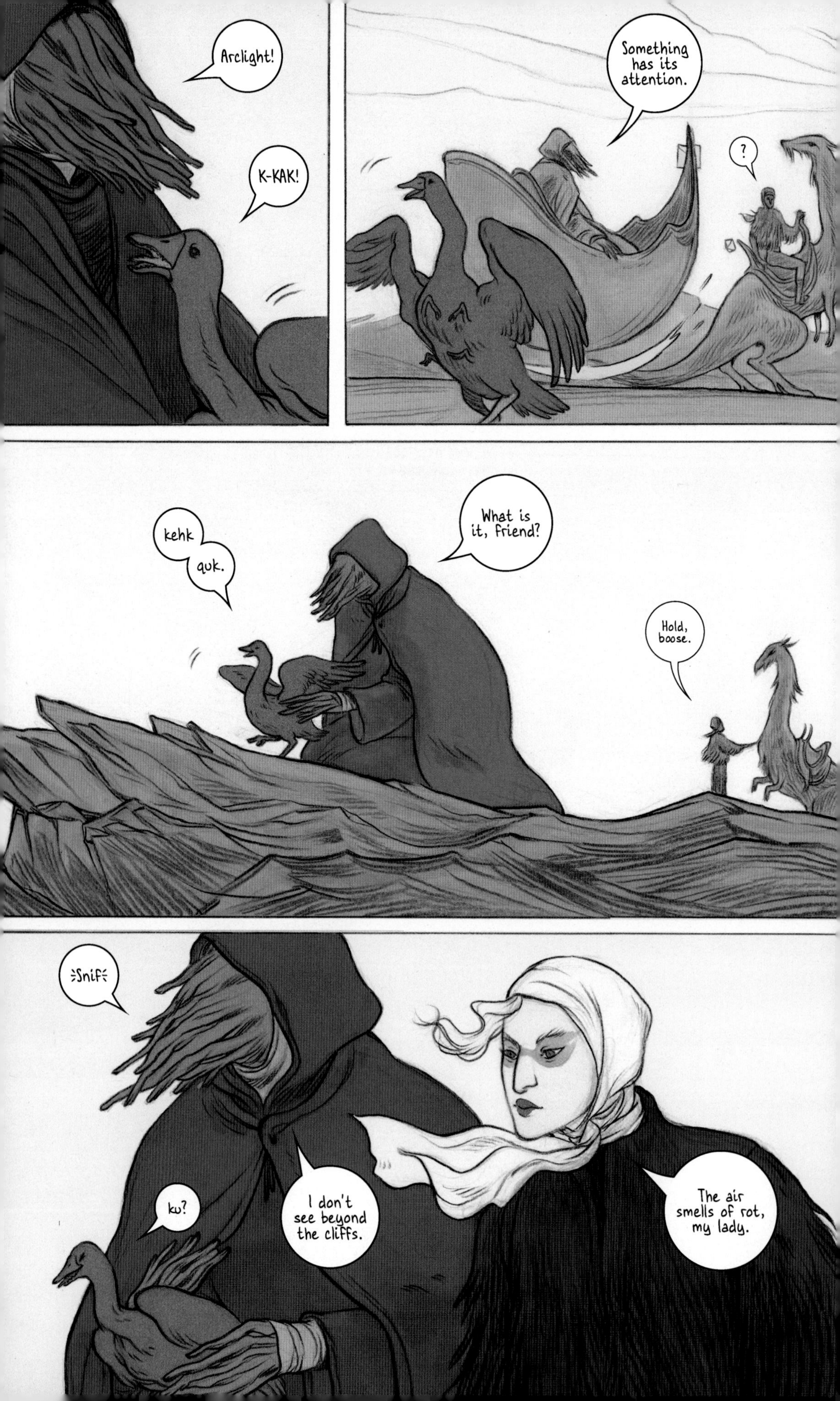
Arclight!
K-KAK!
Something has its attention.
?
kehk
quk.
What is it, friend?
Hold, boose.
≈Snif≈
ku?
I don't see beyond the cliffs.
The air smells of rot, my lady.

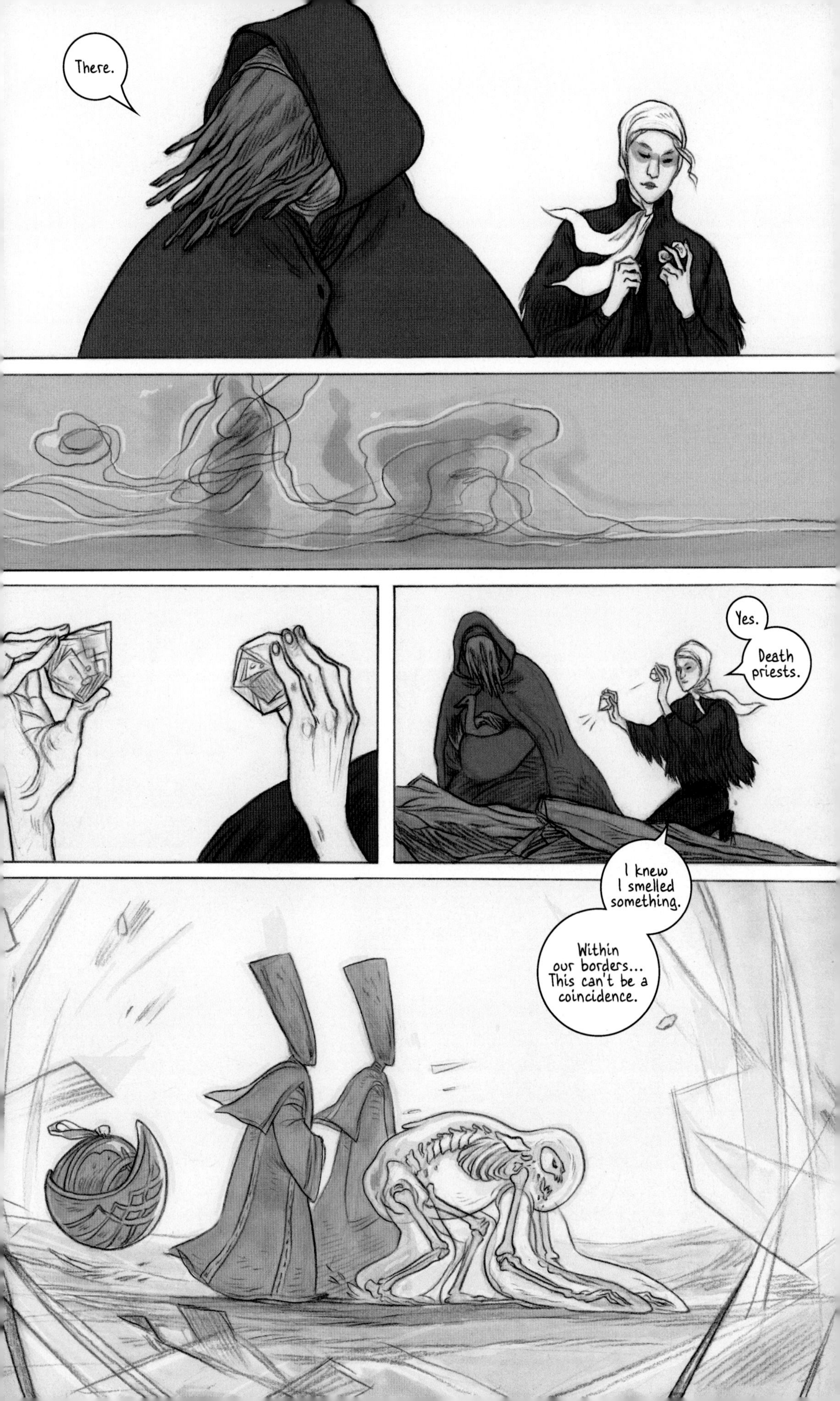
There.
Yes.
Death priests.
I knew I smelled something.
Within our borders... This can't be a coincidence.

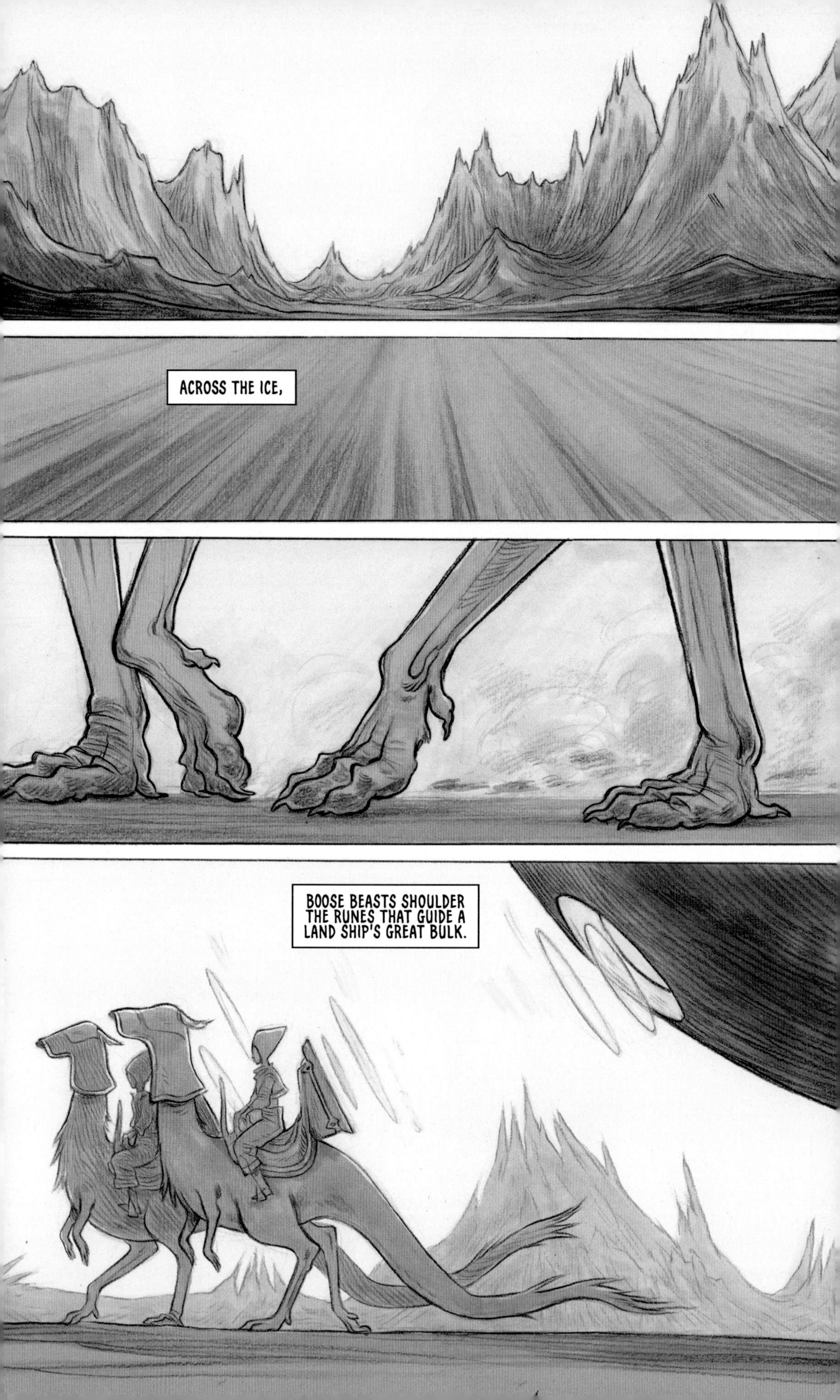
ACROSS THE ICE,
BOOSE BEASTS SHOULDER THE RUNES THAT GUIDE A LAND SHIP'S GREAT BULK.

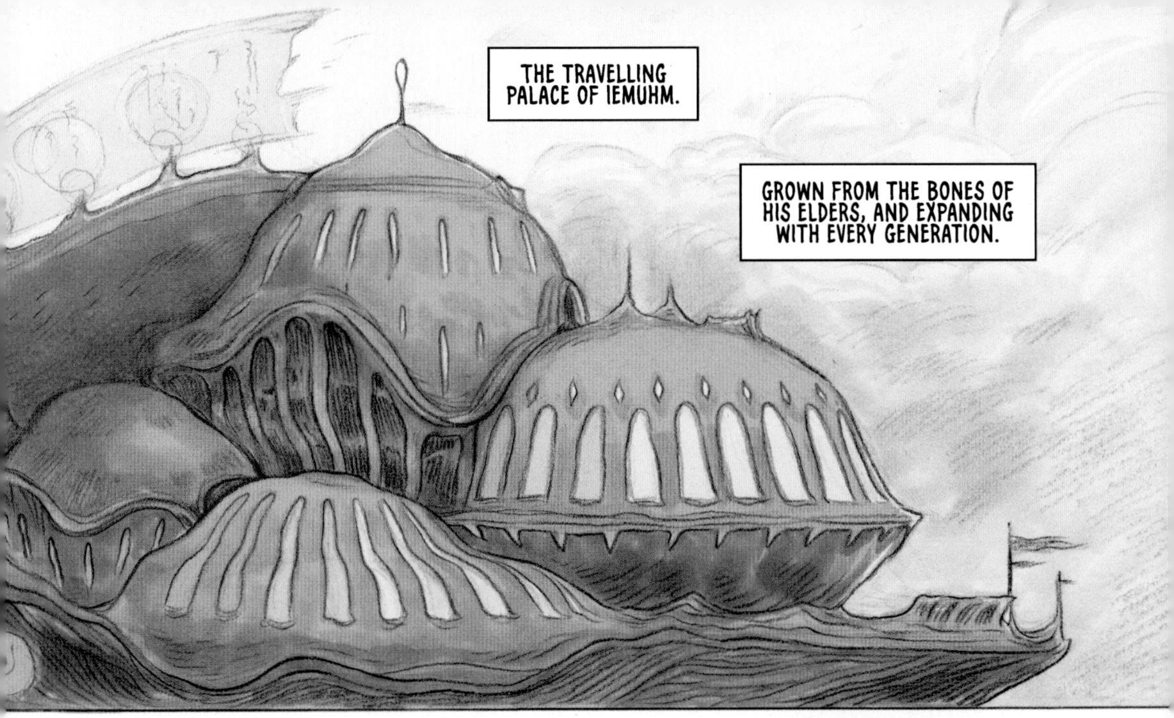
THE TRAVELLING PALACE OF IEMUHM.
GROWN FROM THE BONES OF HIS ELDERS, AND EXPANDING WITH EVERY GENERATION.

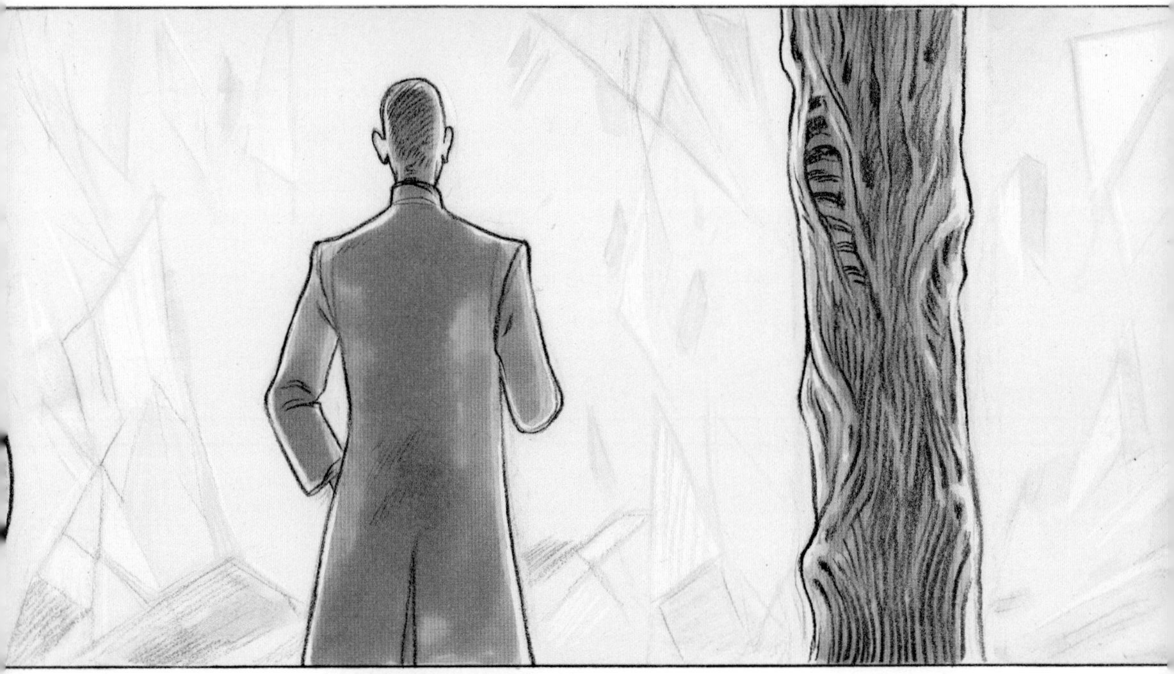

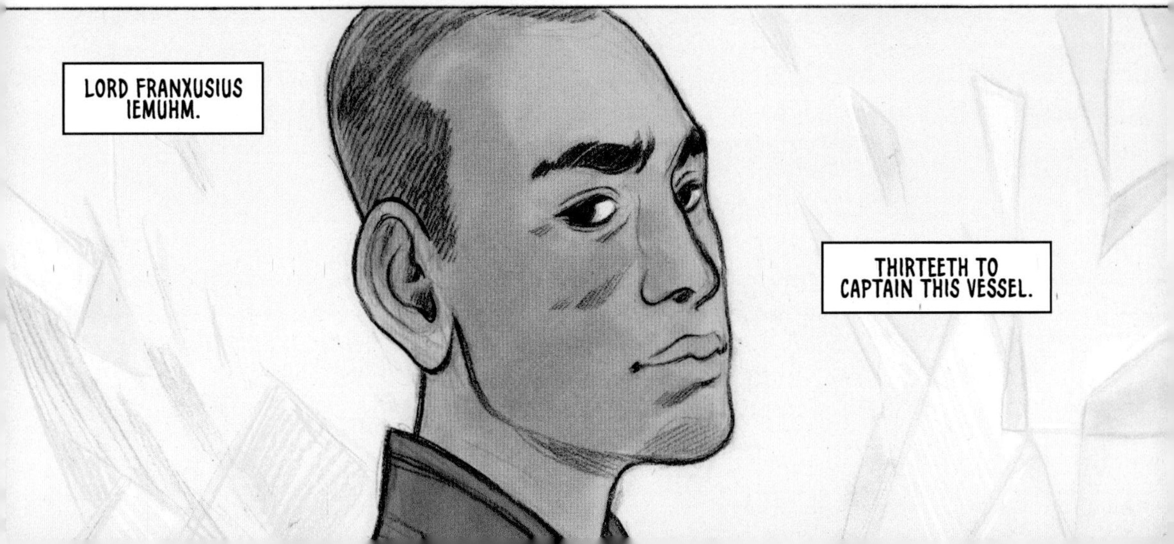
LORD FRANXUSIUS IEMUHM.
THIRTEETH TO CAPTAIN THIS VESSEL.

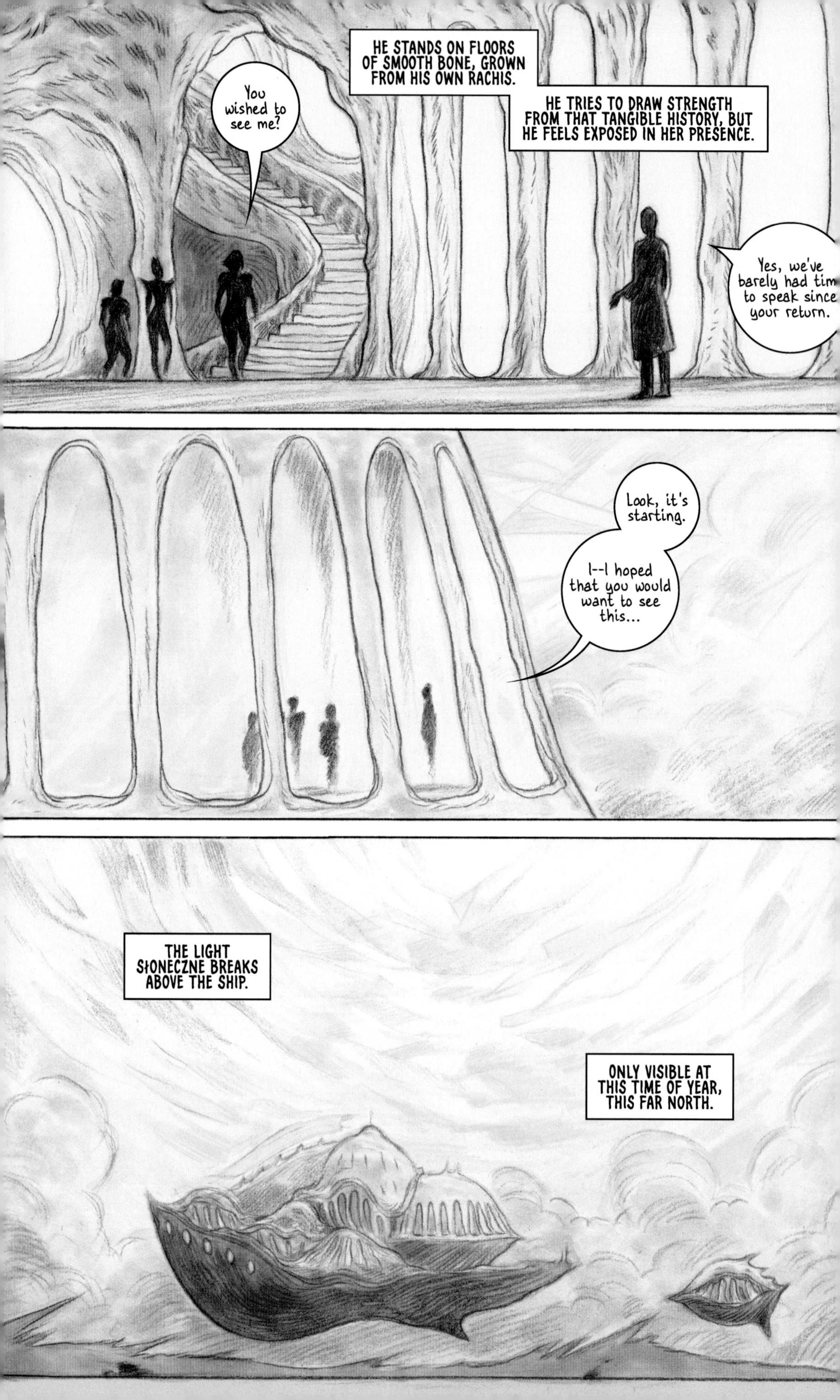
HE STANDS ON FLOORS OF SMOOTH BONE, GROWN FROM HIS OWN RACHIS.
HE TRIES TO DRAW STRENGTH FROM THAT TANGIBLE HISTORY, BUT HE FEELS EXPOSED IN HER PRESENCE.
You wished to see me?
Yes, we've barely had tim to speak since your return.
Look, it's starting.
I--I hoped that you would want to see this...
THE LIGHT SŁONECZNE BREAKS ABOVE THE SHIP.
ONLY VISIBLE AT THIS TIME OF YEAR, THIS FAR NORTH.

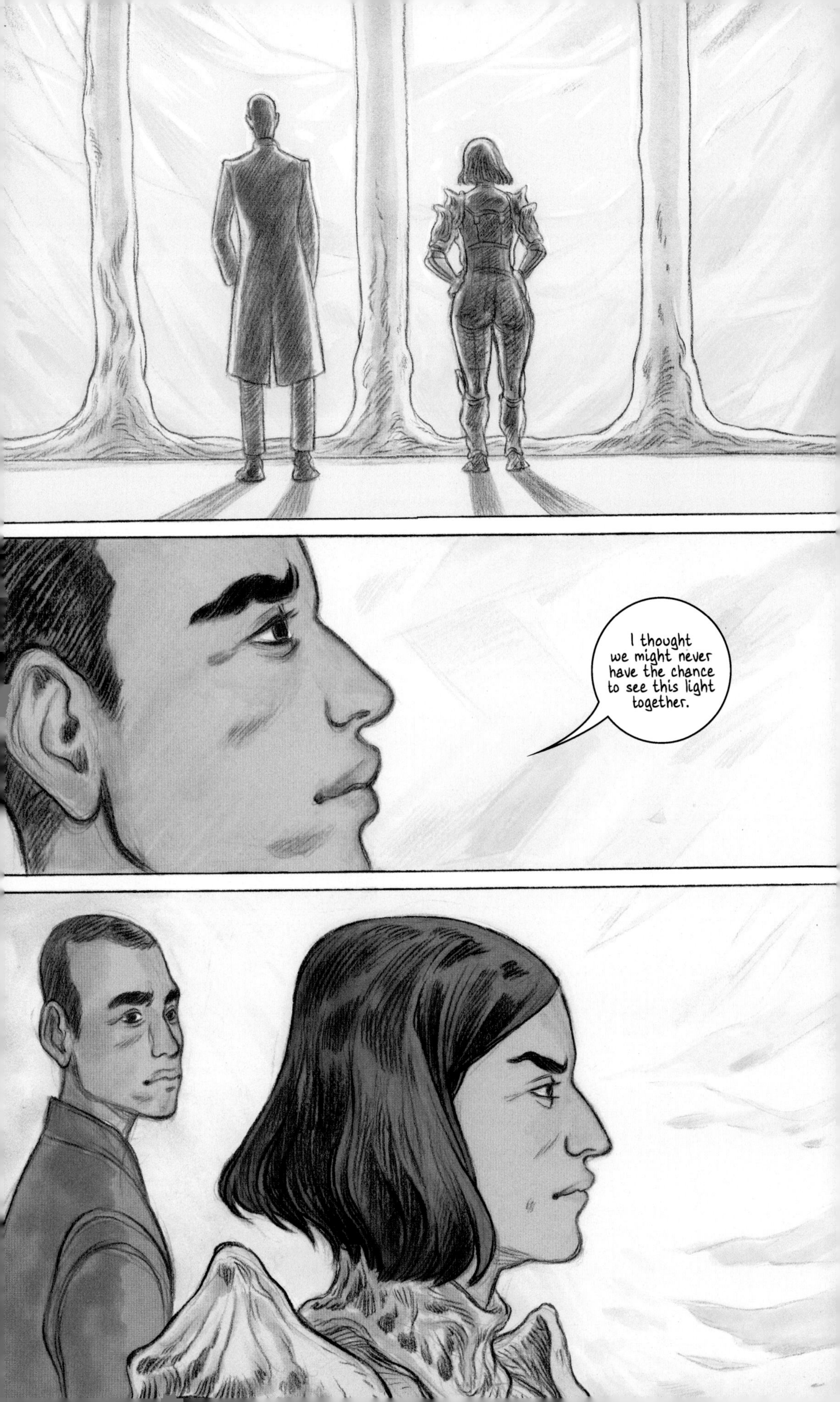
I thought we might never have the chance to see this light together.

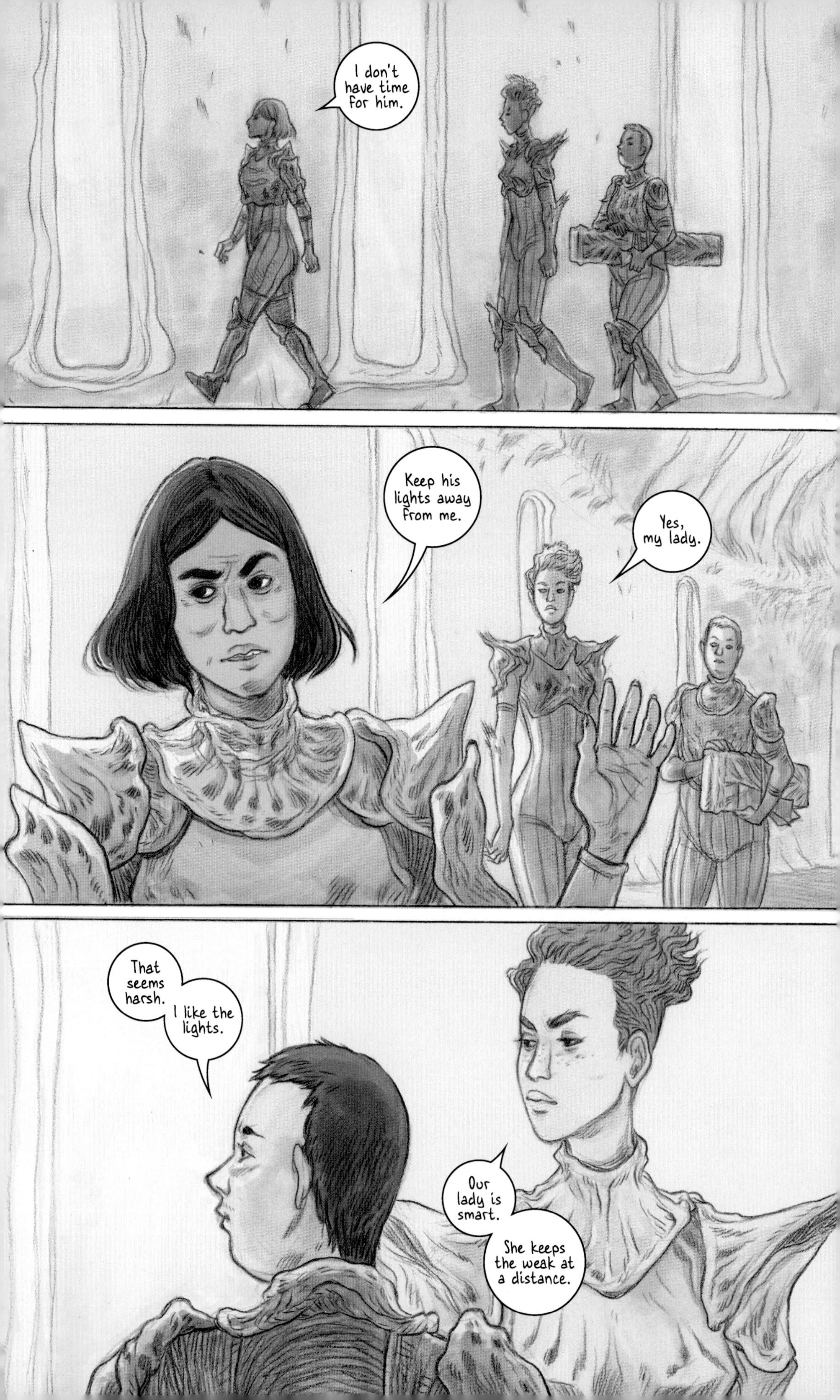
I don't have time for him.
Keep his lights away from me.
Yes, my lady.
That seems harsh.
I like the lights.
Our lady is smart.
She keeps the weak at a distance.

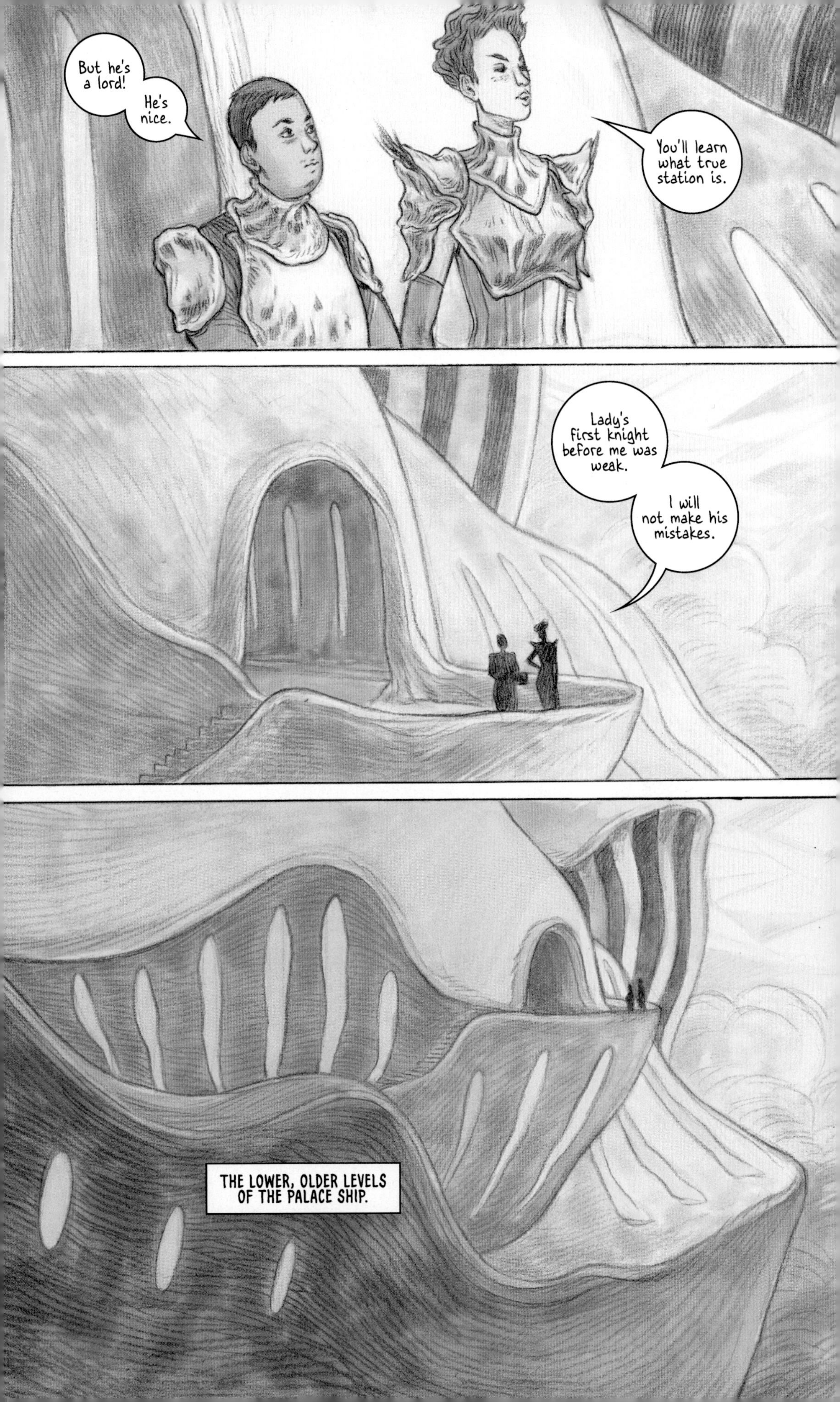
But he's a lord!
He's nice.
You'll learn what true station is.
Lady's first knight before me was weak.
I will not make his mistakes.
THE LOWER, OLDER LEVELS OF THE PALACE SHIP.

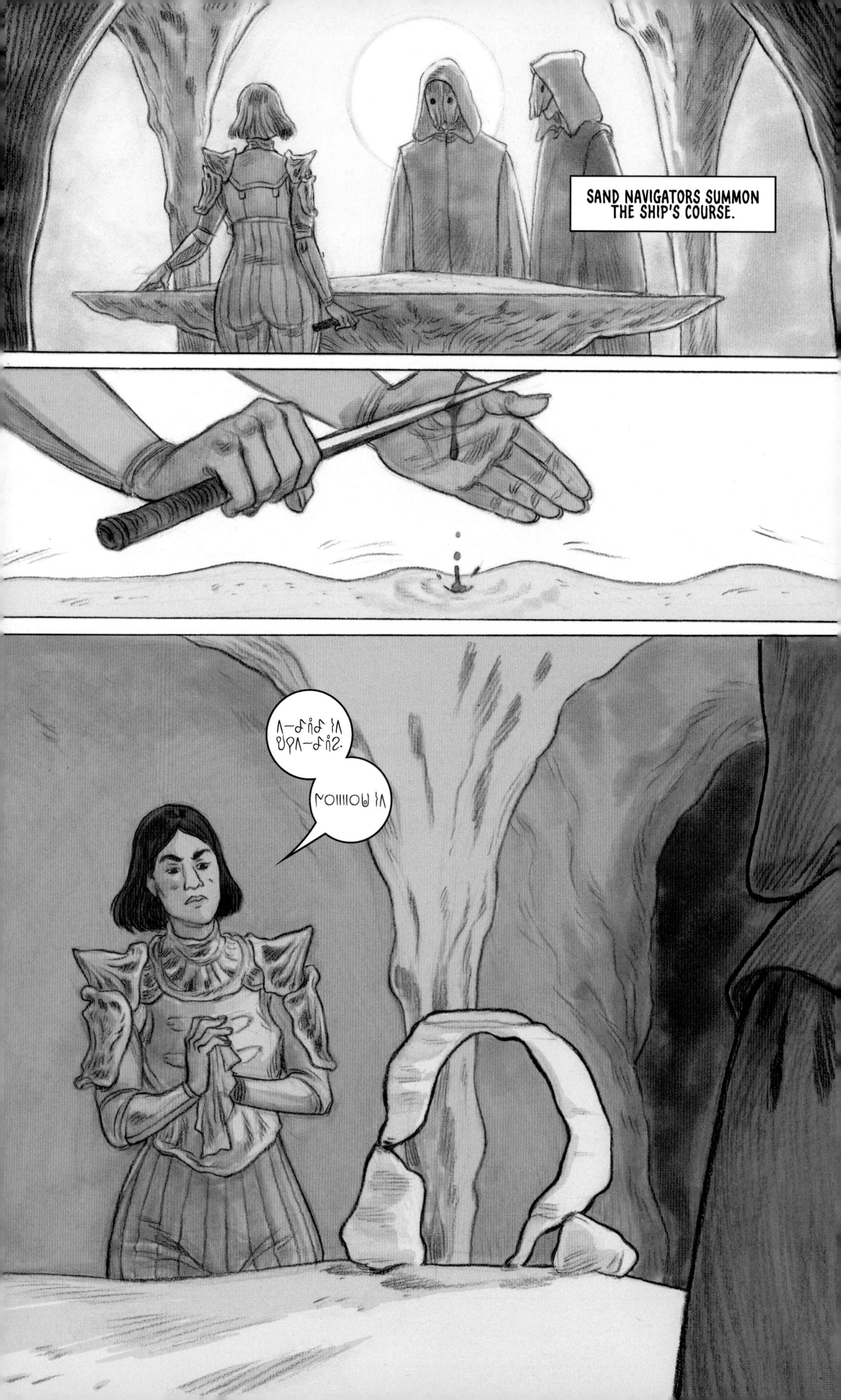
SAND NAVIGATORS SUMMON THE SHIP'S COURSE.

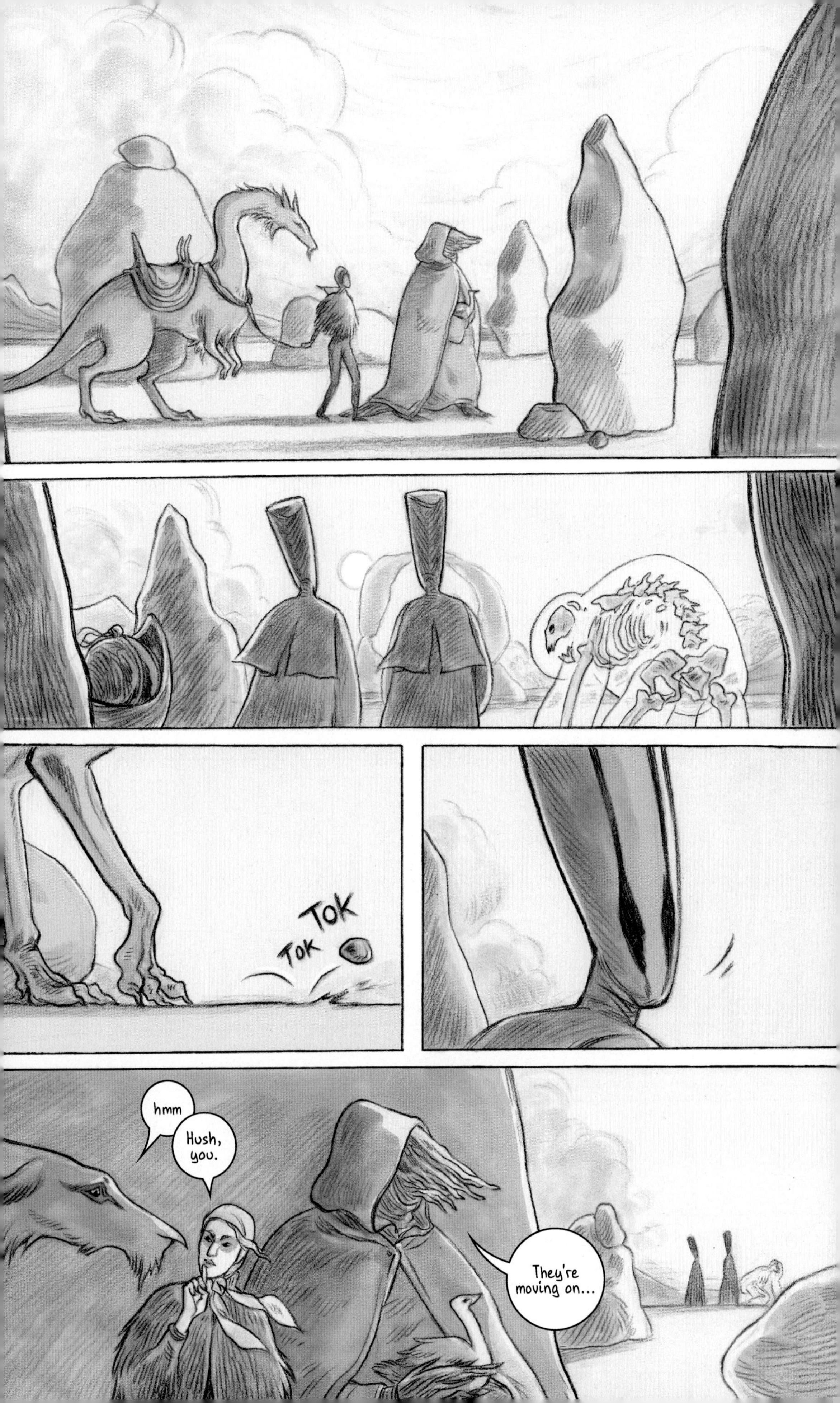
TOK
TOK
hmm
Hush, you.
They're moving on...

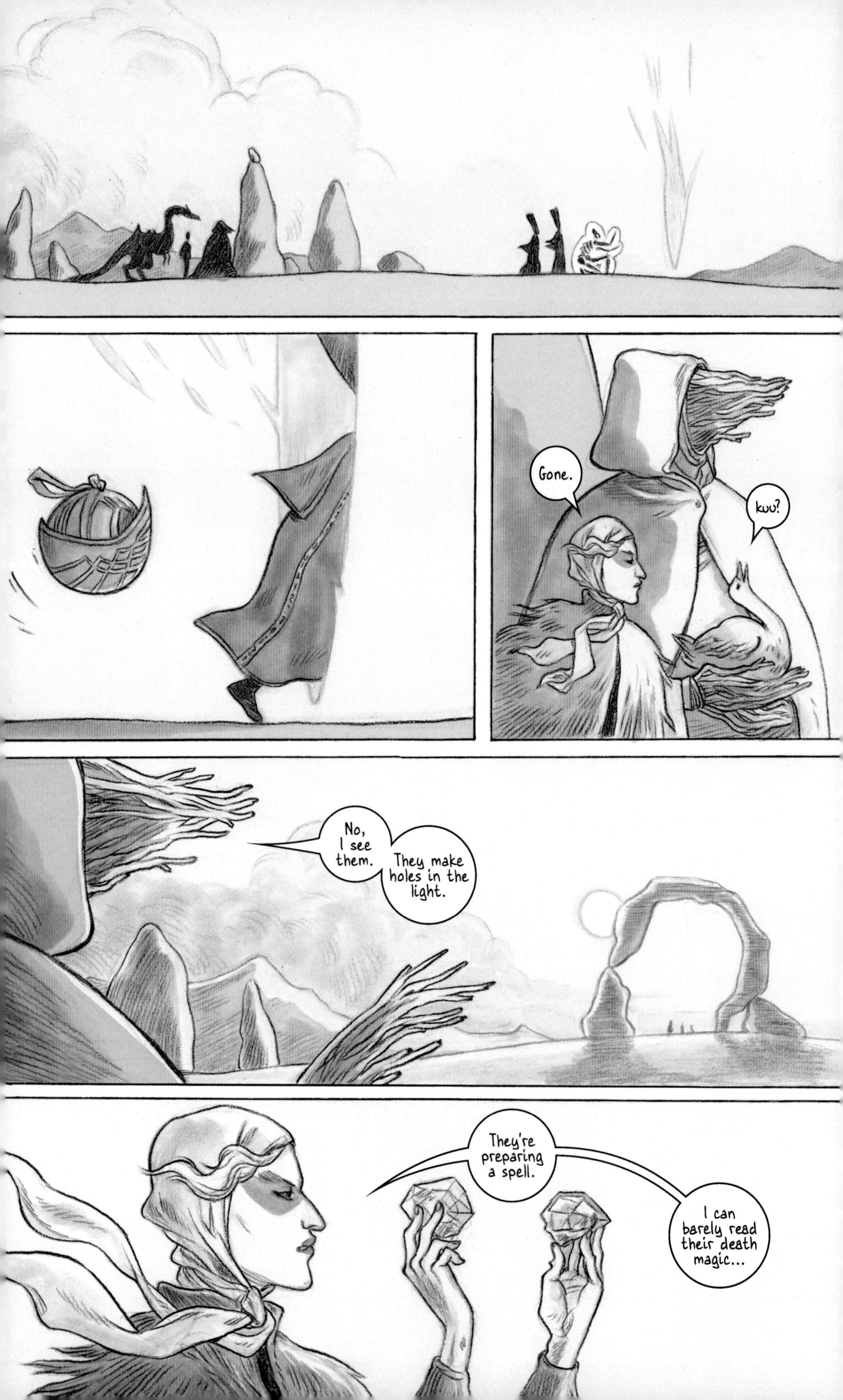
Gone.
kuu?
No, I see them.
They make holes in the light.
They're preparing a spell.
I can barely read their death magic...

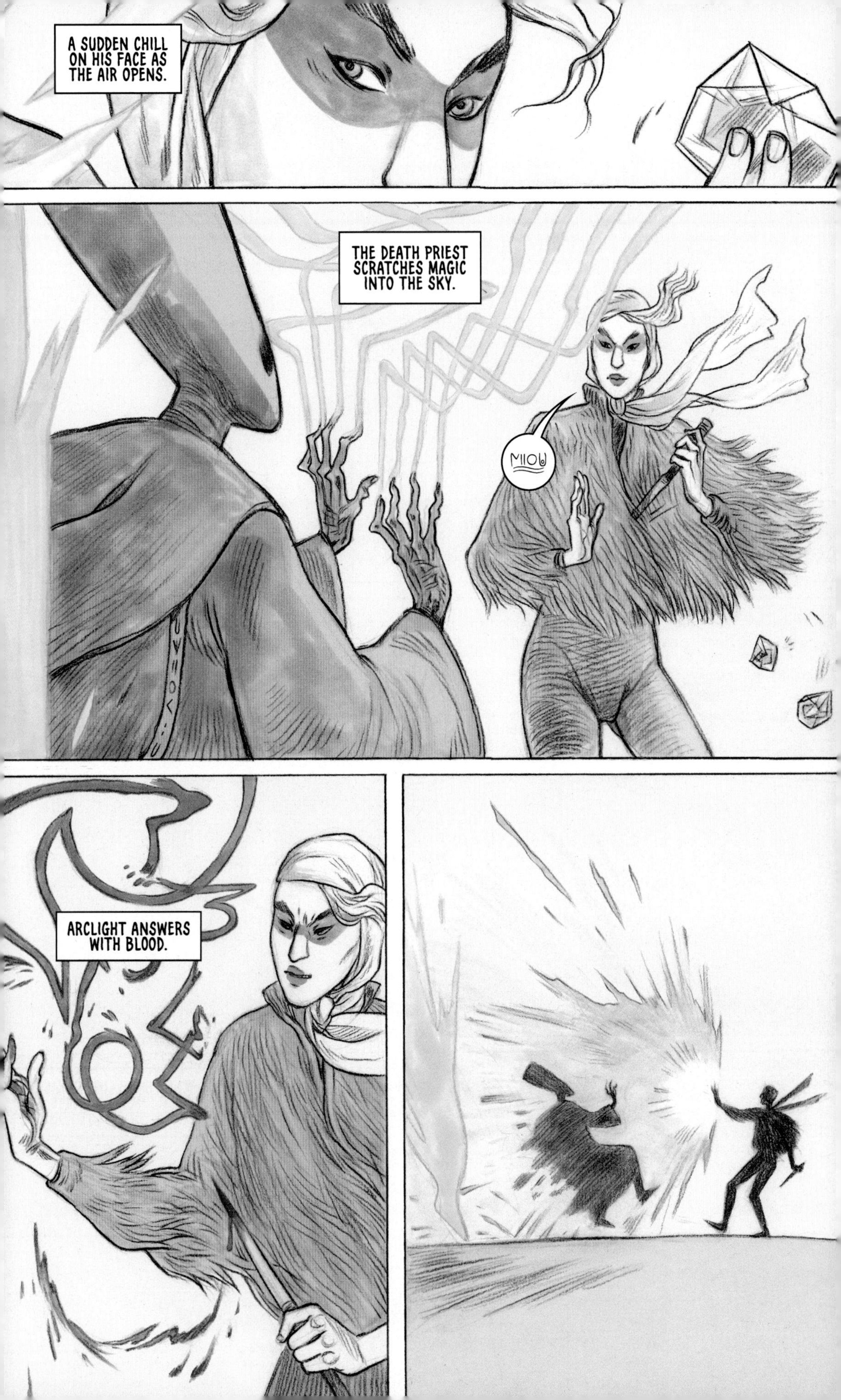
A SUDDEN CHILL ON HIS FACE AS THE AIR OPENS.
THE DEATH PRIEST SCRATCHES MAGIC INTO THE SKY.
MIOU
ARCLIGHT ANSWERS WITH BLOOD.

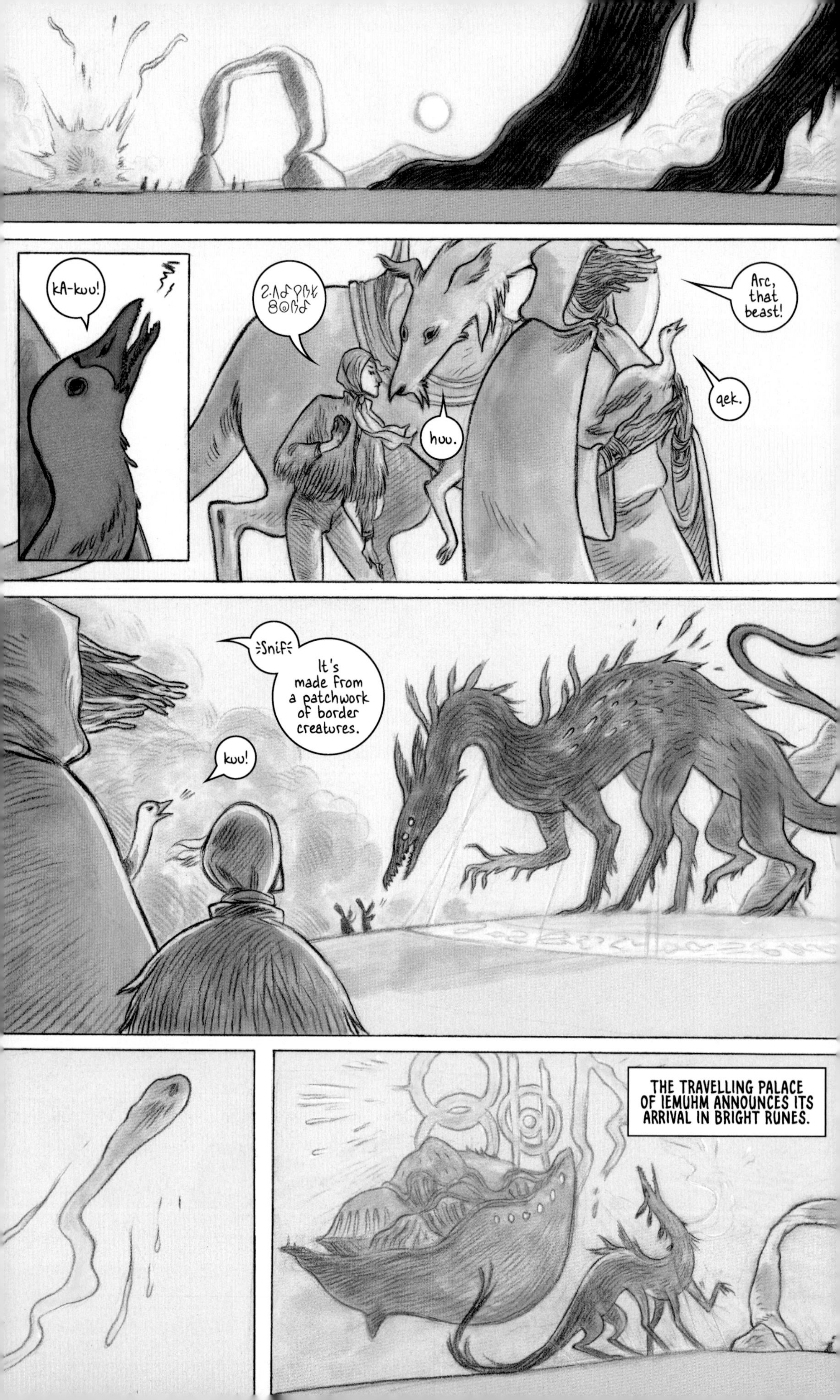
kA-kuu!
Arc, that beast!
qek.
huu.
Snif
It's made from a patchwork of border creatures.
kuu!
THE TRAVELLING PALACE OF IEMUHM ANNOUNCES ITS ARRIVAL IN BRIGHT RUNES.

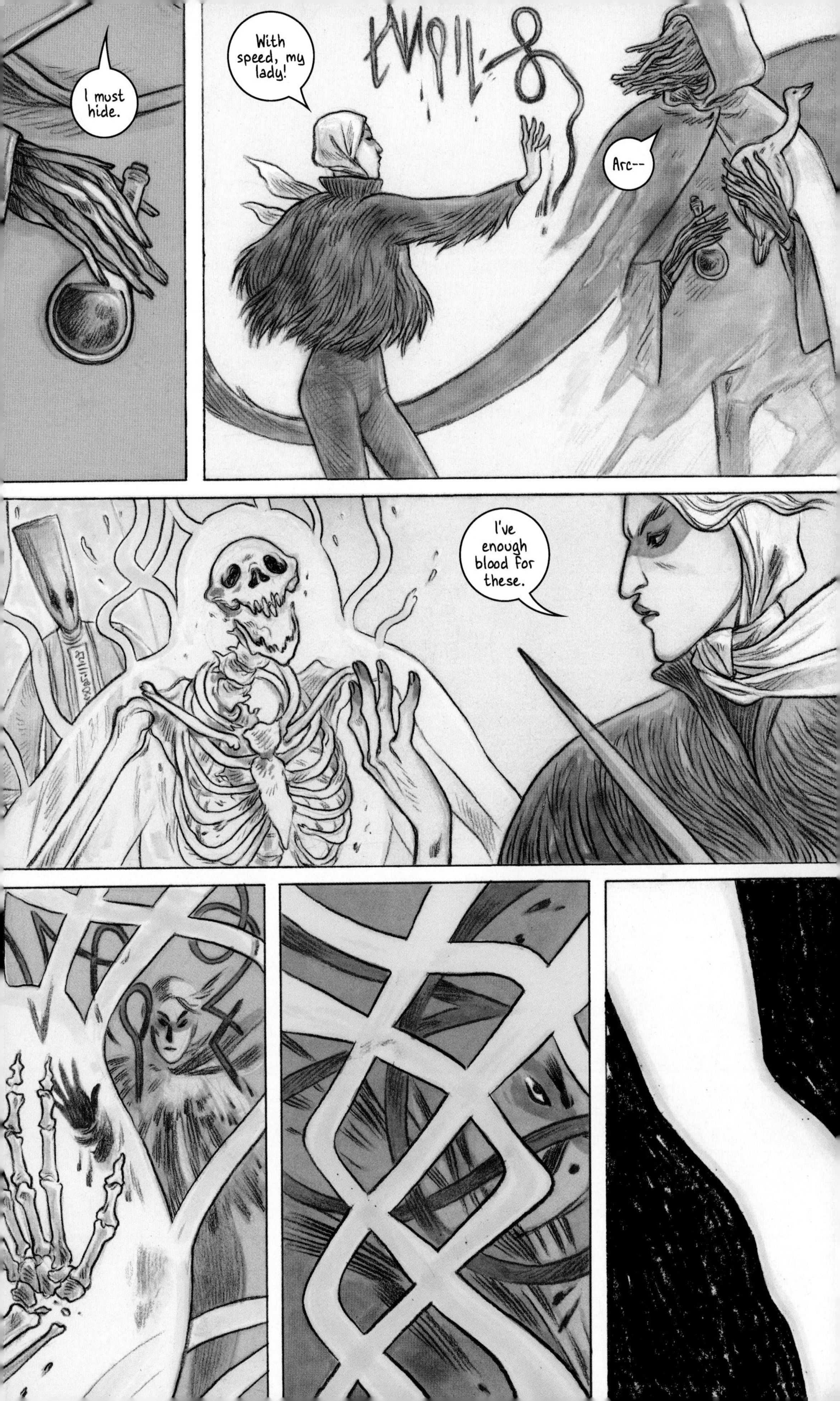
I must hide.
With speed, my lady!
Arc--
I've enough blood for these.

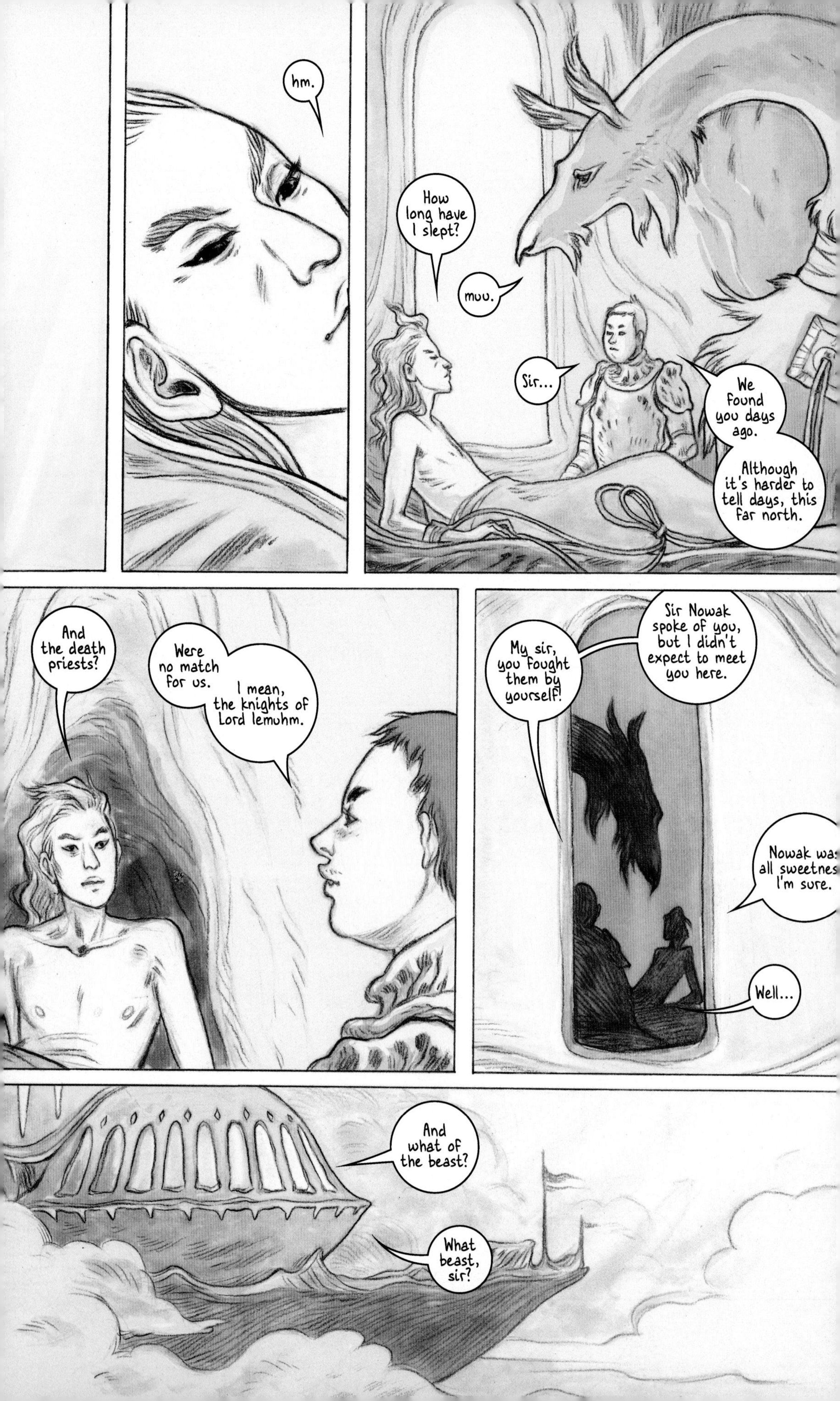
hm.
How long have I slept?
muu.
Sir...
We found you days ago.
Although it's harder to tell days, this far north.
And the death priests?
Were no match for us.
I mean, the knights of Lord Iemuhm.
Sir Nowak spoke of you, but I didn't expect to meet you here.
My sir, you fought them by yourself!
Nowak wa
all sweetnes
I'm sure.
Well...
And what of the beast?
What beast, sir?

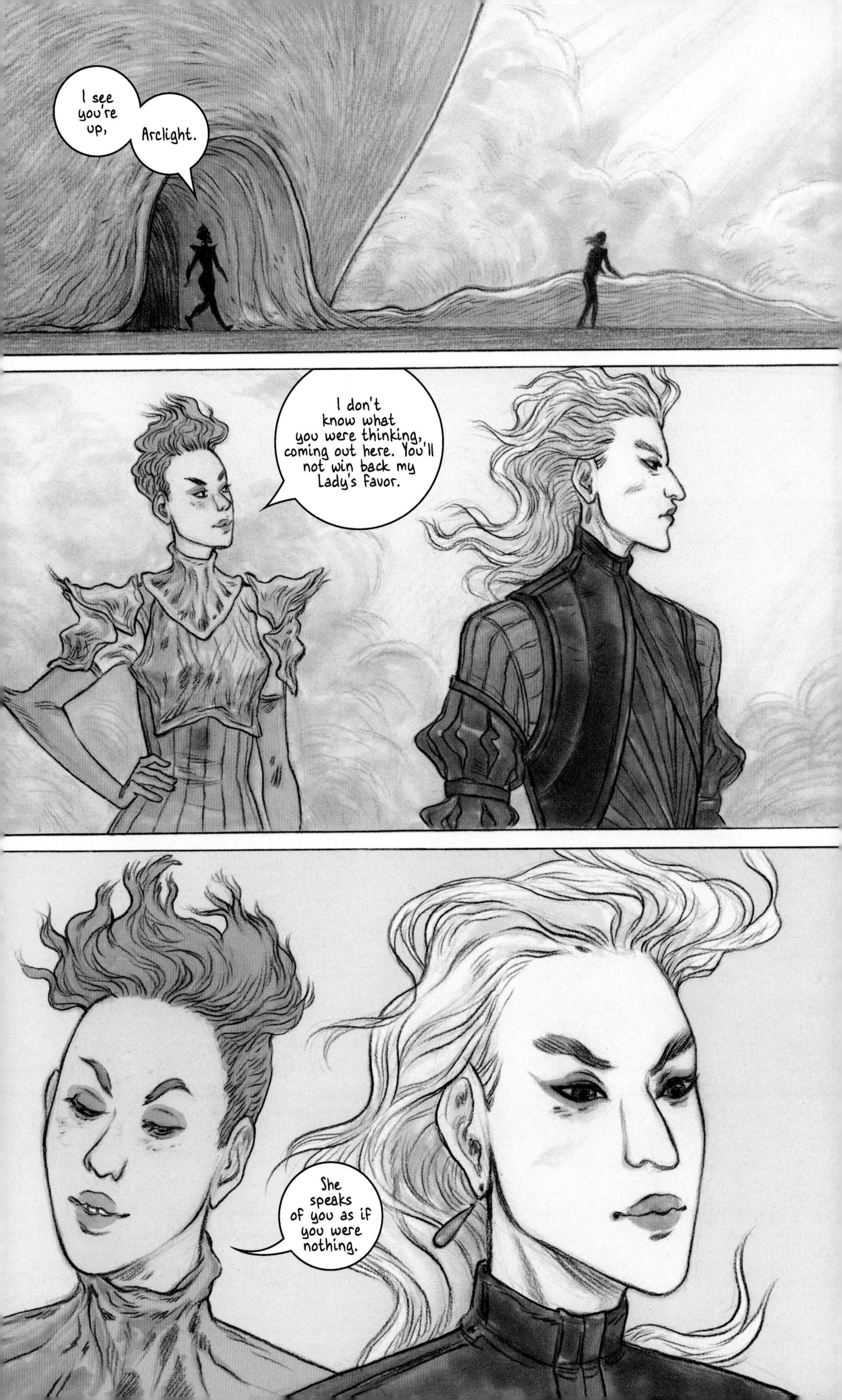
I see you're up,
Arclight.
I don't know what you were thinking, coming out here. You'll not win back my Lady's favor.
She speaks of you as if you were nothing.

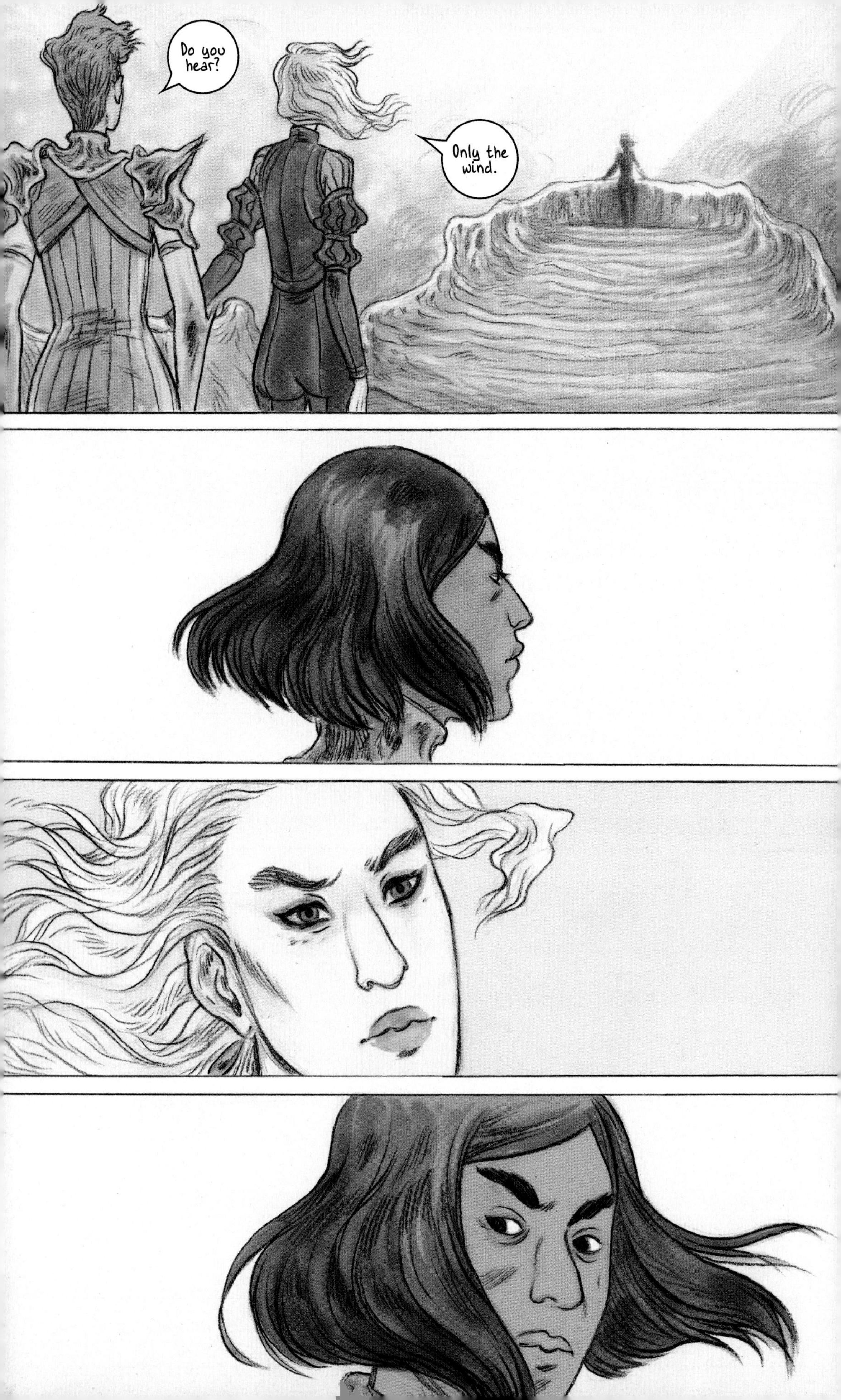
Do you hear?
Only the wind.

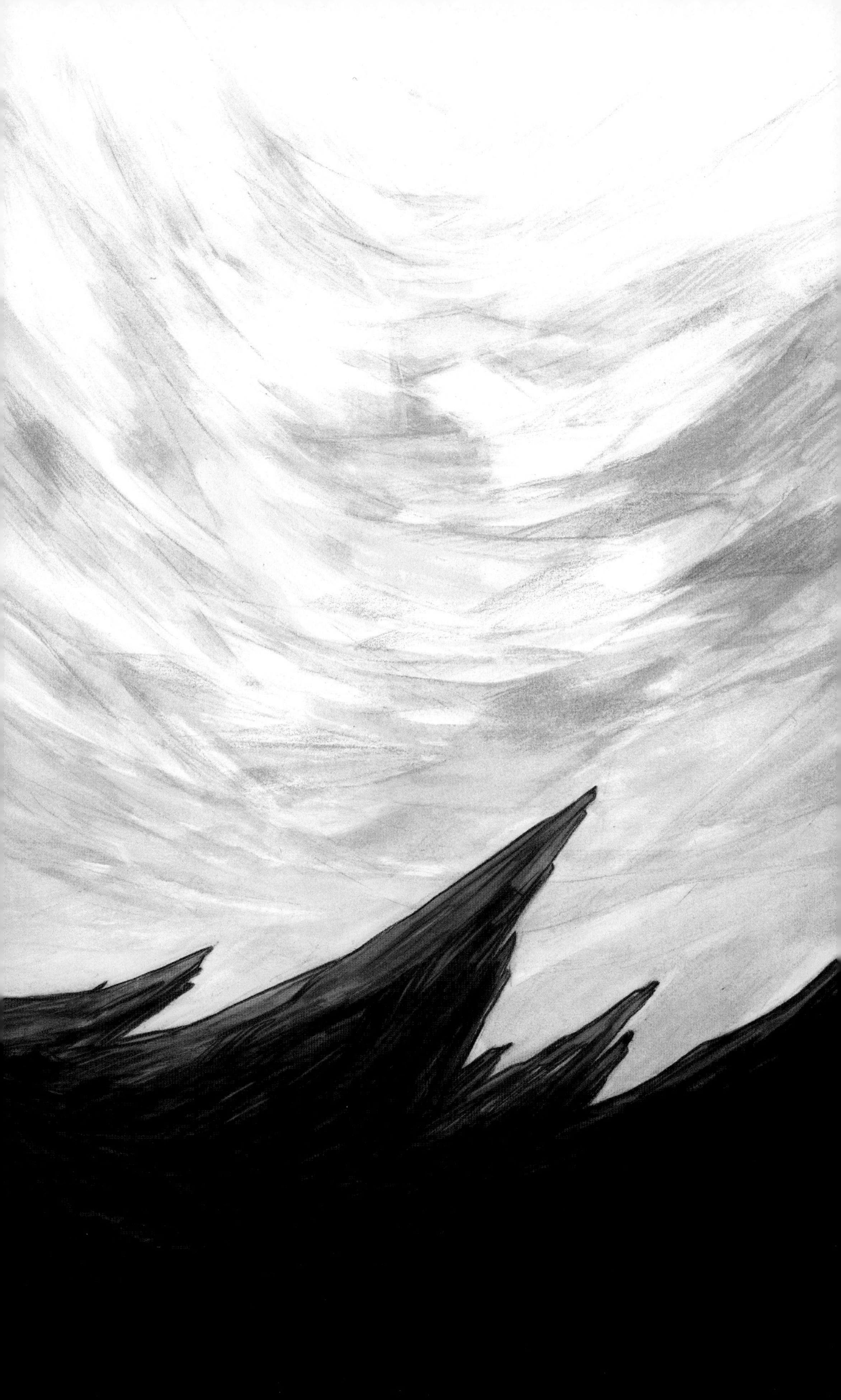

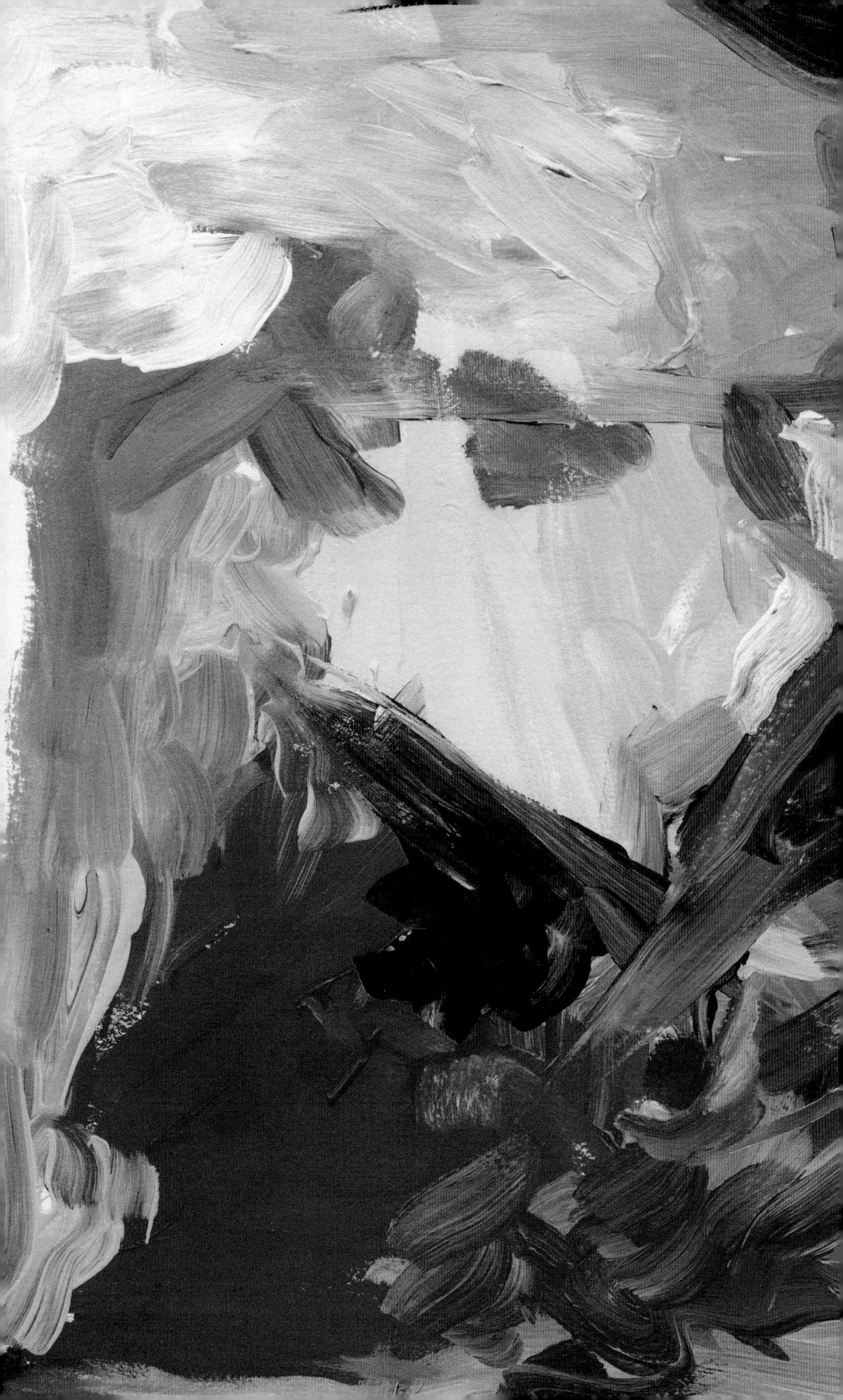

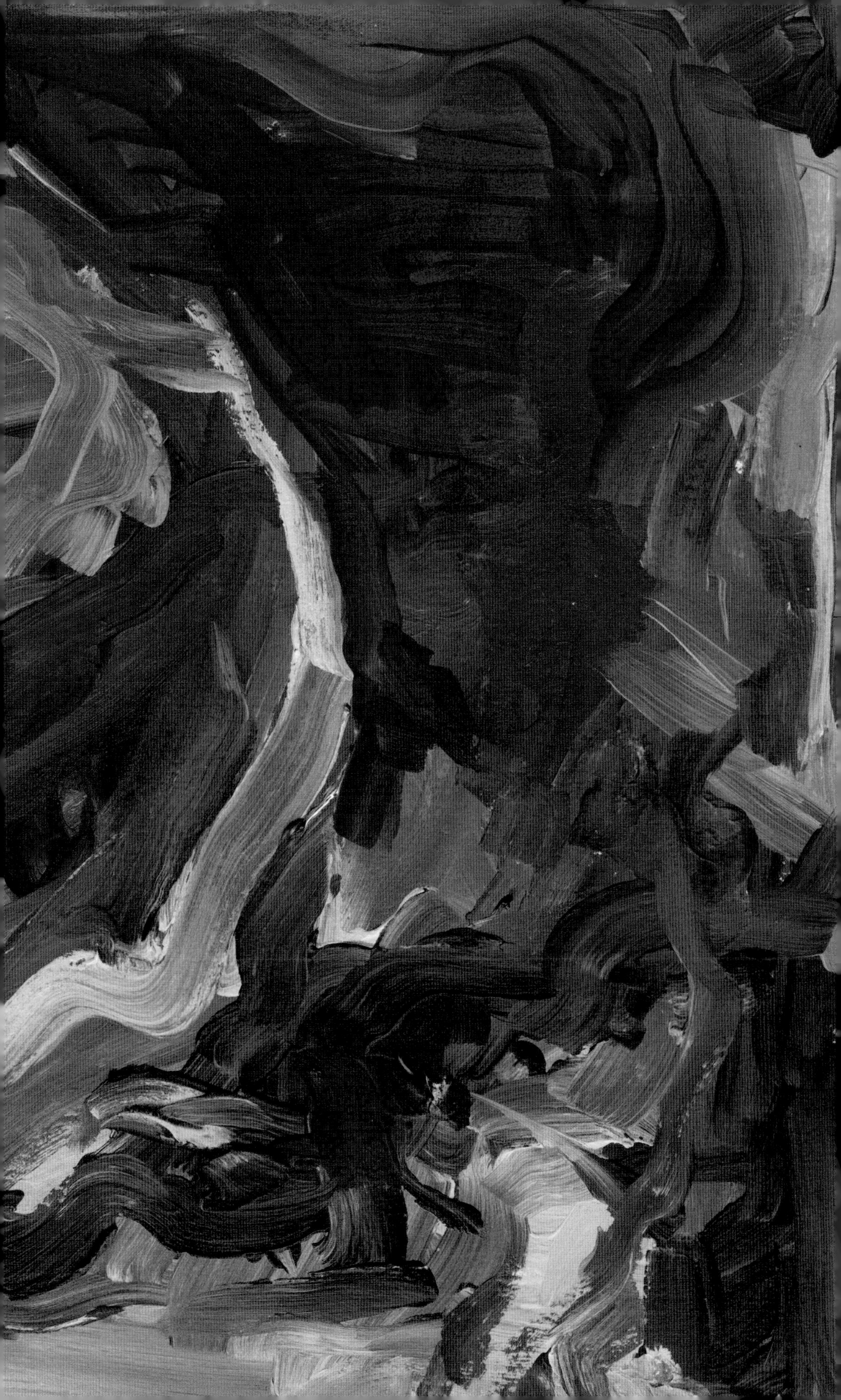

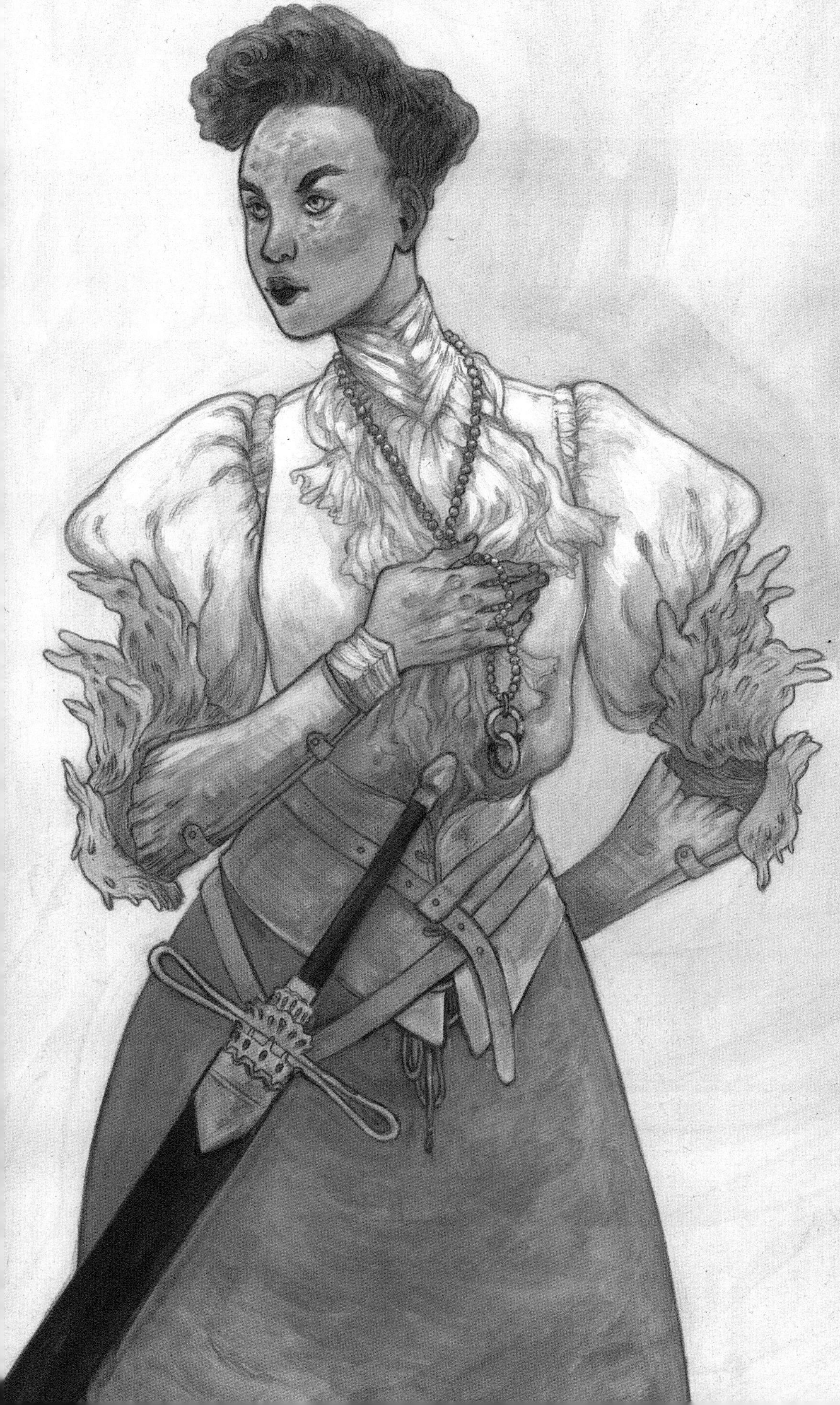

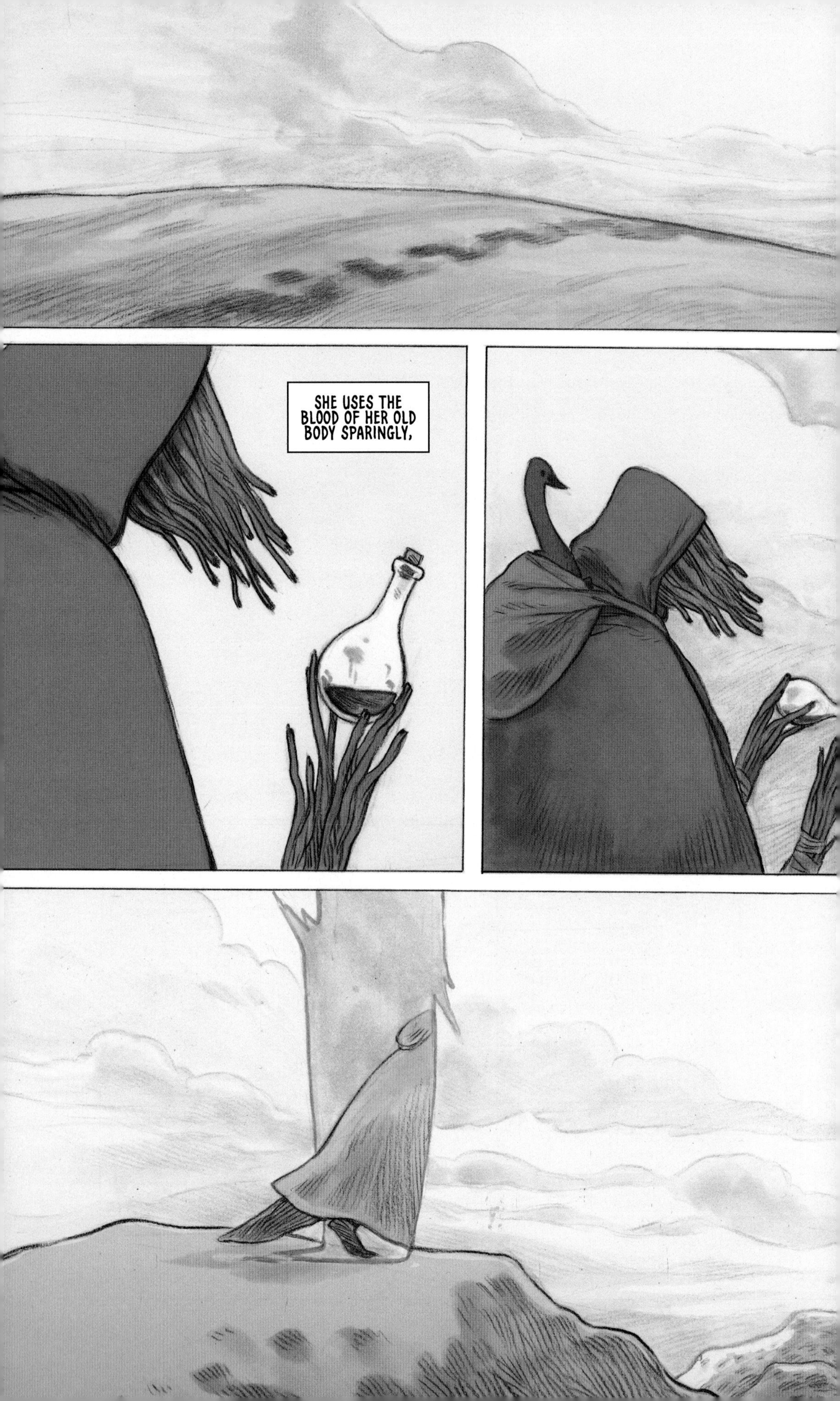
SHE USES THE BLOOD OF HER OLD BODY SPARINGLY,

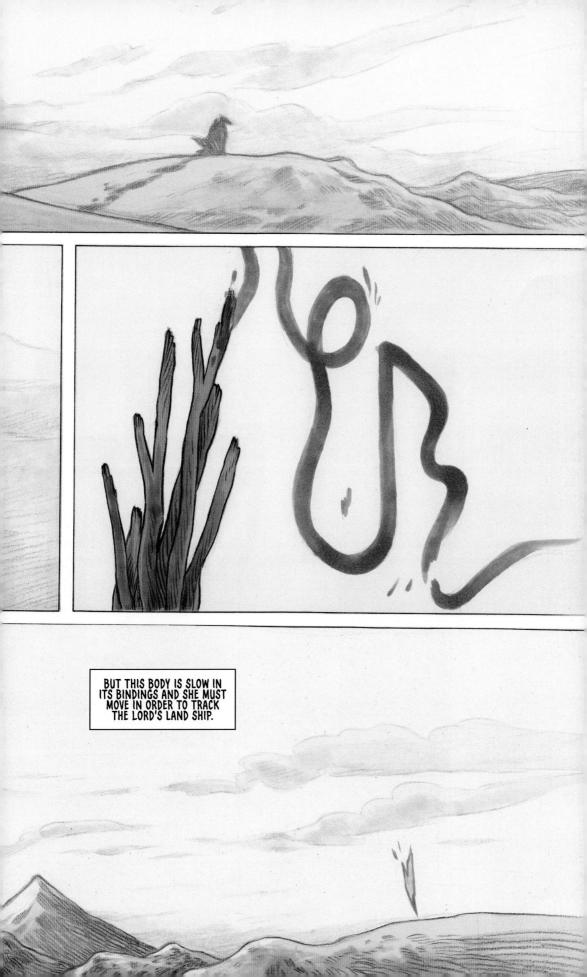

BUT THIS BODY IS SLOW IN
ITS BINDINGS AND SHE MUST
MOVE IN ORDER TO TRACK
THE LORD'S LAND SHIP.

THE LAND SHIP:
IEMUHM.

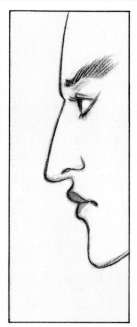

THE DAYS ARE
LONG, INSIDE THE
BONE PALACE;

DAYS SPENT
WATCHING THE THING
IN LADY'S BODY,

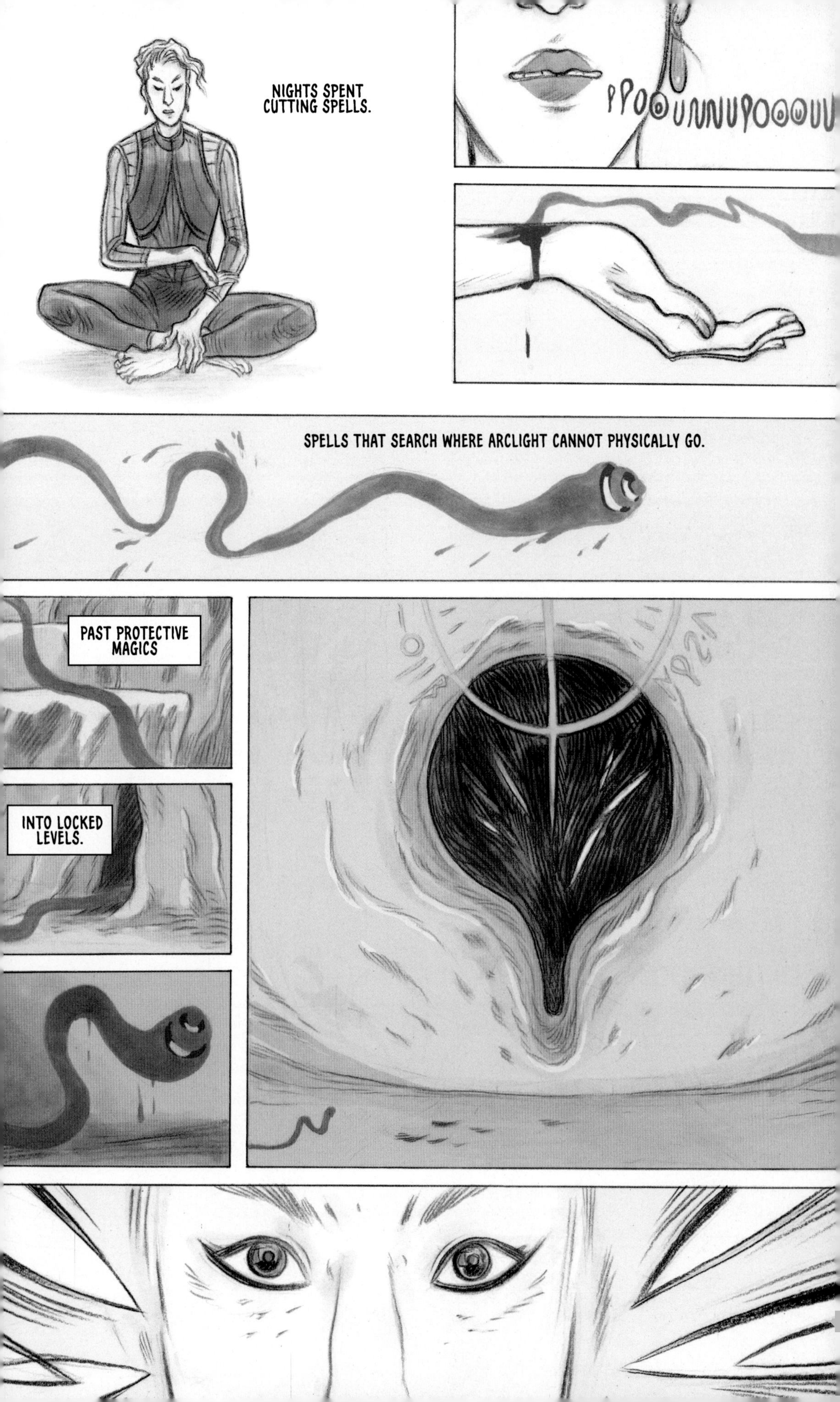

NIGHTS SPENT CUTTING SPELLS.
SPELLS THAT SEARCH WHERE ARCLIGHT CANNOT PHYSICALLY GO.
PAST PROTECTIVE MAGICS
INTO LOCKED LEVELS.

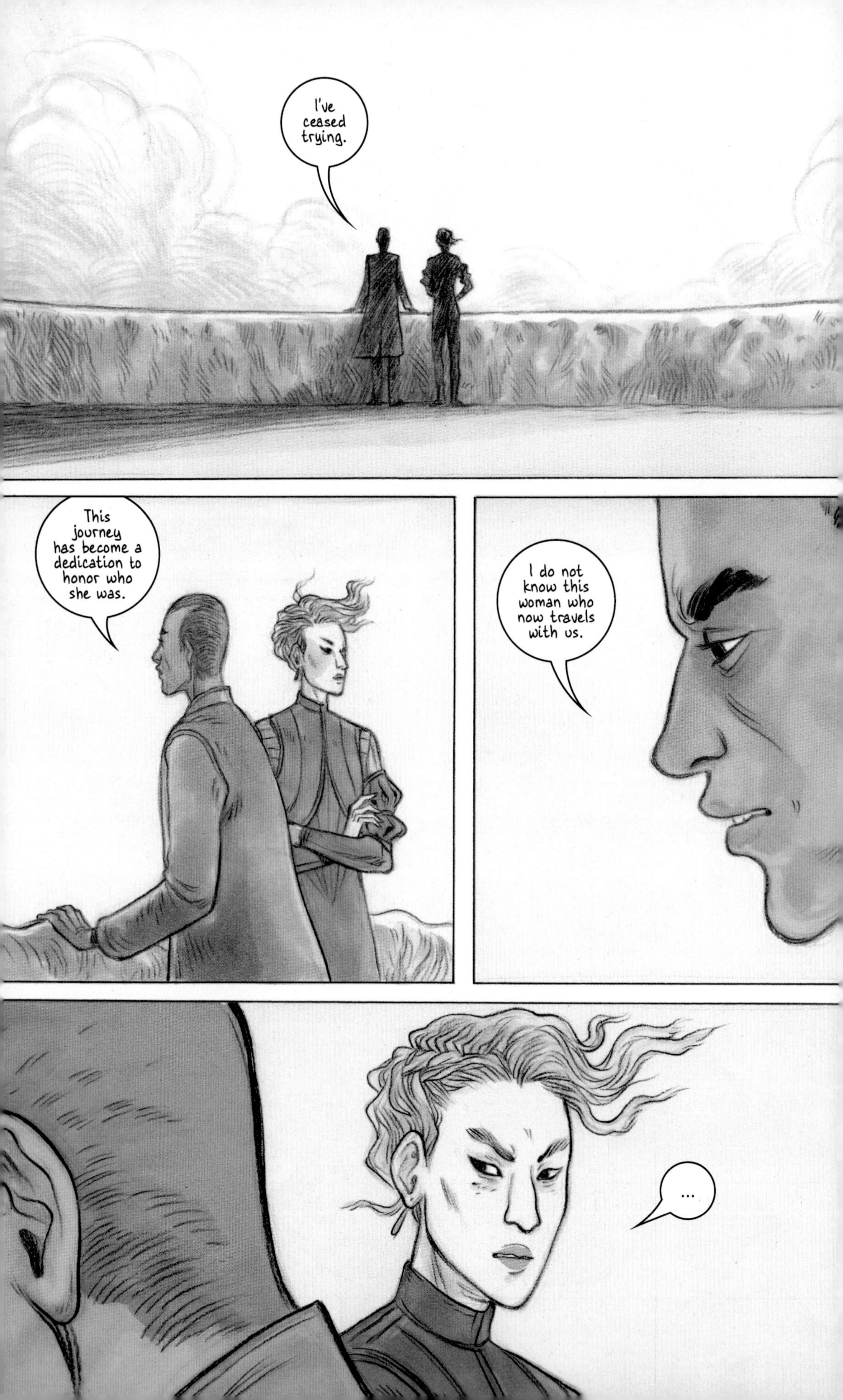
I've ceased trying.
This journey has become a dedication to honor who she was.
I do not know this woman who now travels with us.
...

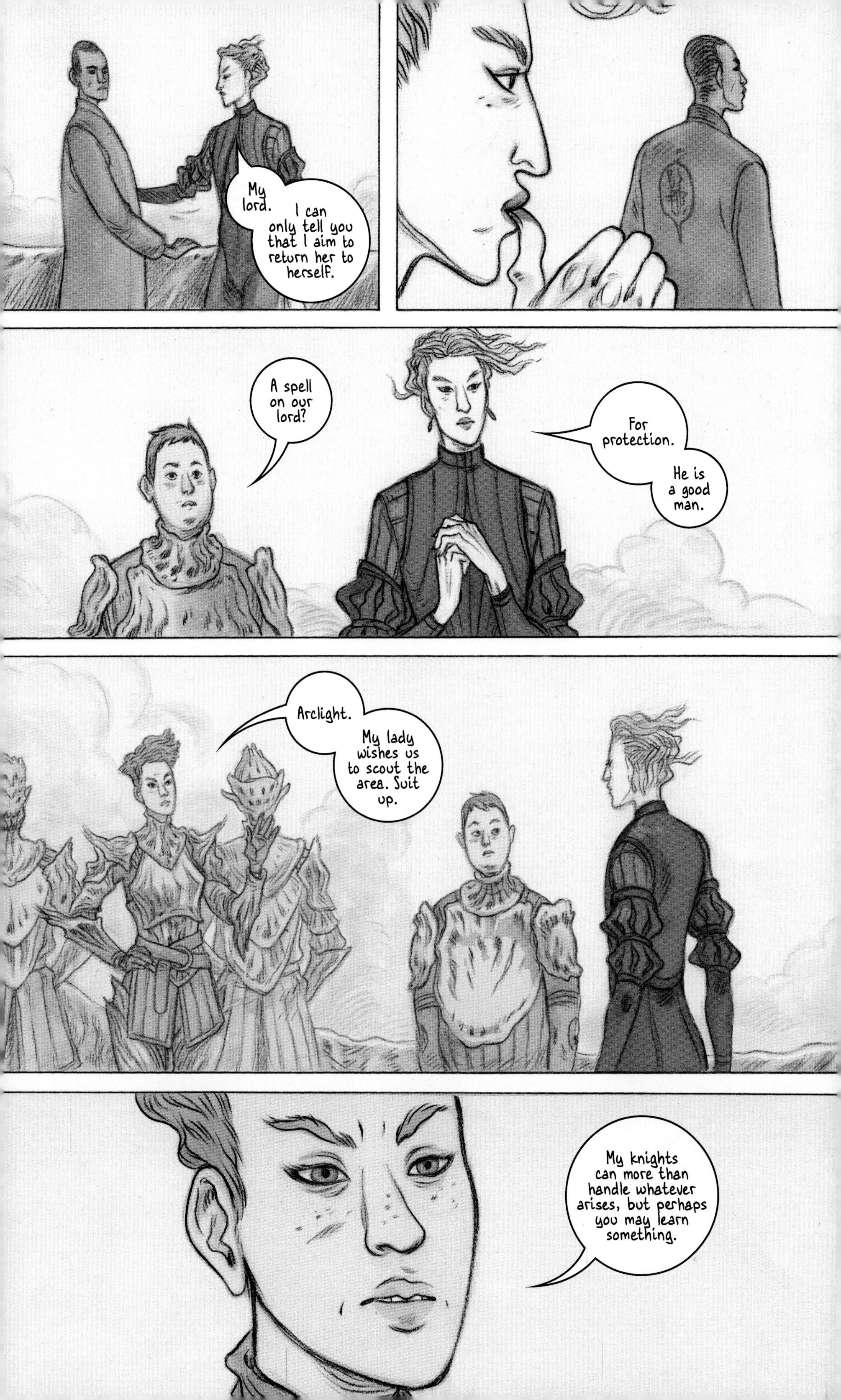
My lord.
I can only tell you that I aim to return her to herself.
A spell on our lord?
For protection.
He is a good man.
Arclight.
My lady wishes us to scout the area. Suit up.
My knights can more than handle whatever arises, but perhaps you may learn something.

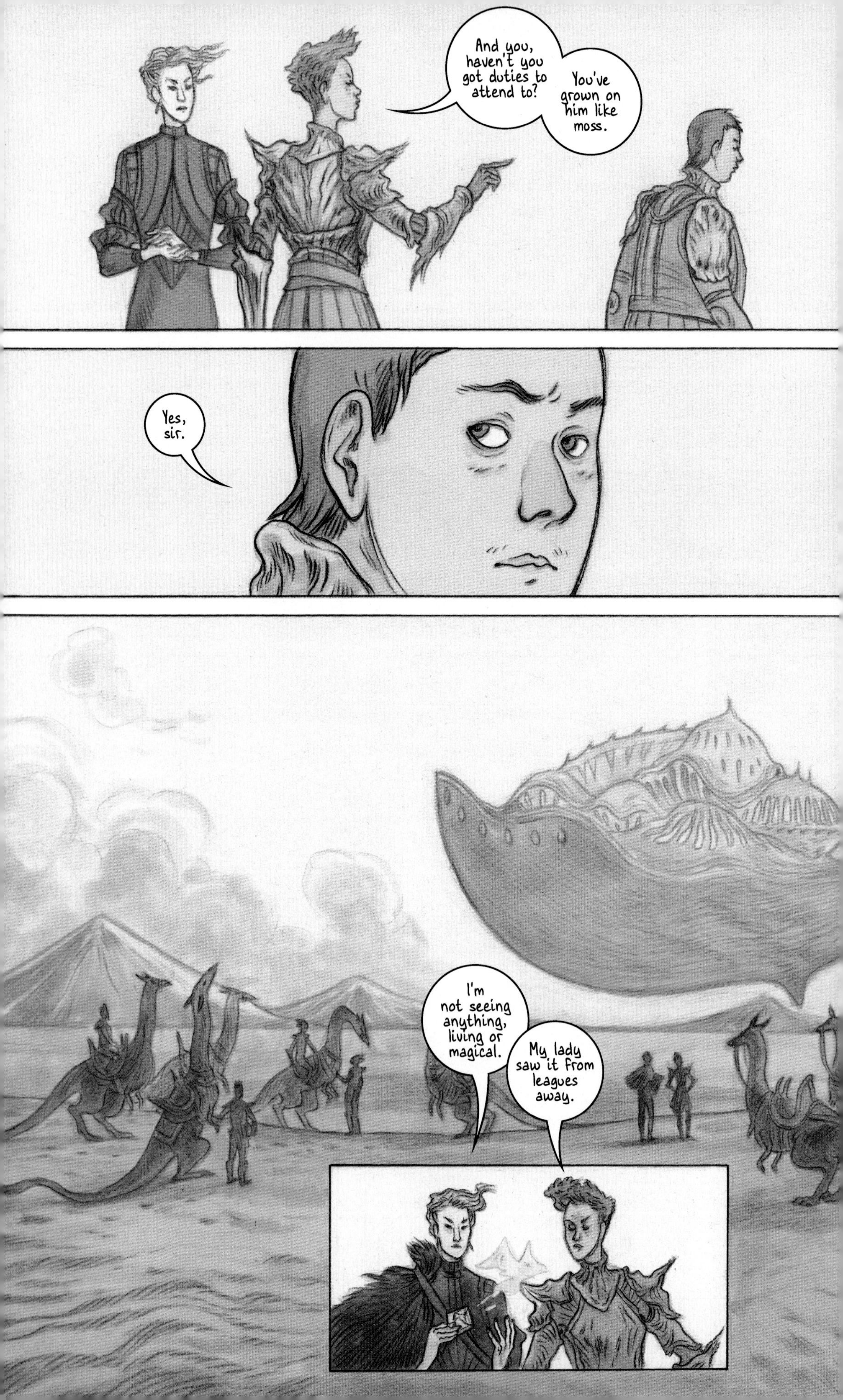
And you, haven't you got duties to attend to?
You've grown on him like moss.
Yes, sir.
I'm not seeing anything, living or magical.
My lady saw it from leagues away.

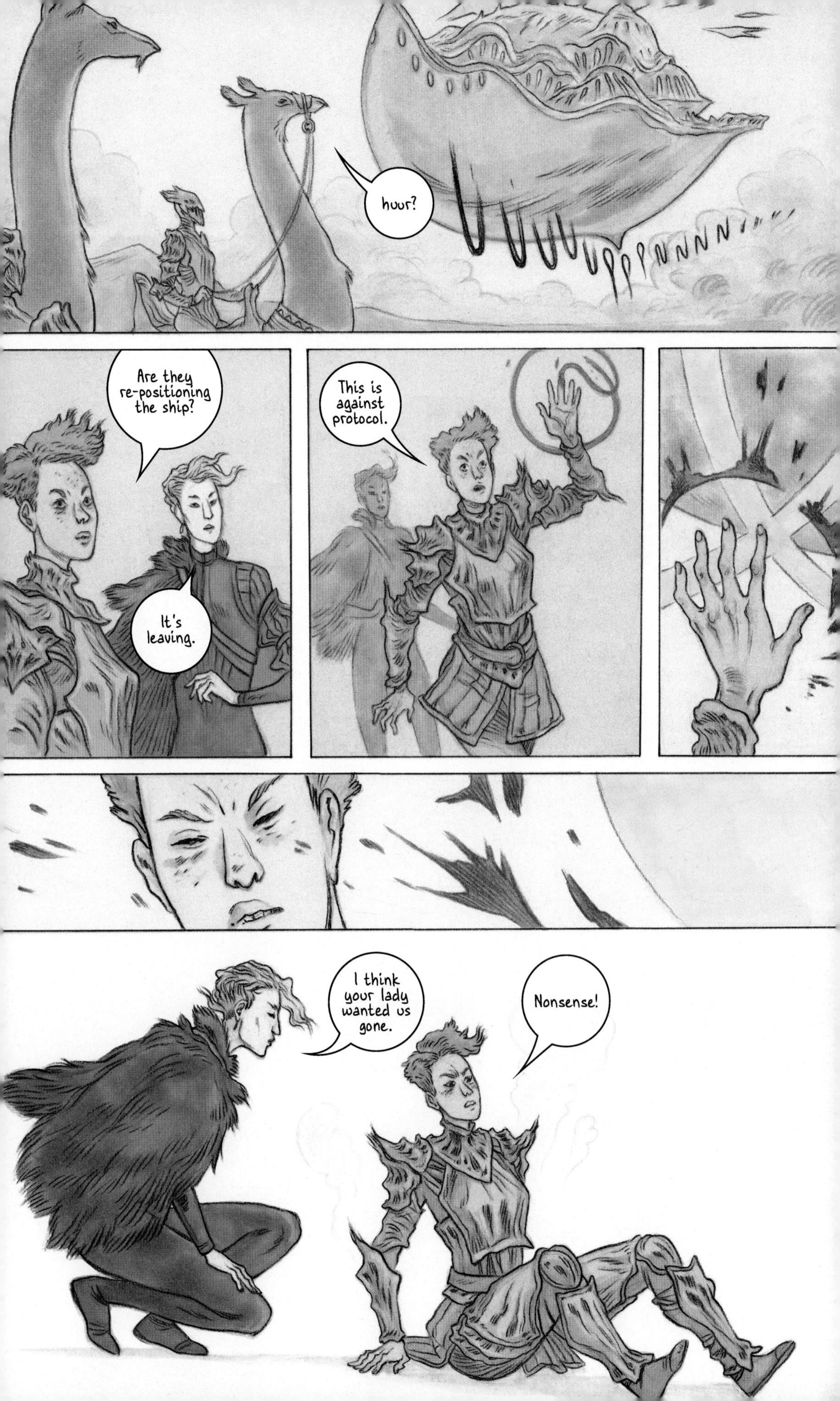

huur?
UUUUUpppNNNN...
Are they re-positioning the ship?
It's leaving.
This is against protocol.
I think your lady wanted us gone.
Nonsense!

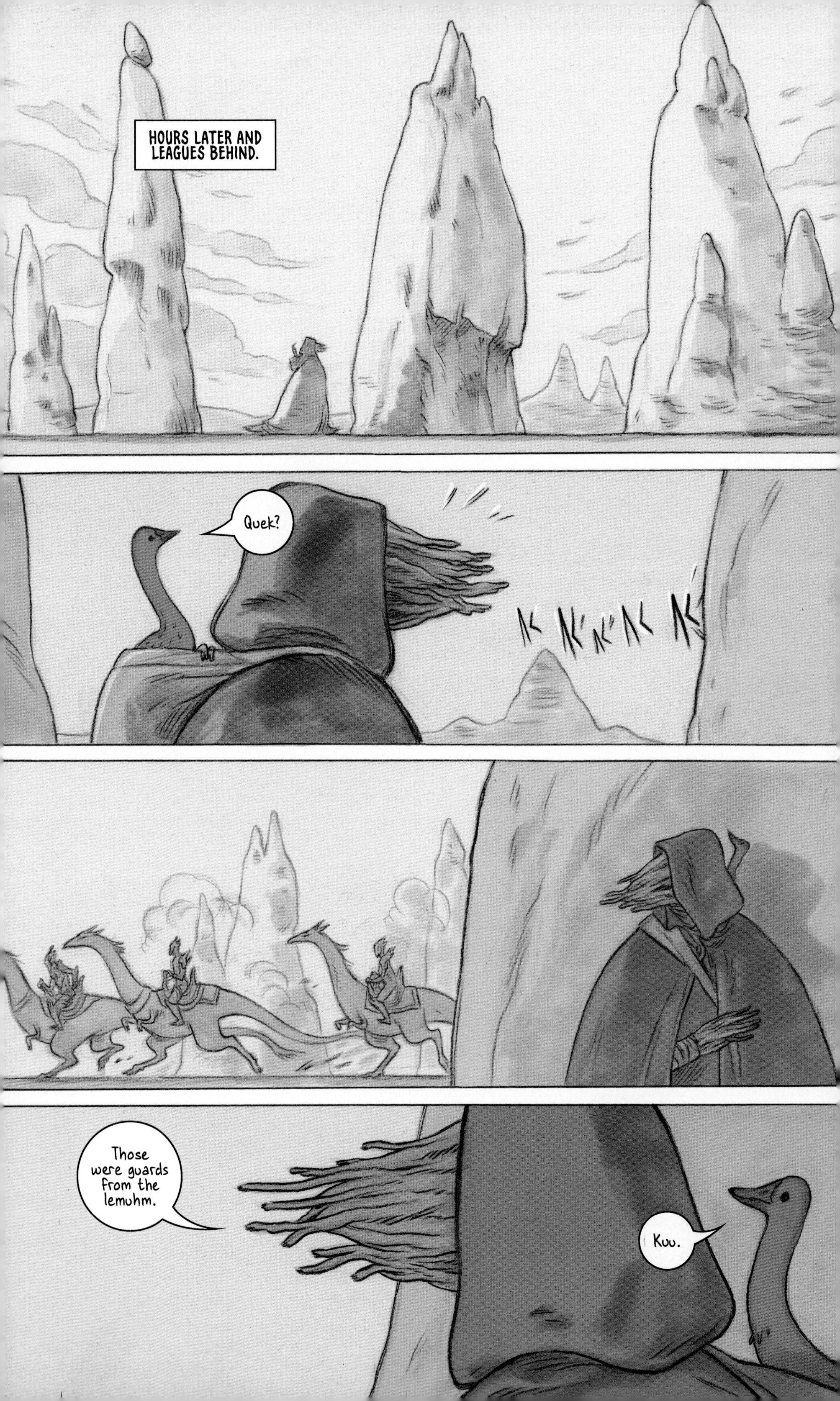
HOURS LATER AND LEAGUES BEHIND.
Quek?
Those were guards from the lemuhm.
Kuu.

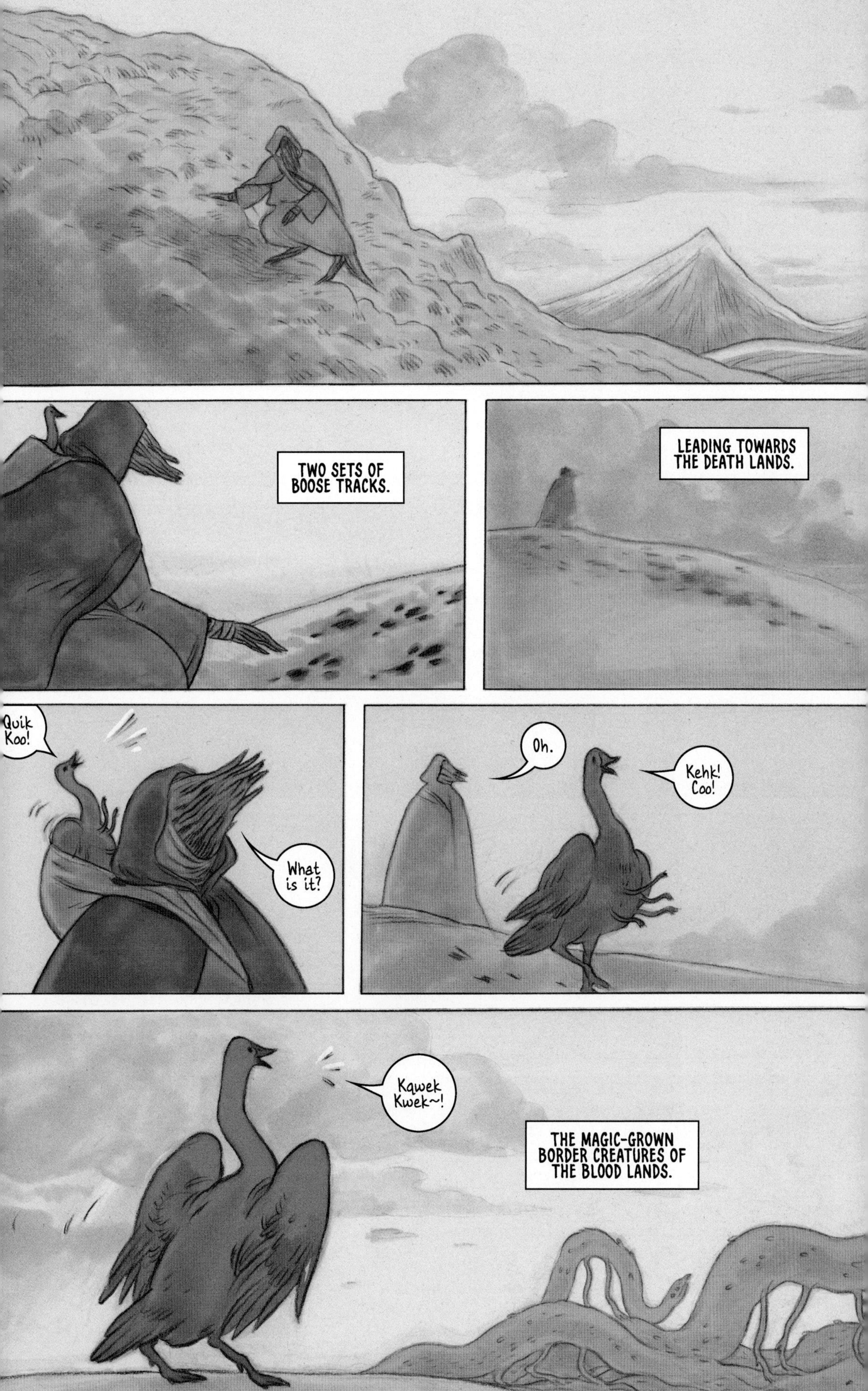
TWO SETS OF BOOSE TRACKS.
LEADING TOWARDS THE DEATH LANDS.
Quik Koo!
What is it?
Oh.
Kehk! Coo!
Kqwek Kwek~!
THE MAGIC-GROWN BORDER CREATURES OF THE BLOOD LANDS.

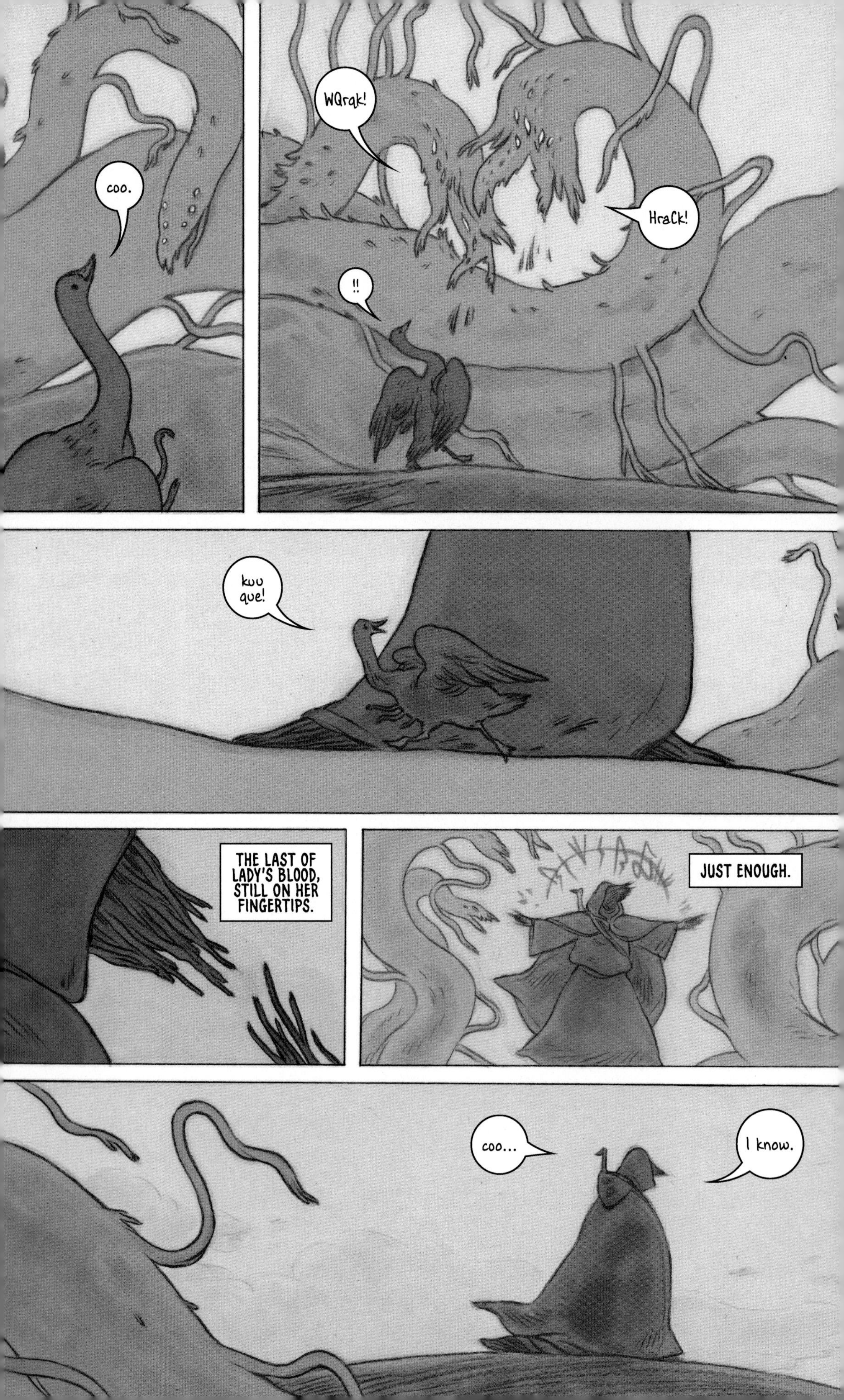
coo.
WQrqk!
HraCk!
!!
kuu que!
THE LAST OF LADY'S BLOOD, STILL ON HER FINGERTIPS.
JUST ENOUGH.
coo...
I know.

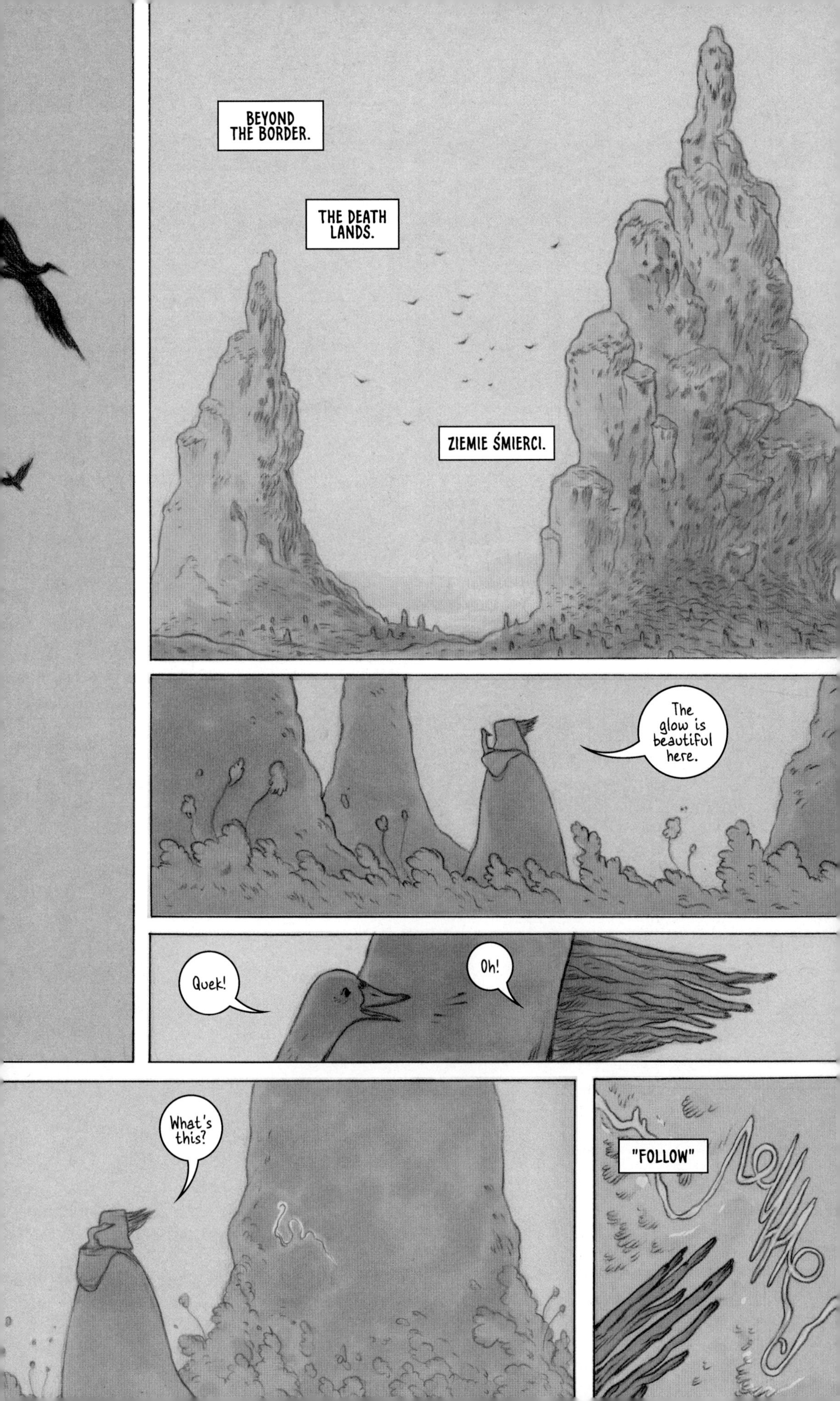

BEYOND THE BORDER.
THE DEATH LANDS.
ZIEMIE ŚMIERCI.
The glow is beautiful here.
Quek!
Oh!
What's this?
"FOLLOW"

THE LIGHT SPILLS FROM THE ROCKFACE AND DANCES ACROSS THE LICHEN.

Quee!

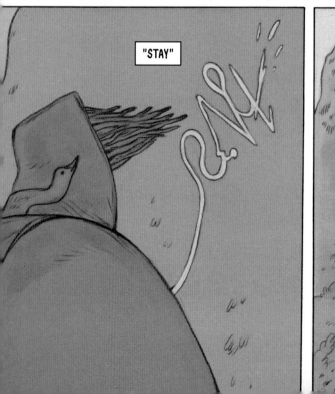

"STAY"

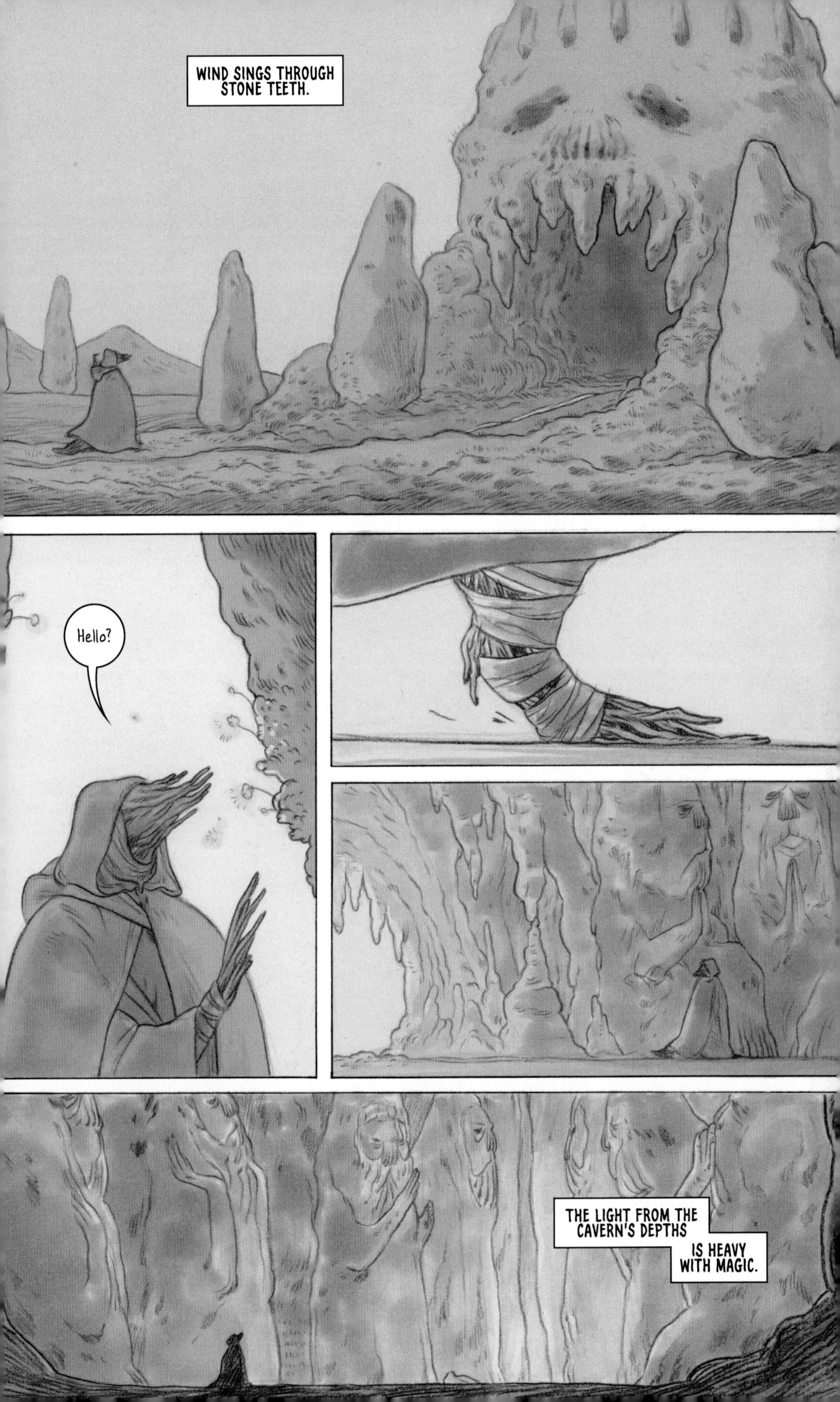
WIND SINGS THROUGH STONE TEETH.
Hello?
THE LIGHT FROM THE CAVERN'S DEPTHS
IS HEAVY WITH MAGIC.

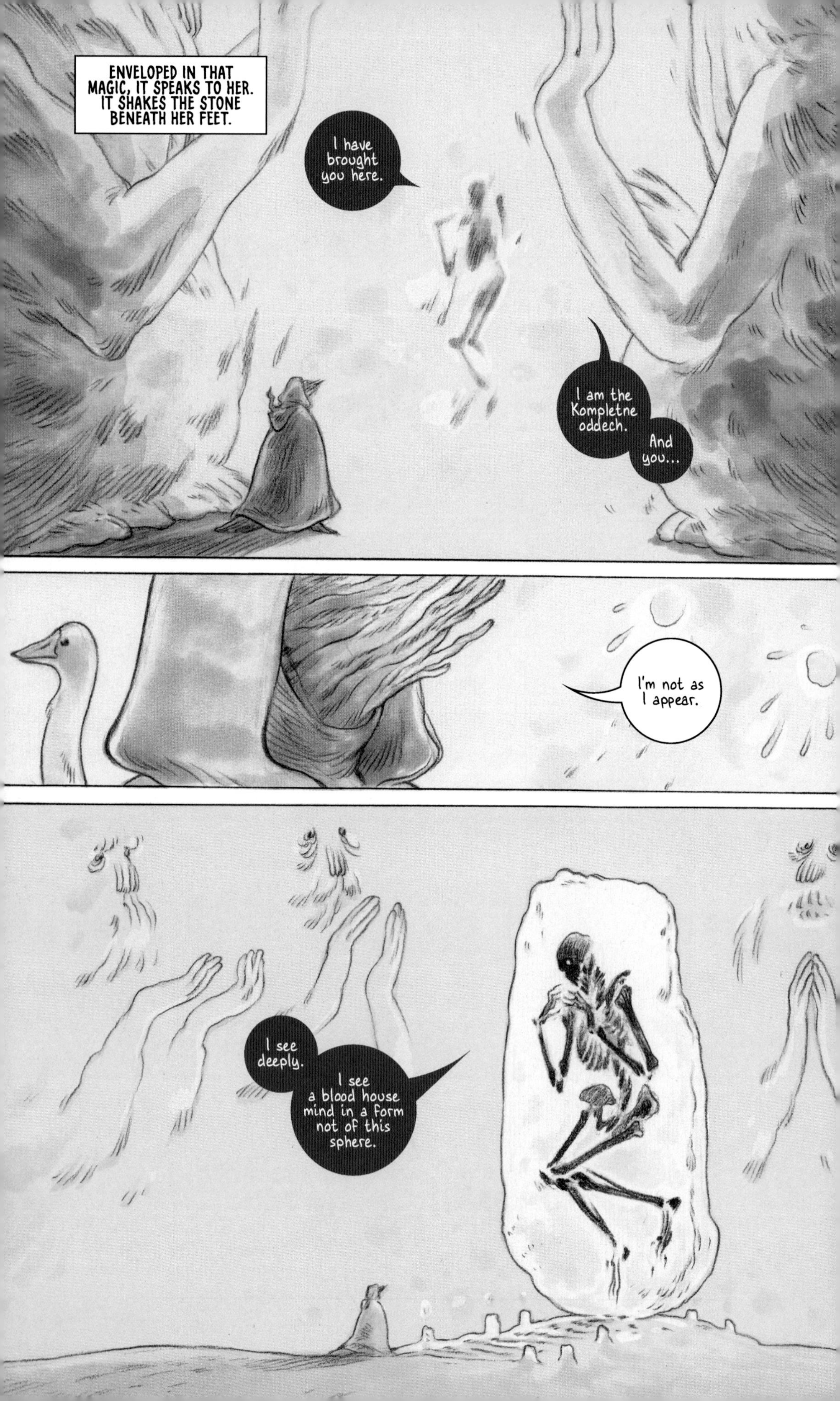
ENVELOPED IN THAT MAGIC, IT SPEAKS TO HER. IT SHAKES THE STONE BENEATH HER FEET.
I have brought you here.
I am the Kompletne oddech.
And you...
I'm not as I appear.
I see deeply.
I see a blood house mind in a form not of this sphere.

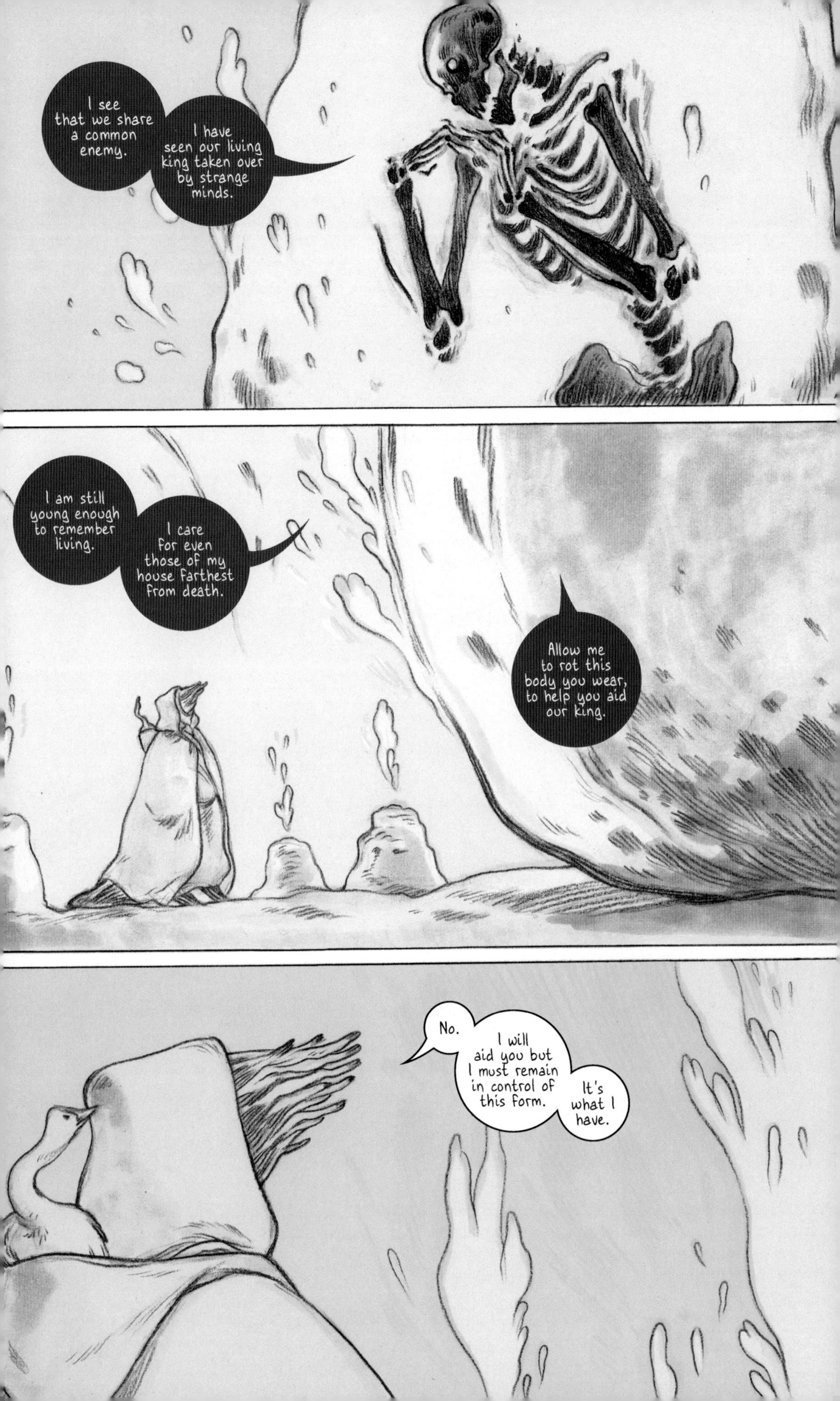
I see that we share a common enemy.
I have seen our living king taken over by strange minds.
I am still young enough to remember living.
I care for even those of my house farthest from death.
Allow me to rot this body you wear, to help you aid our king.
No.
I will aid you but I must remain in control of this form.
It's what I have.

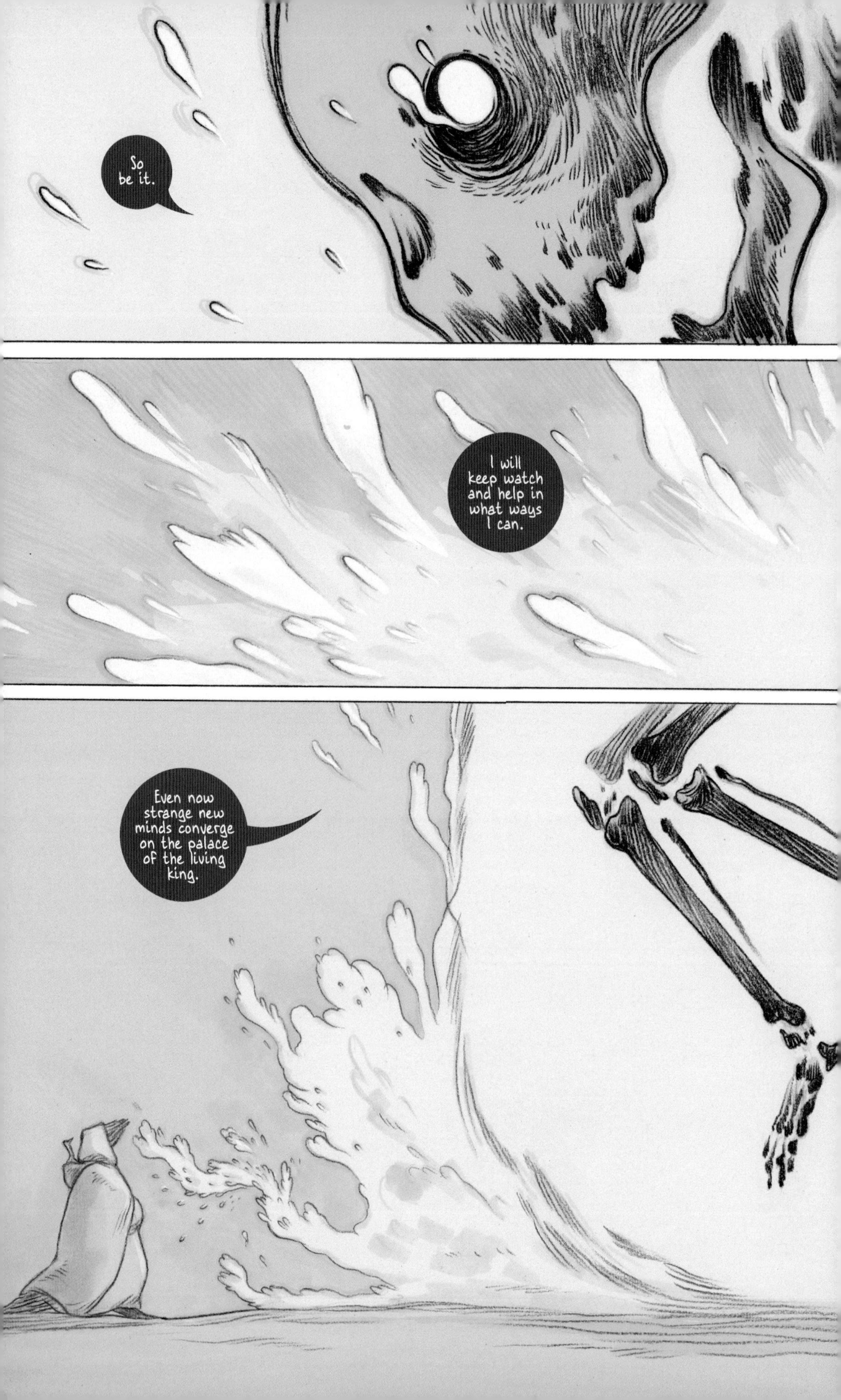

So be it.
I will keep watch and help in what ways I can.
Even now strange new minds converge on the palace of the living king.

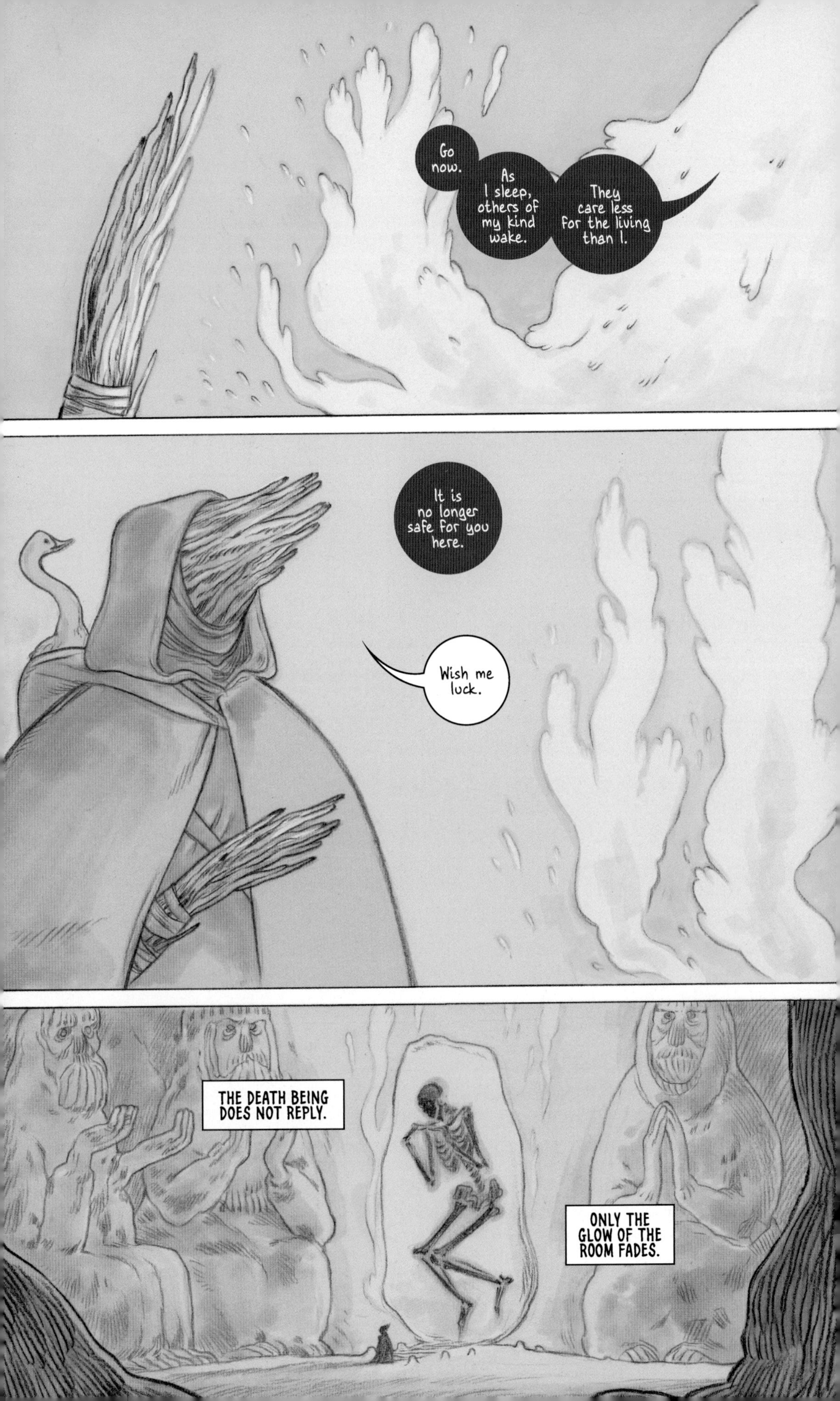
Go now.
As I sleep, others of my kind wake.
They care less for the living than I.
It is no longer safe for you here.
Wish me luck.
THE DEATH BEING DOES NOT REPLY.
ONLY THE GLOW OF THE ROOM FADES.

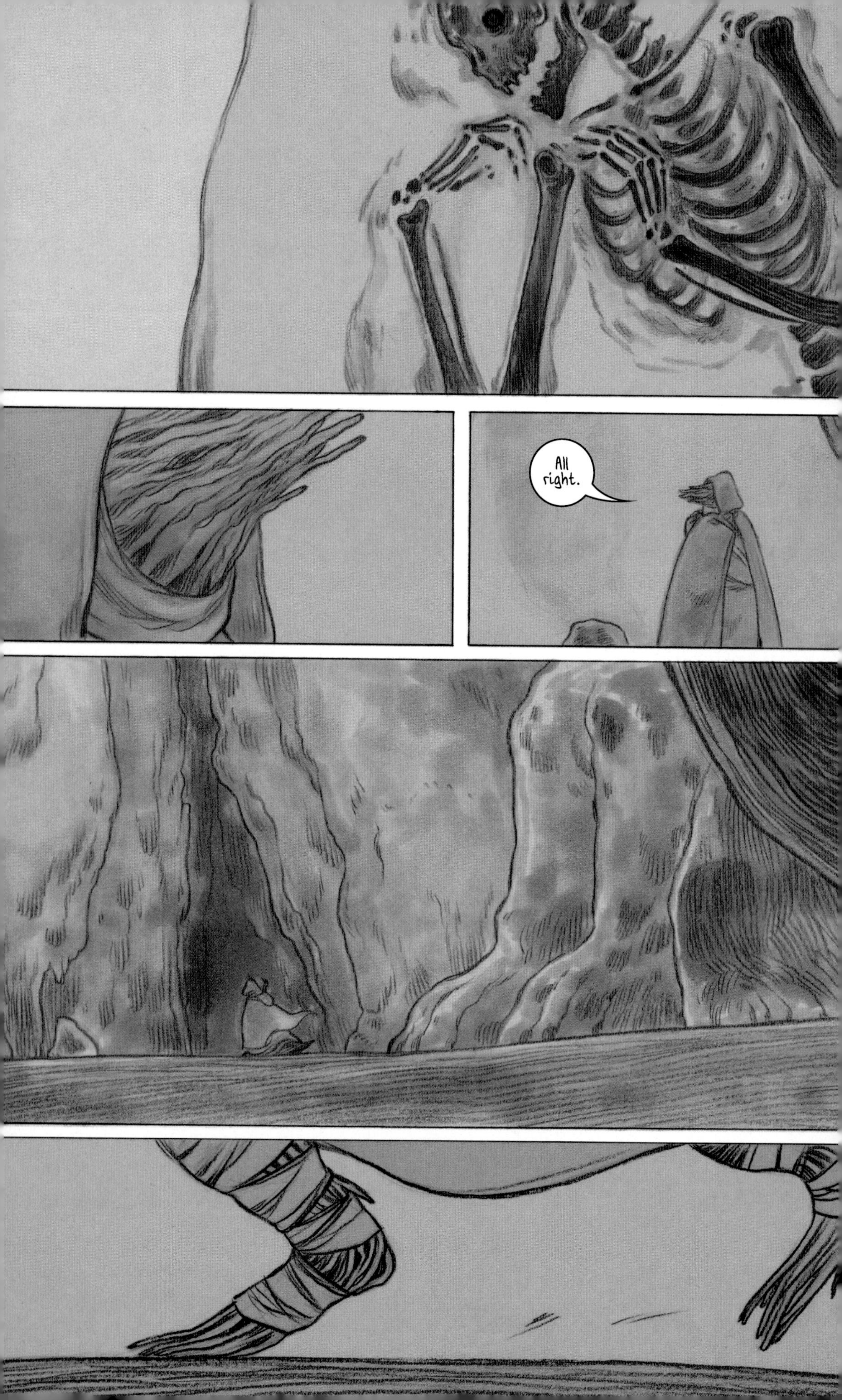
All right.

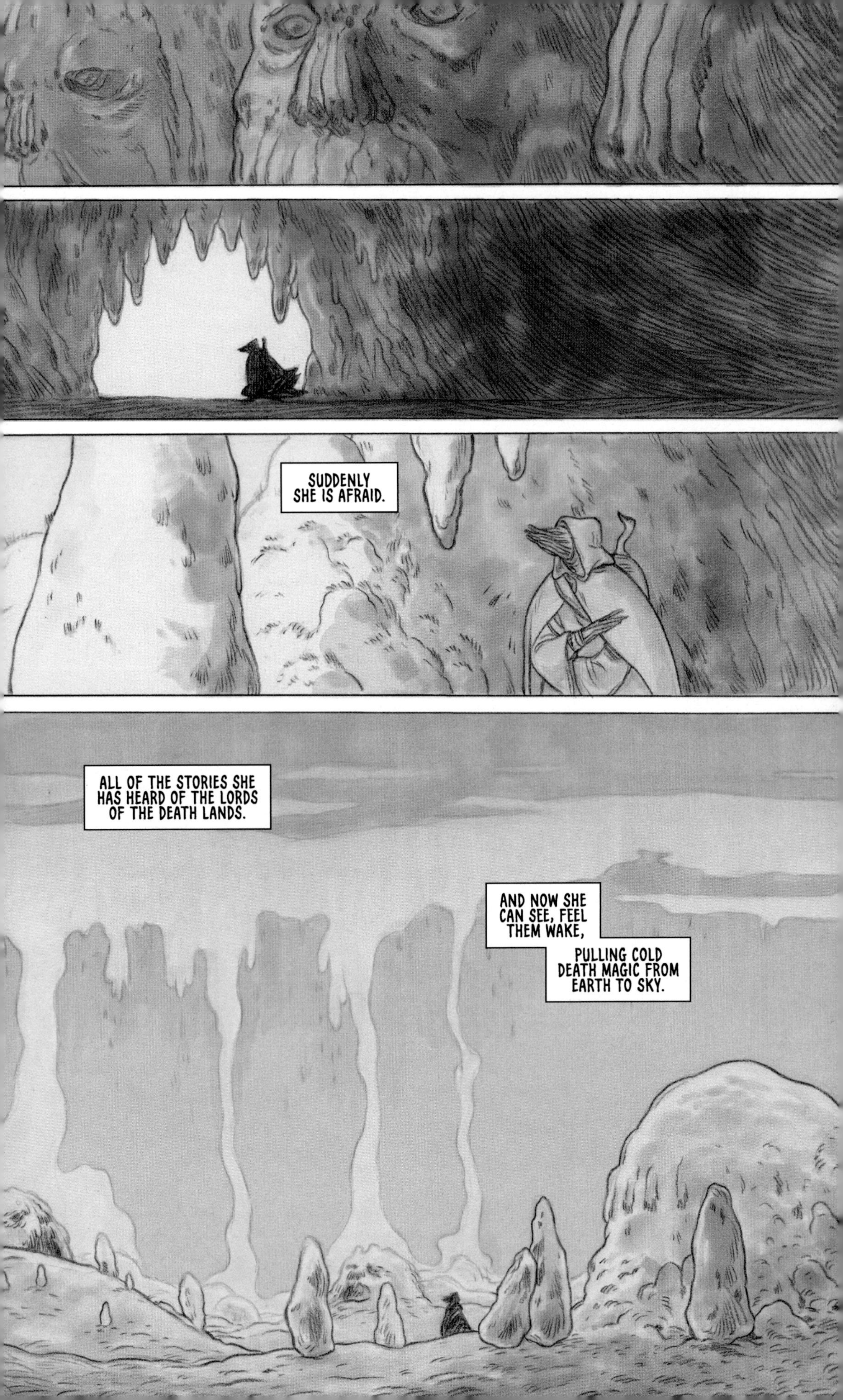
SUDDENLY SHE IS AFRAID.
ALL OF THE STORIES SHE HAS HEARD OF THE LORDS OF THE DEATH LANDS.
AND NOW SHE CAN SEE, FEEL THEM WAKE,
PULLING COLD DEATH MAGIC FROM EARTH TO SKY.

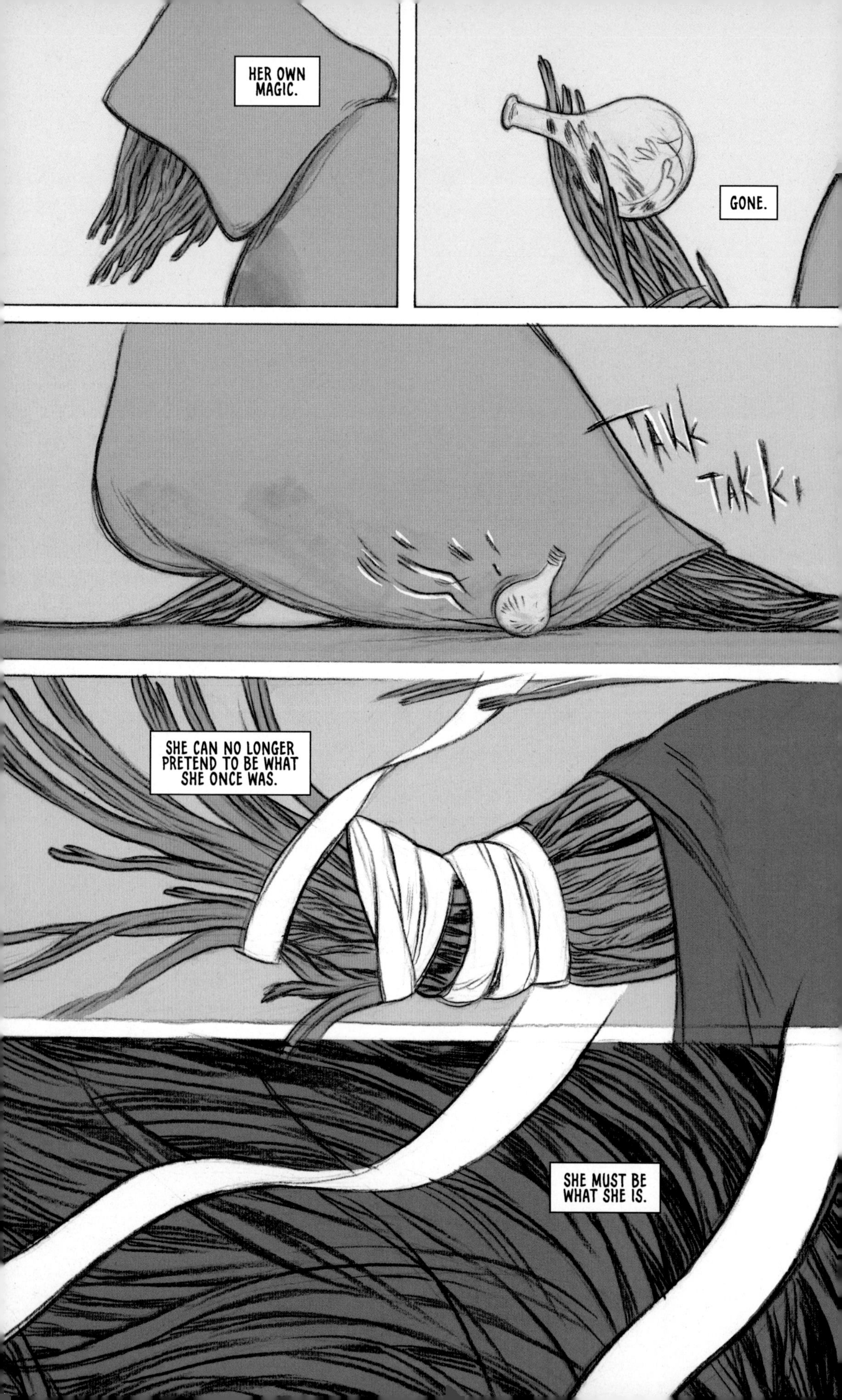
HER OWN MAGIC.
GONE.
TAKK
TAKK
SHE CAN NO LONGER PRETEND TO BE WHAT SHE ONCE WAS.
SHE MUST BE WHAT SHE IS.

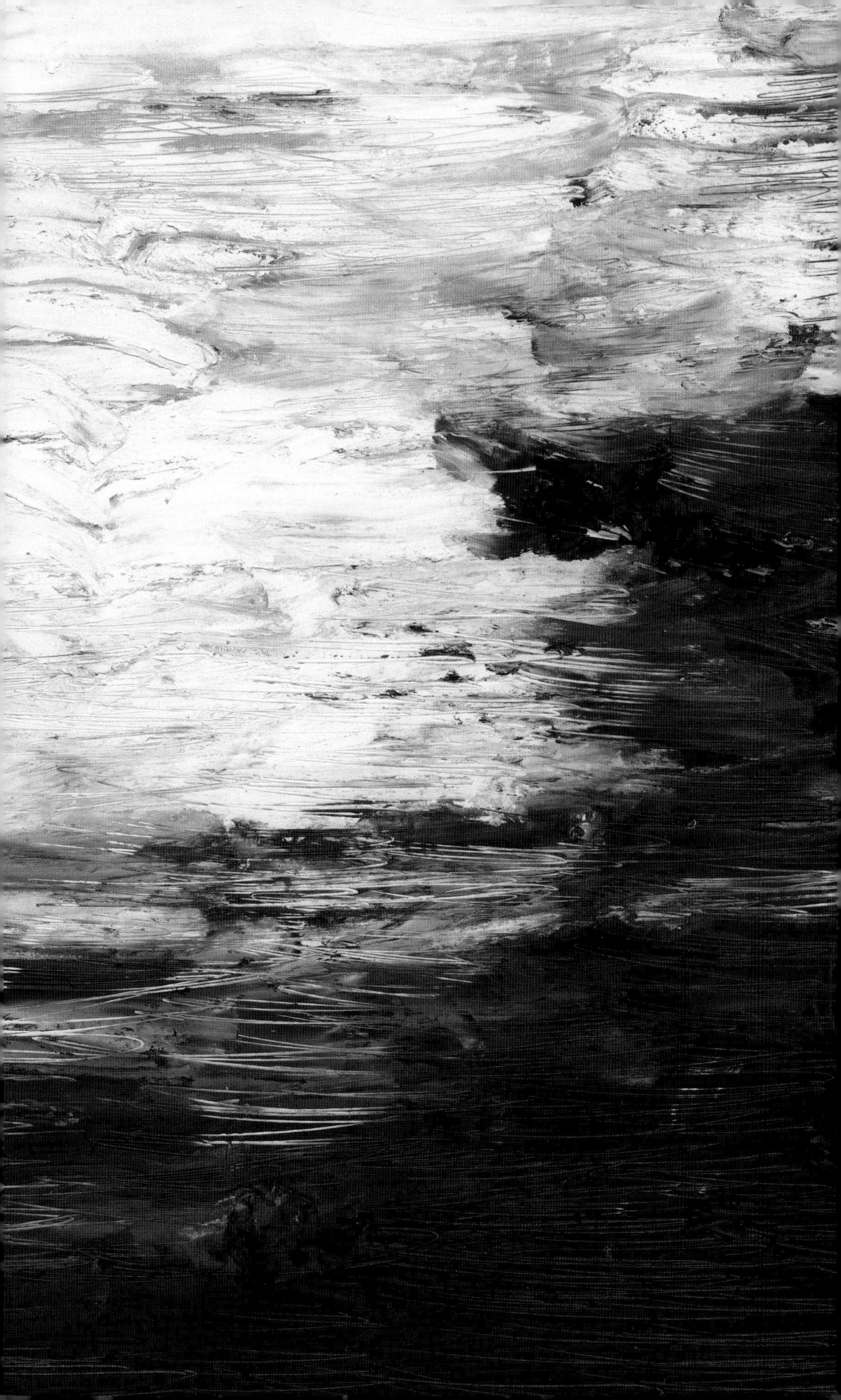

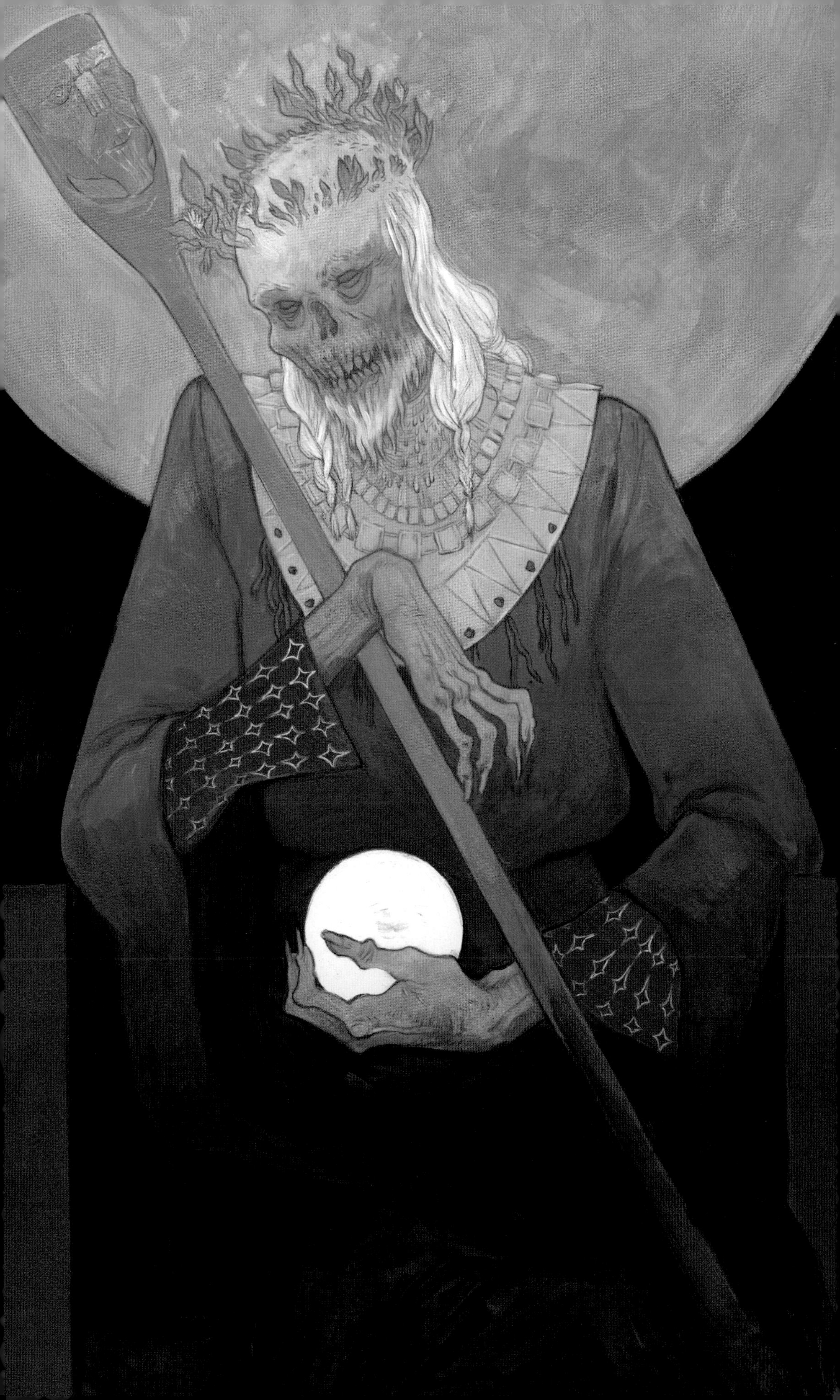

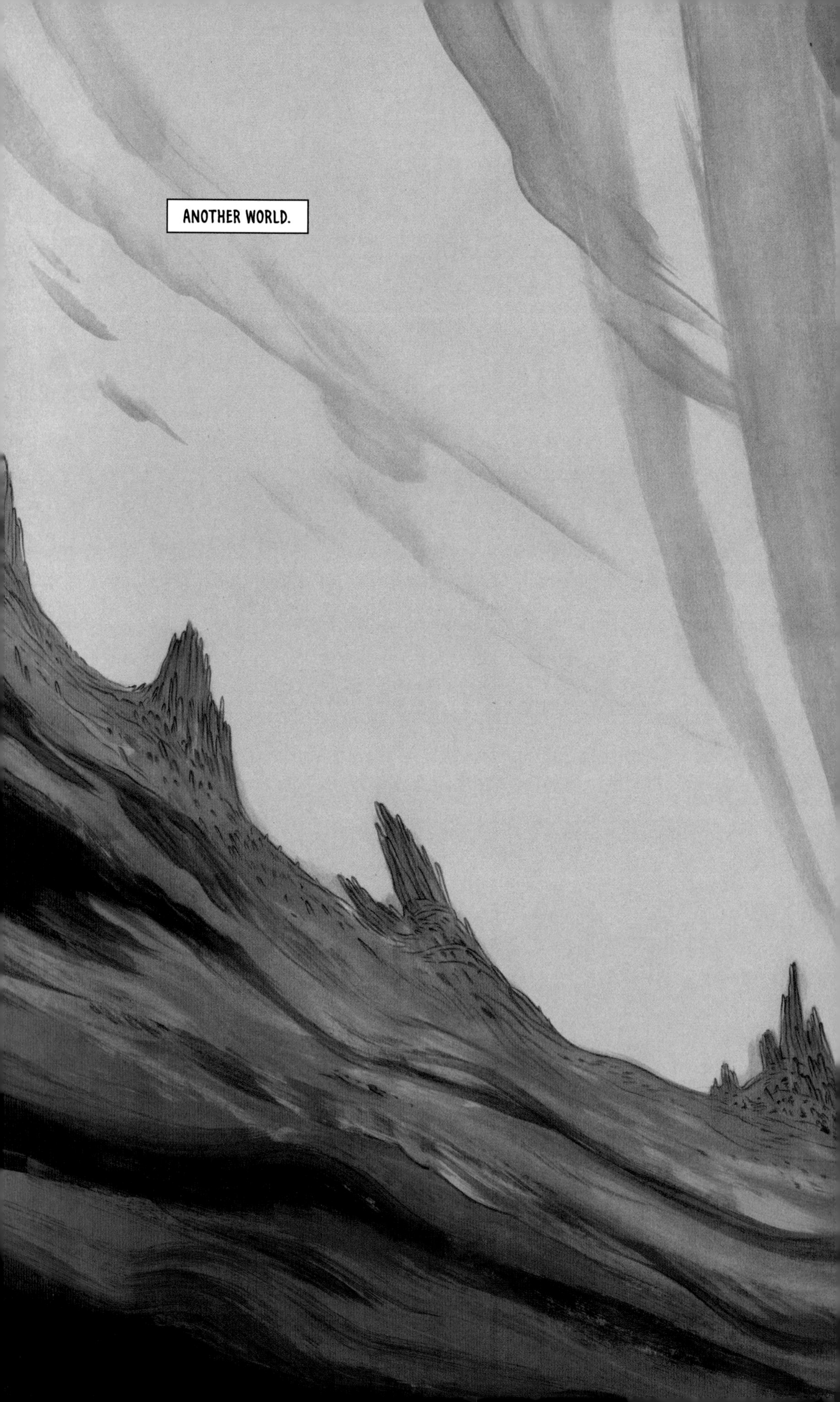
ANOTHER WORLD.

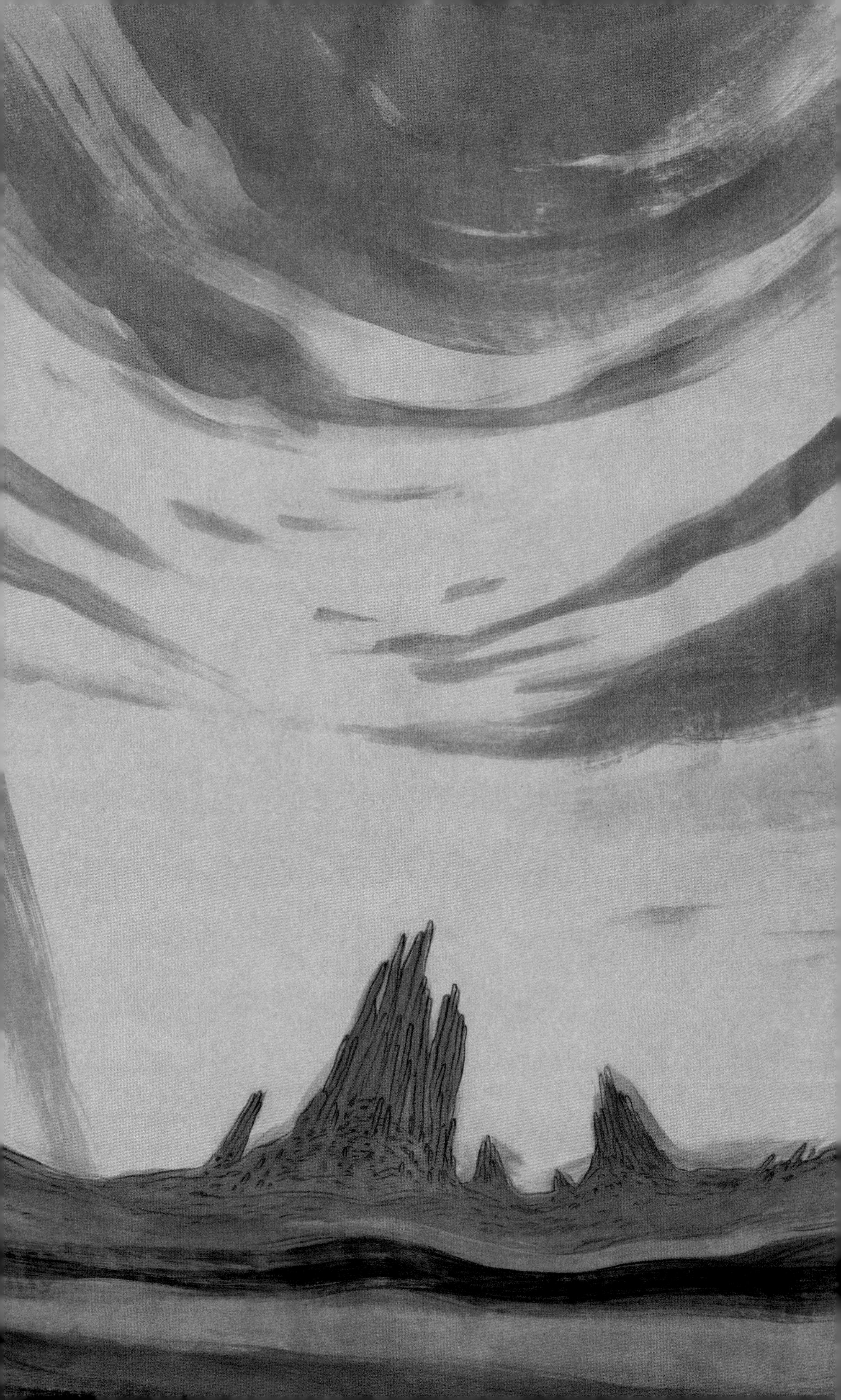

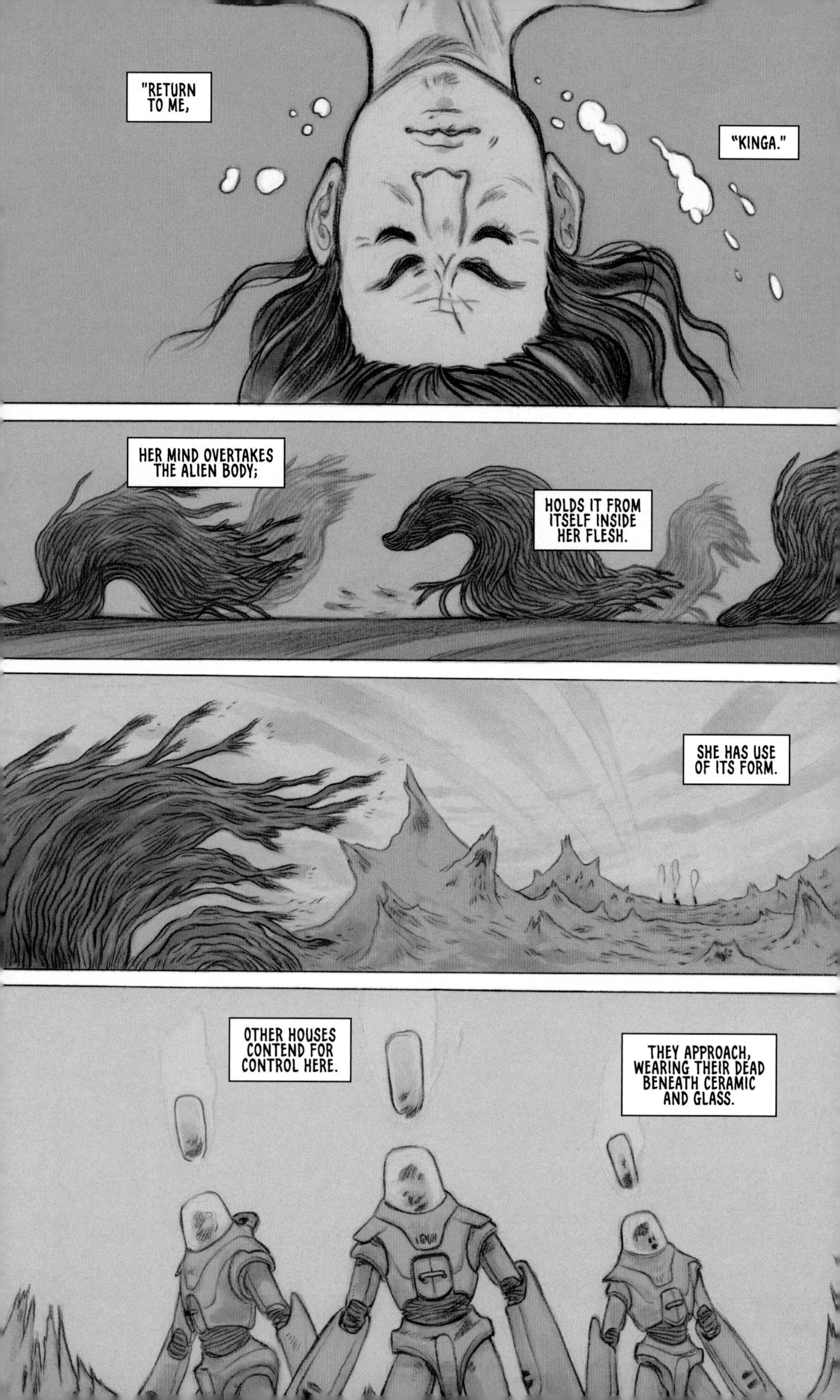
"RETURN TO ME,
"KINGA."
HER MIND OVERTAKES THE ALIEN BODY;
HOLDS IT FROM ITSELF INSIDE HER FLESH.
SHE HAS USE OF ITS FORM.
OTHER HOUSES CONTEND FOR CONTROL HERE.
THEY APPROACH, WEARING THEIR DEAD BENEATH CERAMIC AND GLASS.

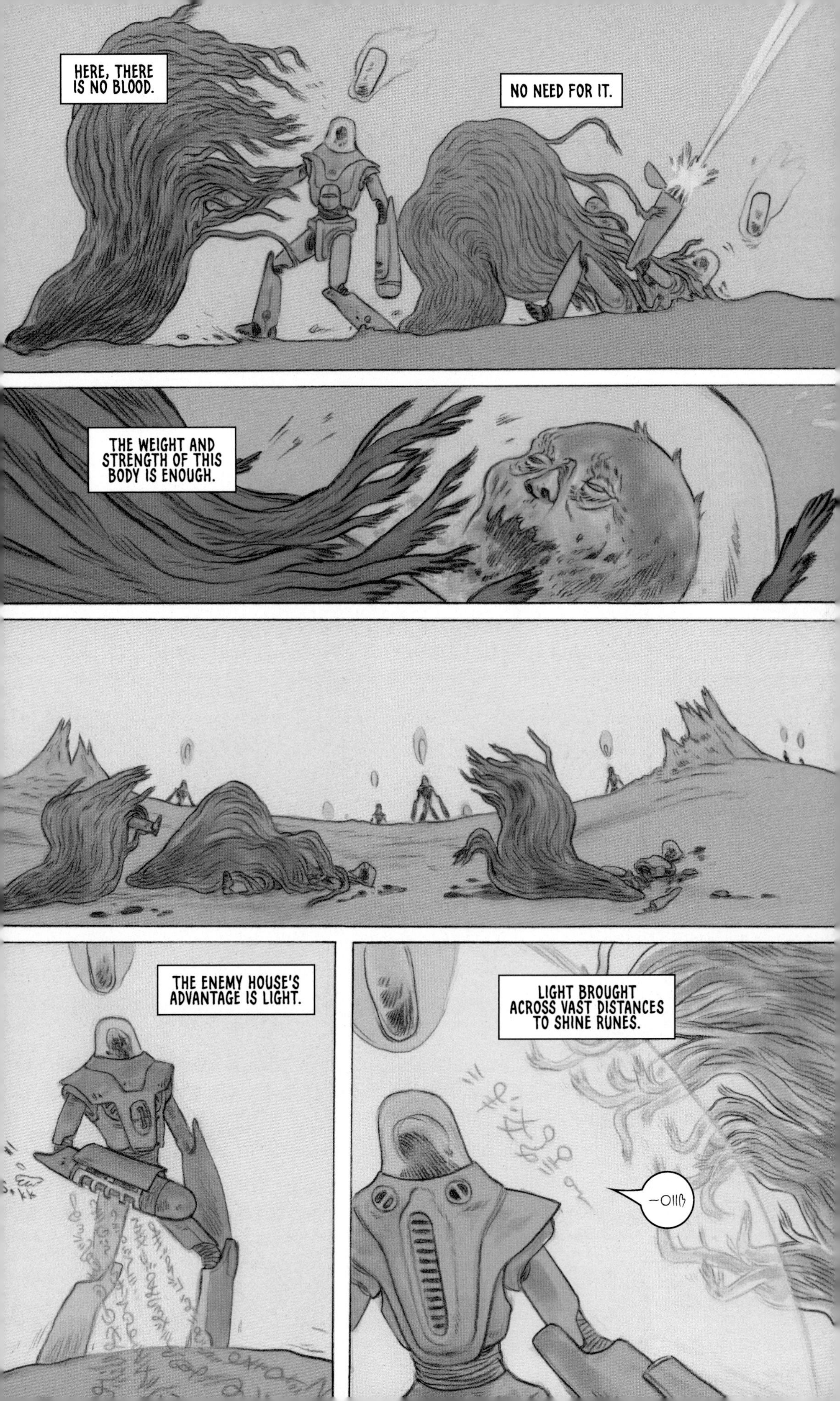
HERE, THERE IS NO BLOOD.
NO NEED FOR IT.
THE WEIGHT AND STRENGTH OF THIS BODY IS ENOUGH.
THE ENEMY HOUSE'S ADVANTAGE IS LIGHT.
LIGHT BROUGHT ACROSS VAST DISTANCES TO SHINE RUNES.

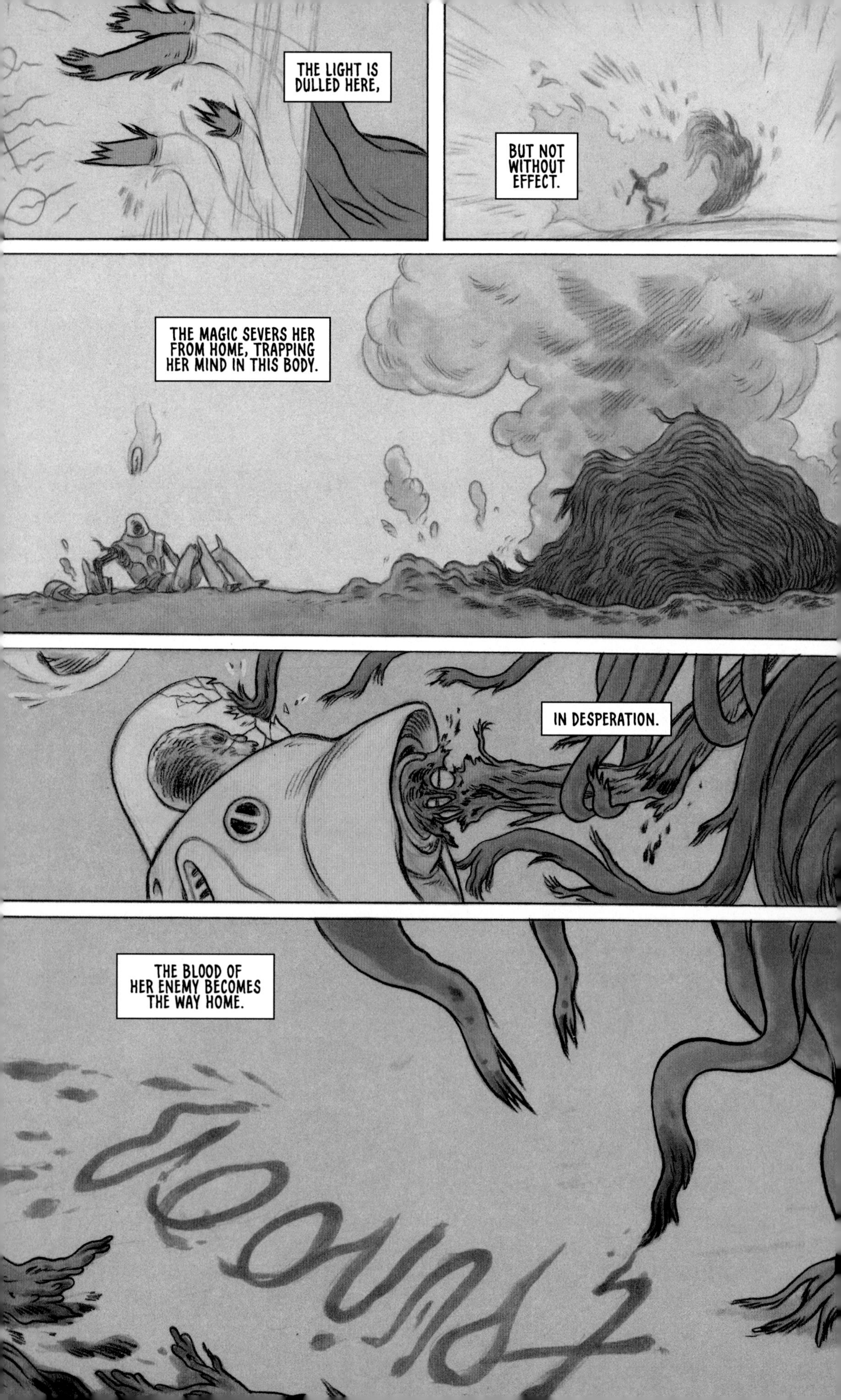
THE LIGHT IS DULLED HERE,
BUT NOT WITHOUT EFFECT.
THE MAGIC SEVERS HER FROM HOME, TRAPPING HER MIND IN THIS BODY.
IN DESPERATION.
THE BLOOD OF HER ENEMY BECOMES THE WAY HOME.

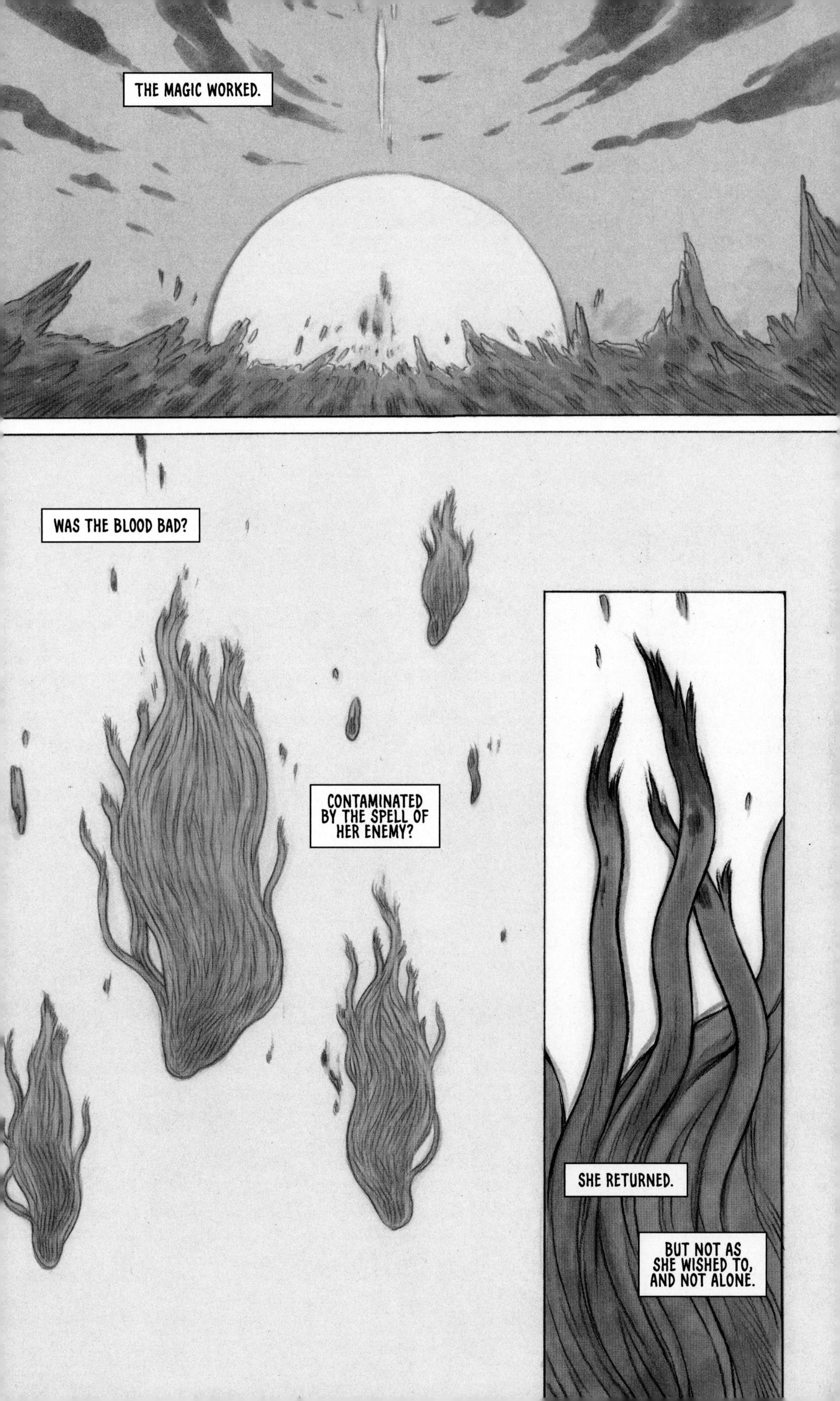
THE MAGIC WORKED.
WAS THE BLOOD BAD?
CONTAMINATED BY THE SPELL OF HER ENEMY?
SHE RETURNED.
BUT NOT AS SHE WISHED TO, AND NOT ALONE.

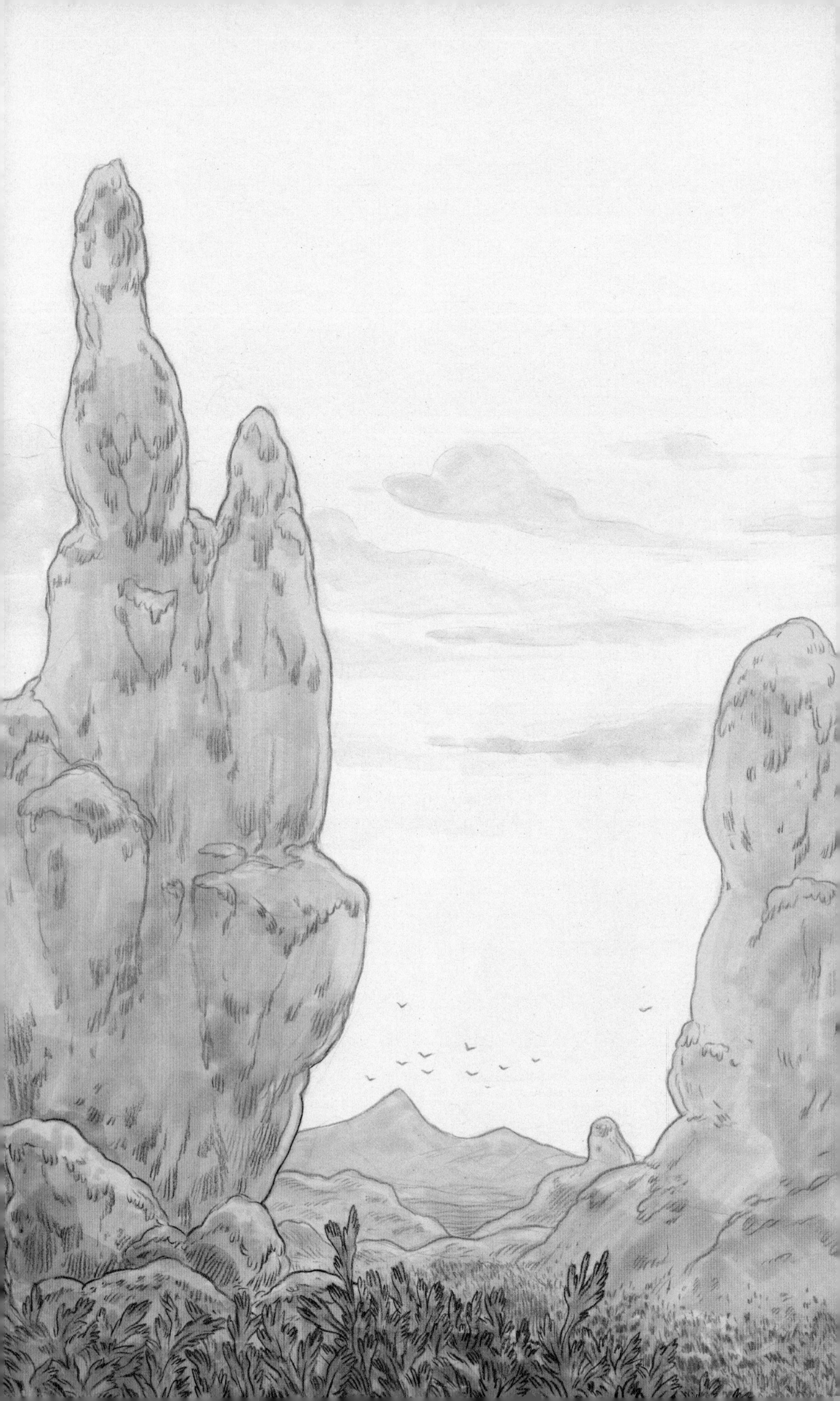

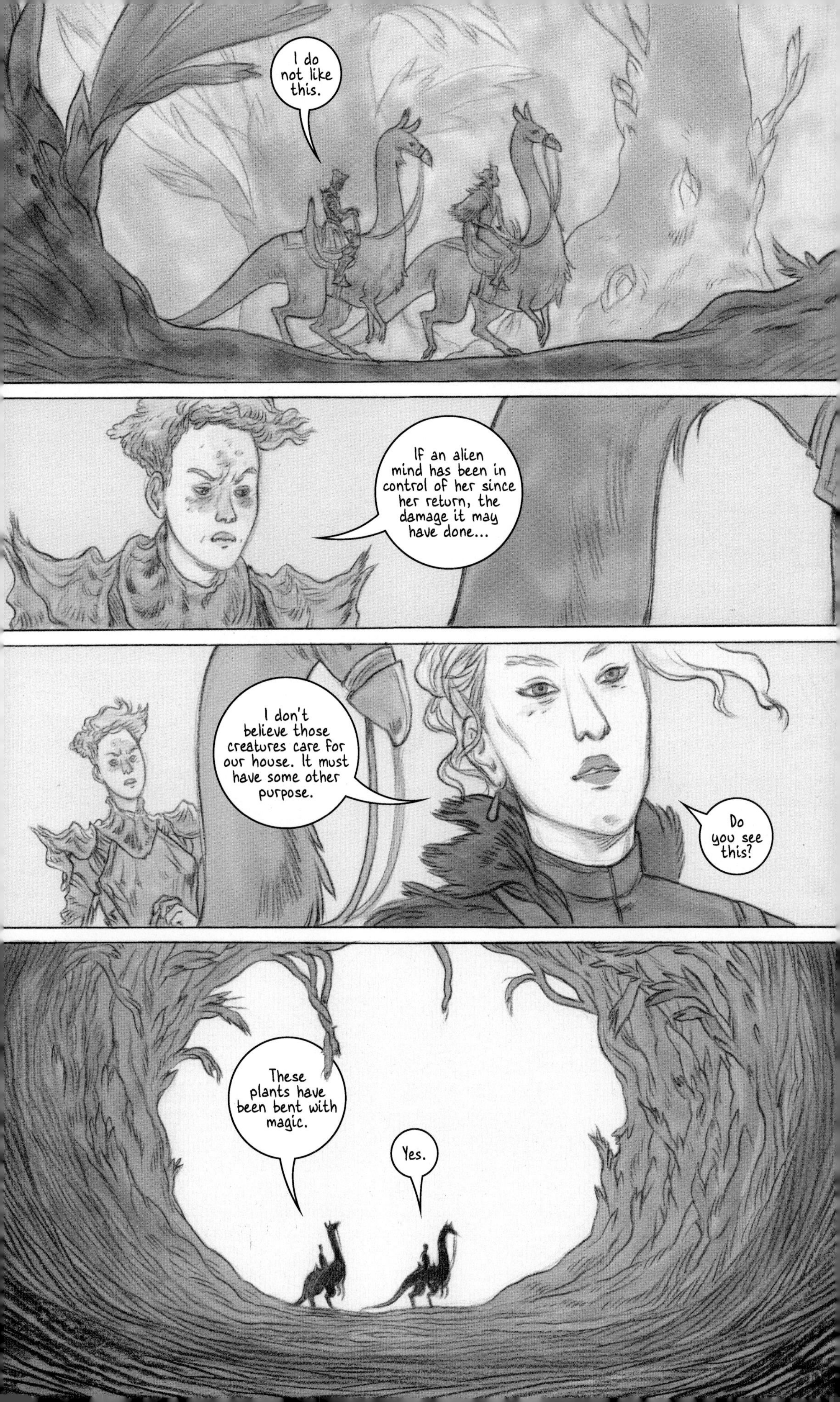
I do not like this.
If an alien mind has been in control of her since her return, the damage it may have done...
I don't believe those creatures care for our house. It must have some other purpose.
Do you see this?
These plants have been bent with magic.
Yes.

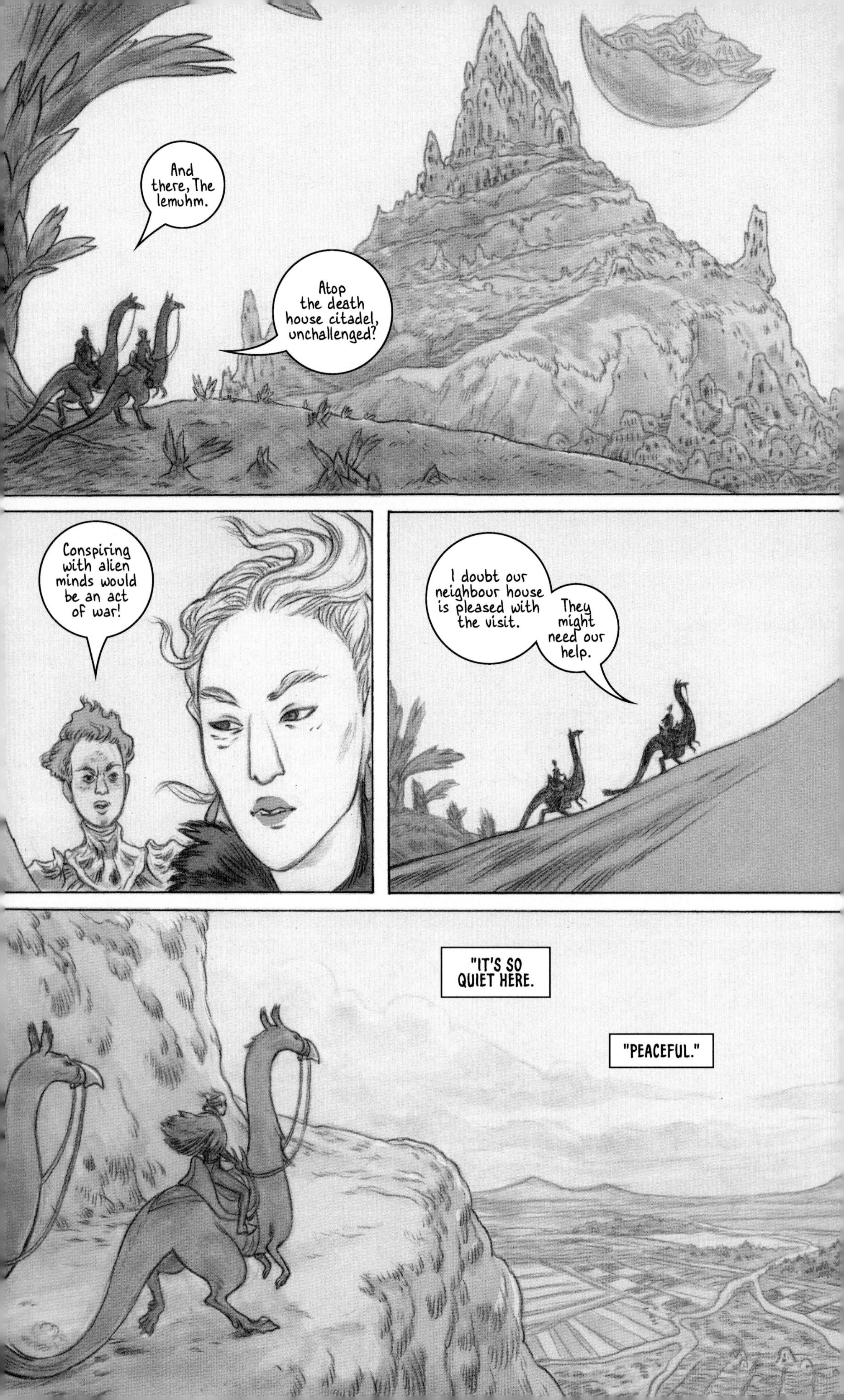
And there, The lemuhm.
Atop the death house citadel, unchallenged?
Conspiring with alien minds would be an act of war!
I doubt our neighbour house is pleased with the visit.
They might need our help.
"IT'S SO QUIET HERE.
"PEACEFUL."

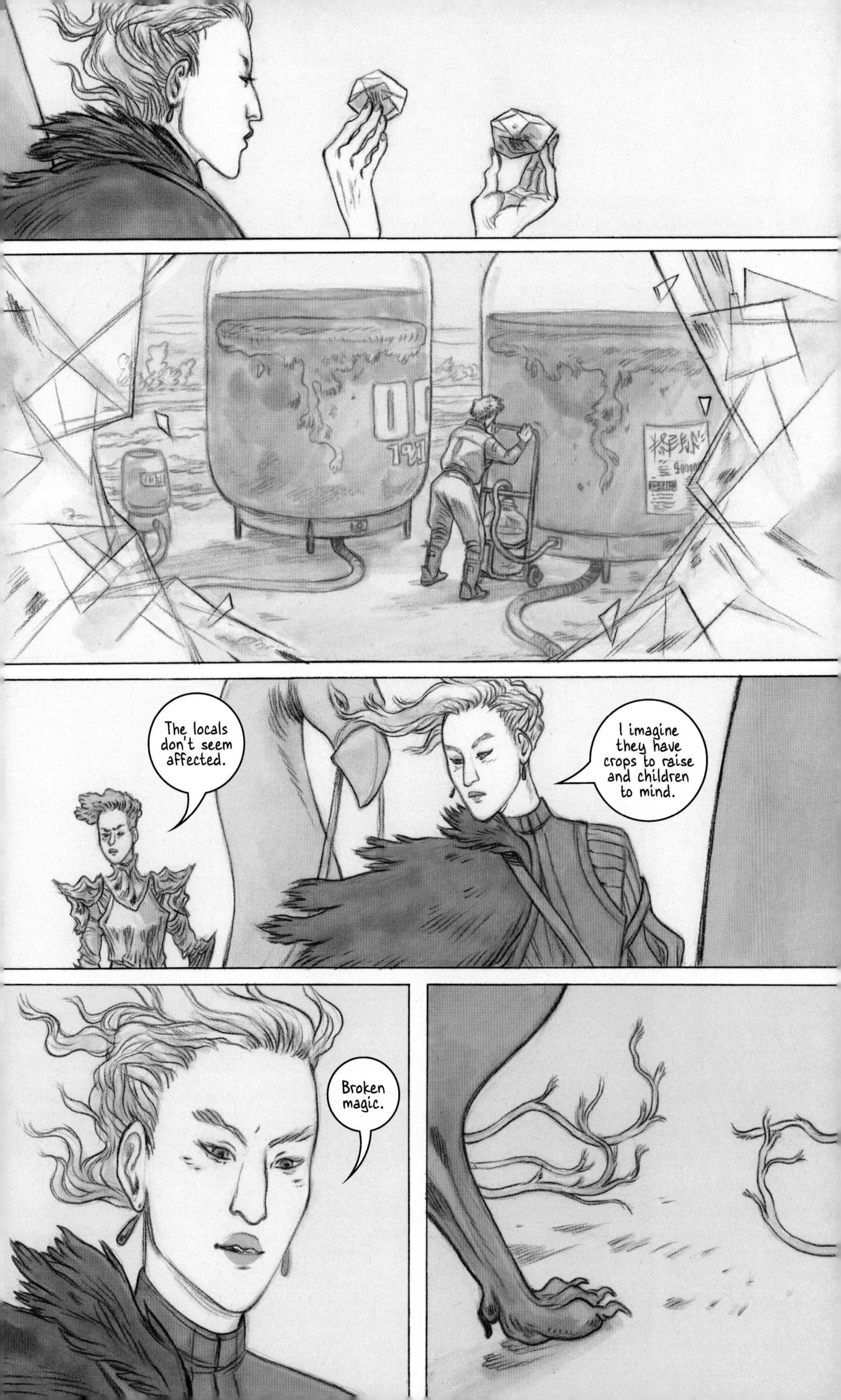
The locals don't seem affected.
I imagine they have crops to raise and children to mind.
Broken magic.

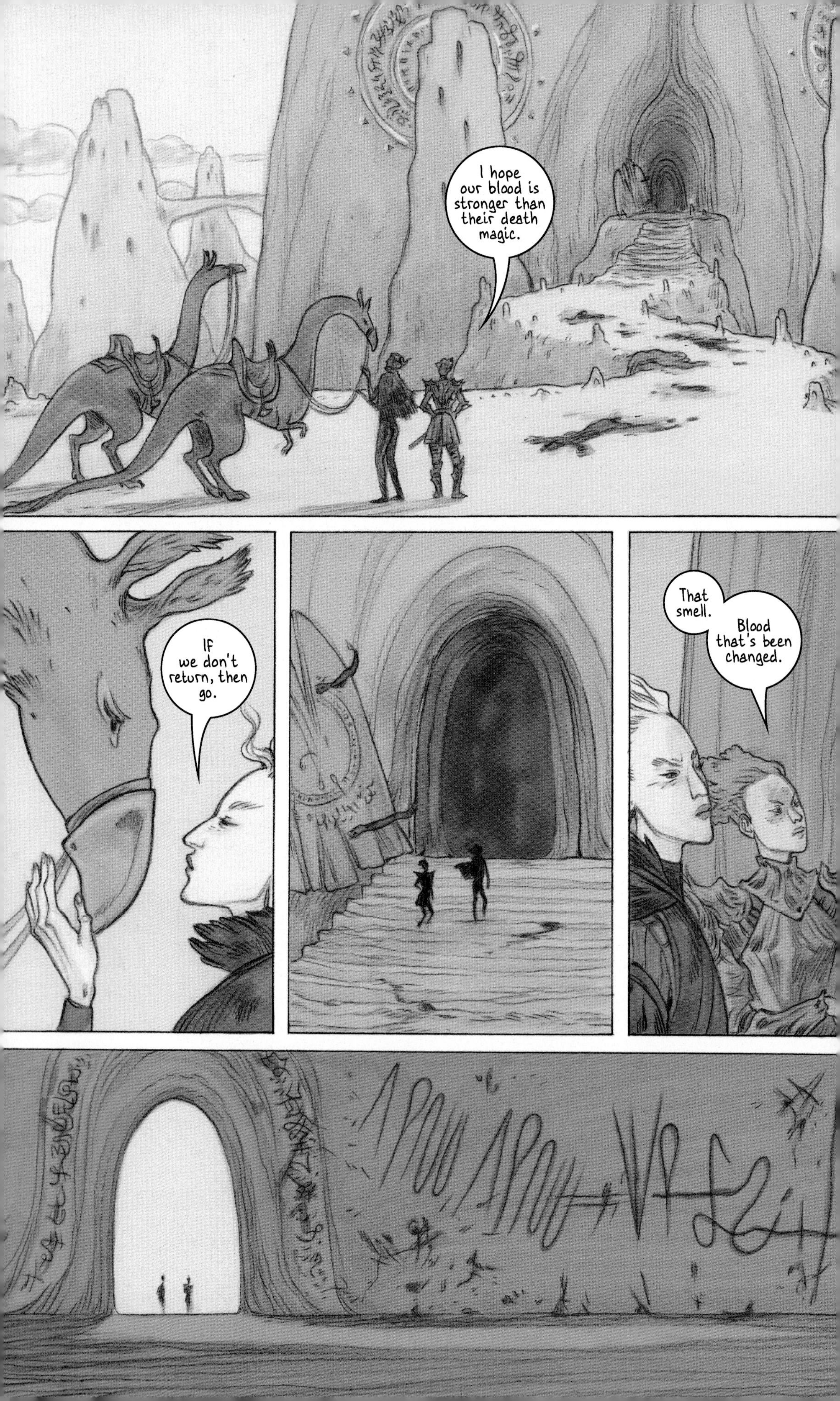
I hope our blood is stronger than their death magic.
If we don't return, then go.
That smell.
Blood that's been changed.

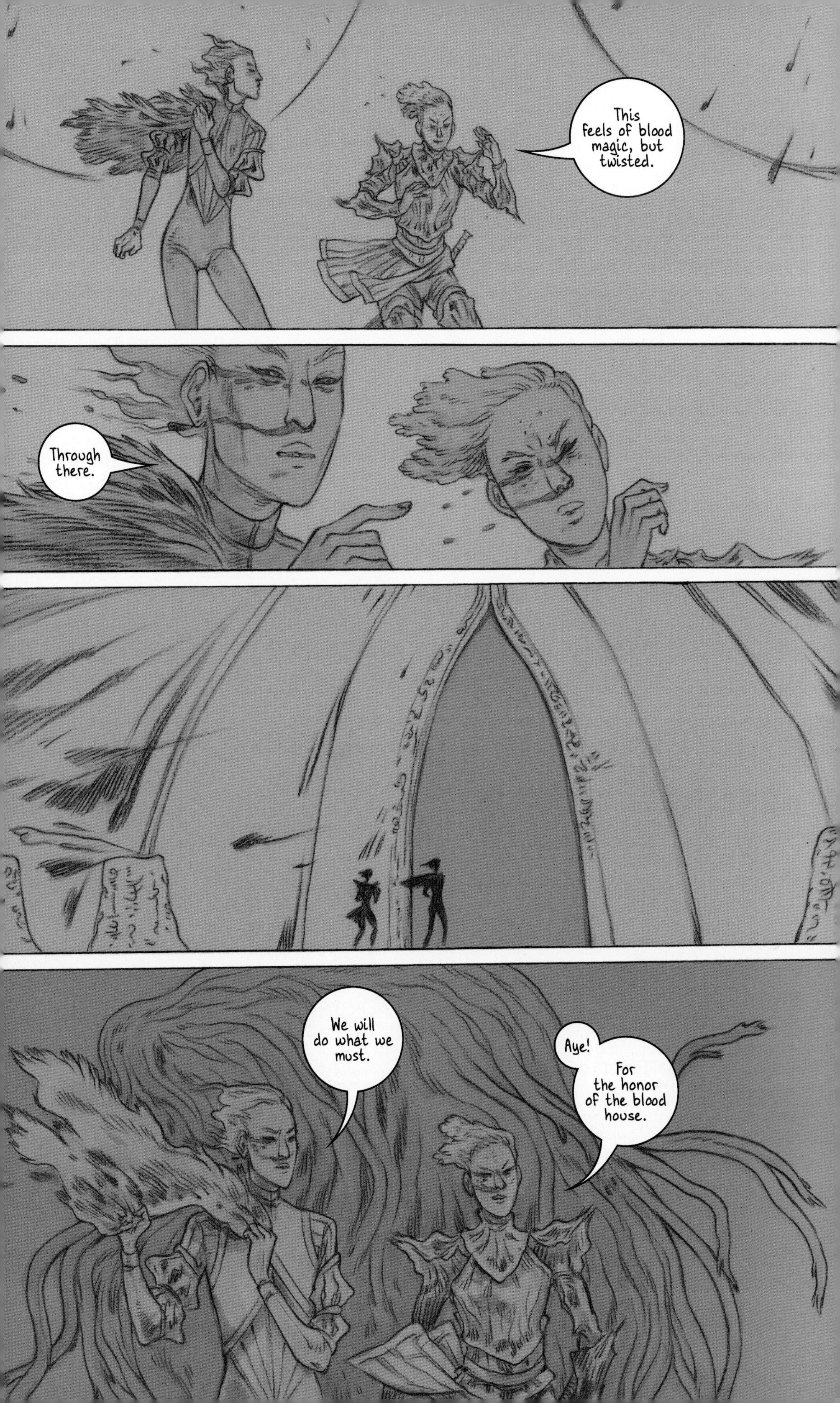
This feels of blood magic, but twisted.
Through there.
We will do what we must.
Aye!
For the honor of the blood house.

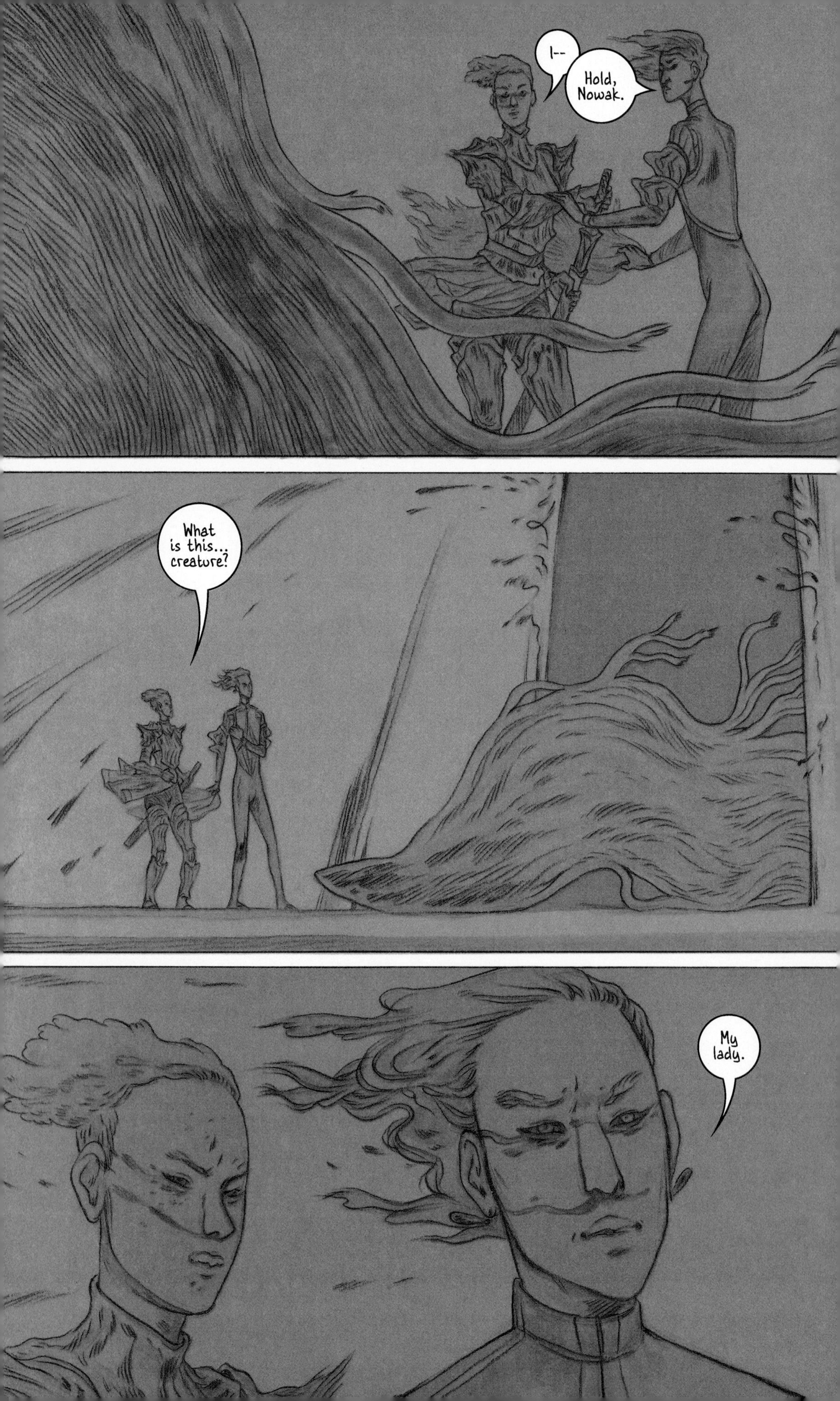
I--
Hold, Nowak.
What is this... creature?
My lady.

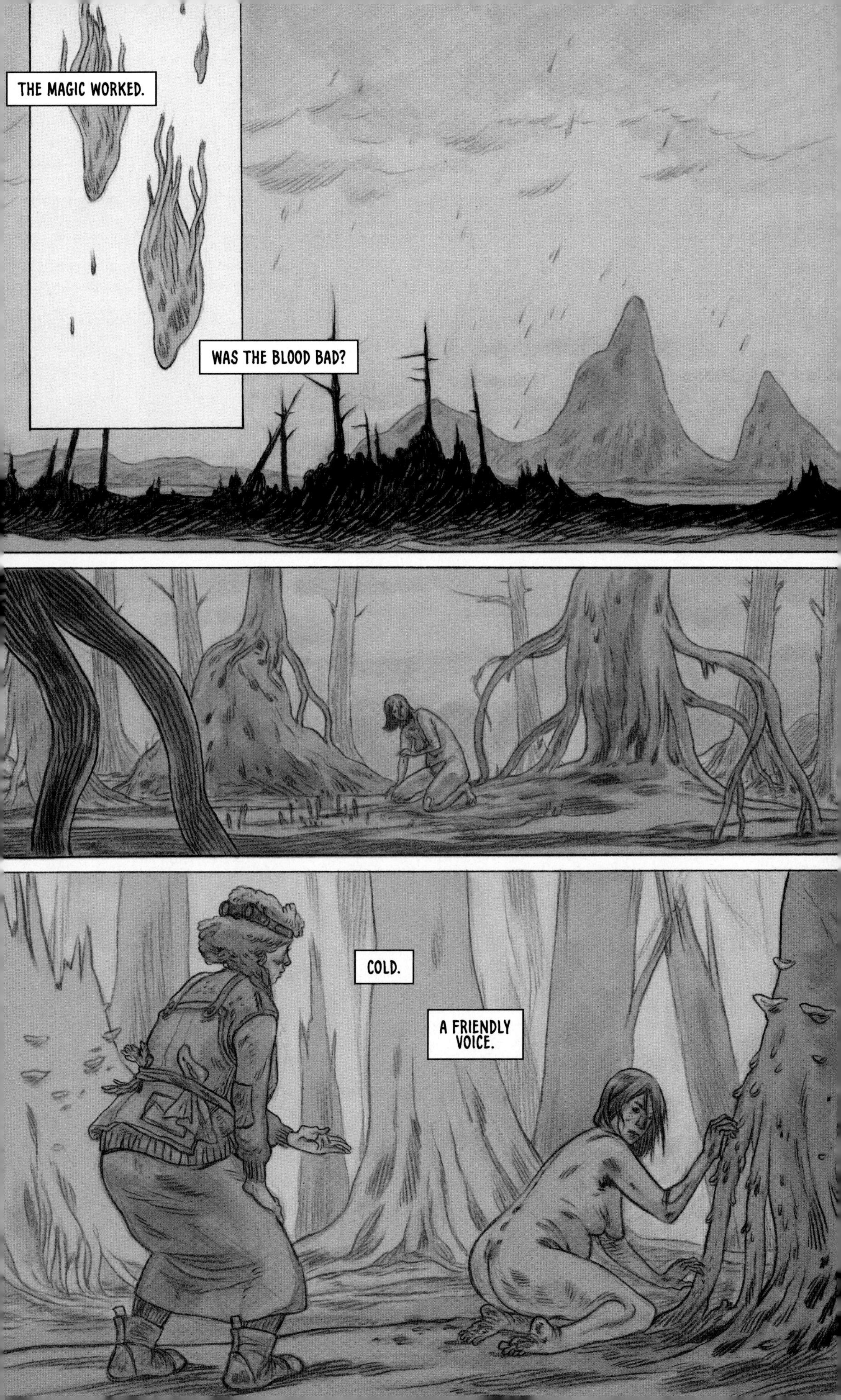
THE MAGIC WORKED.
WAS THE BLOOD BAD?
COLD.
A FRIENDLY VOICE.

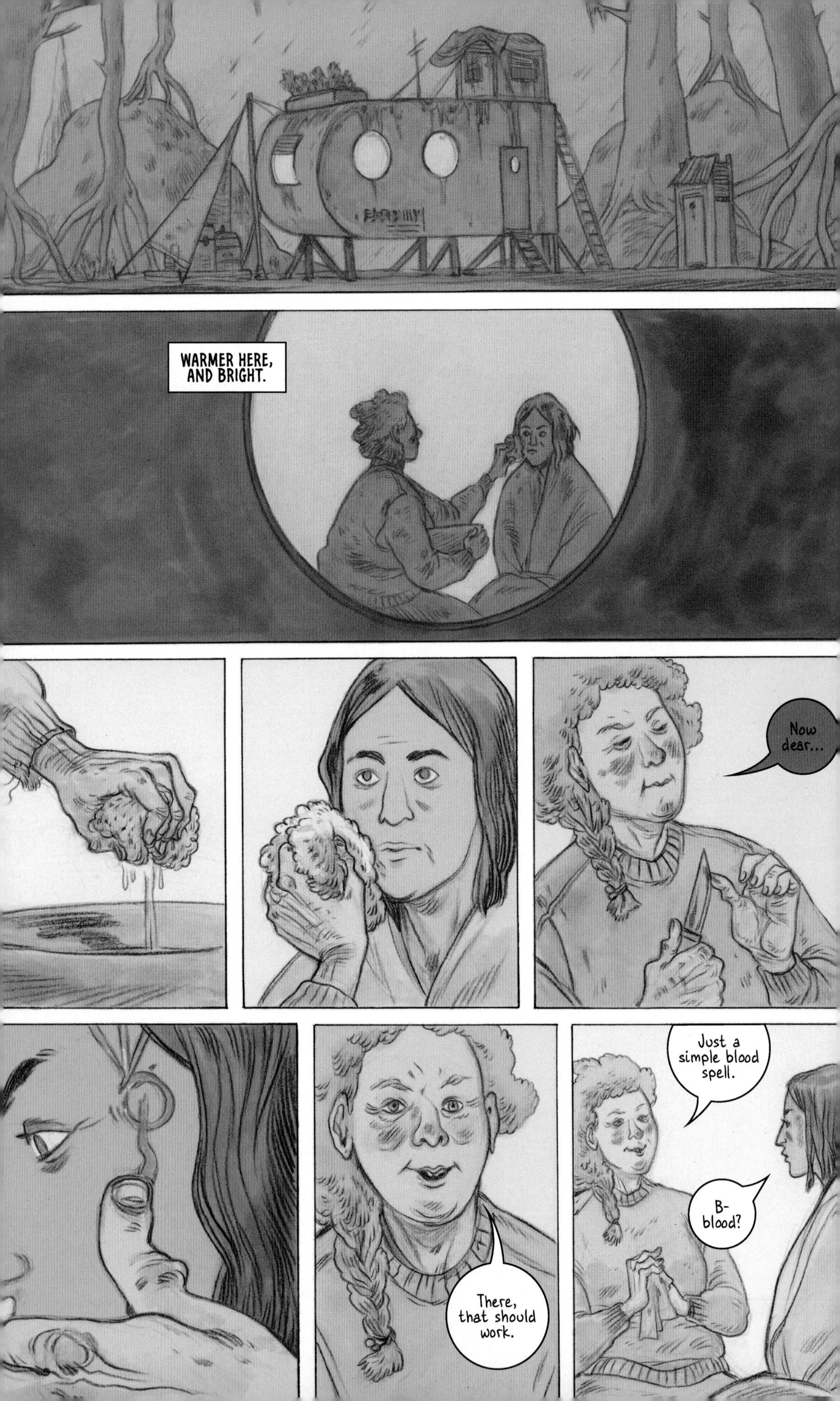
WARMER HERE, AND BRIGHT.
Now dear...
Just a simple blood spell.
There, that should work.
B- blood?

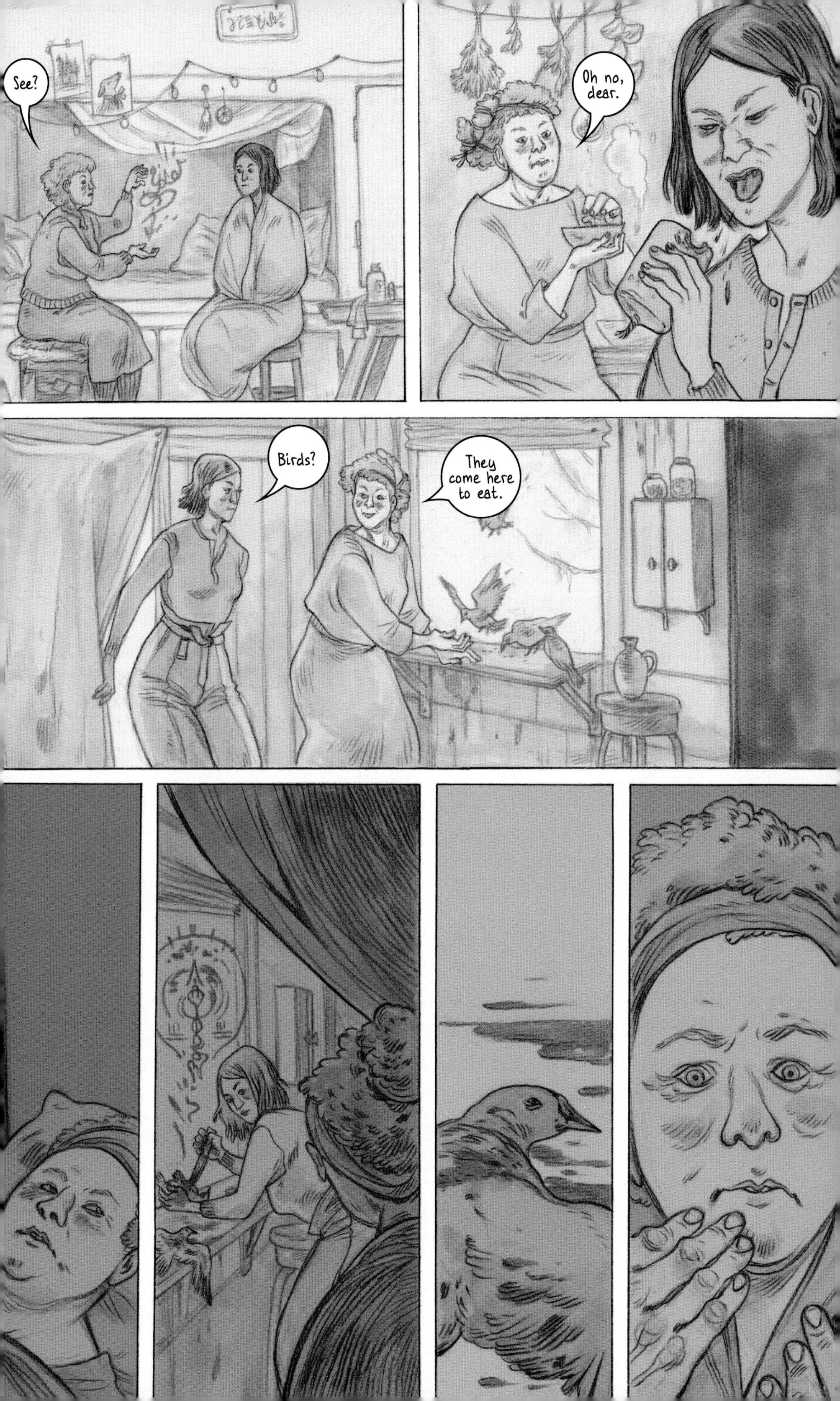
See?
Oh no, dear.
Birds?
They come here to eat.

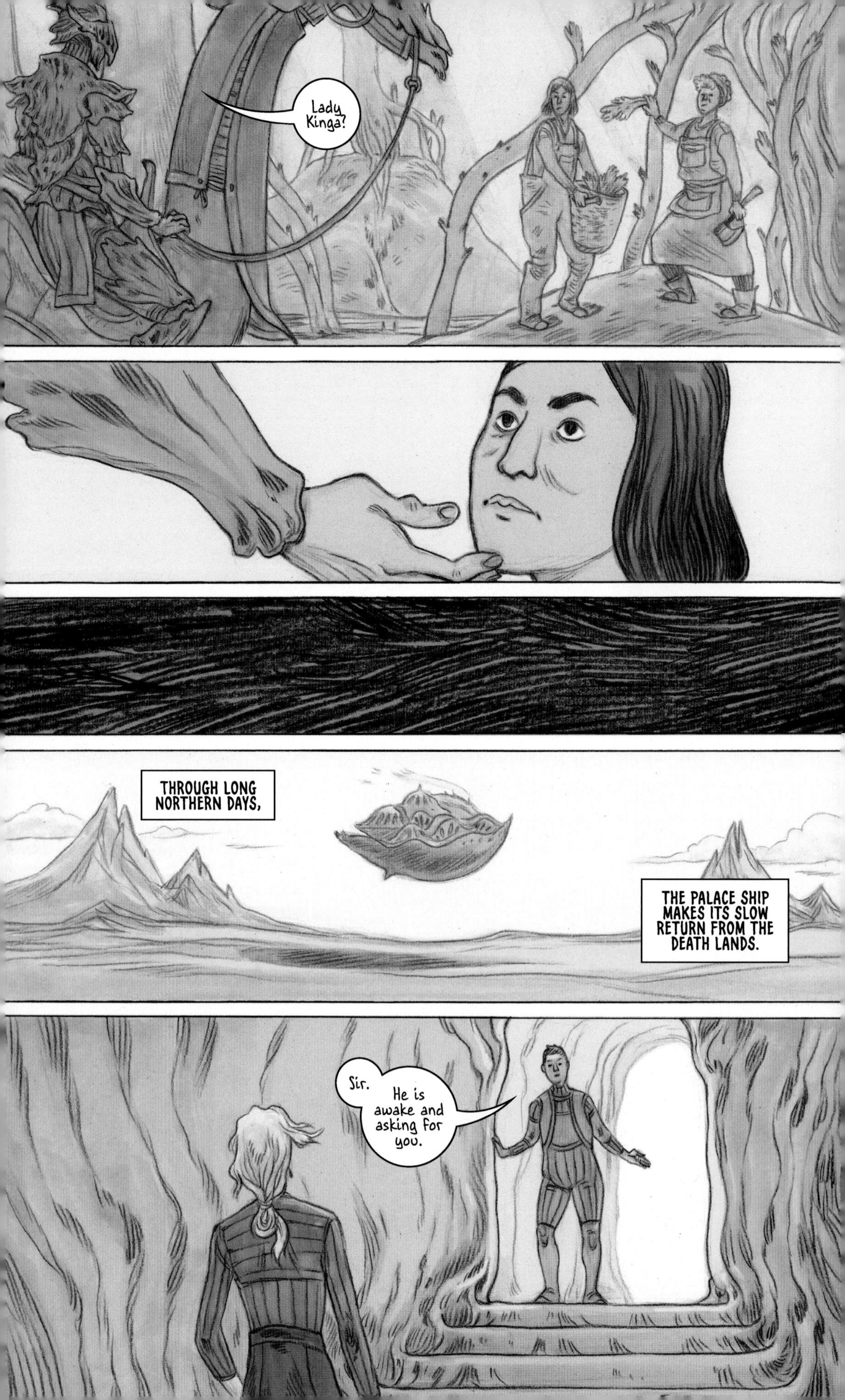
Lady Kinga?
THROUGH LONG NORTHERN DAYS,
THE PALACE SHIP MAKES ITS SLOW RETURN FROM THE DEATH LANDS.
Sir.
He is awake and asking for you.

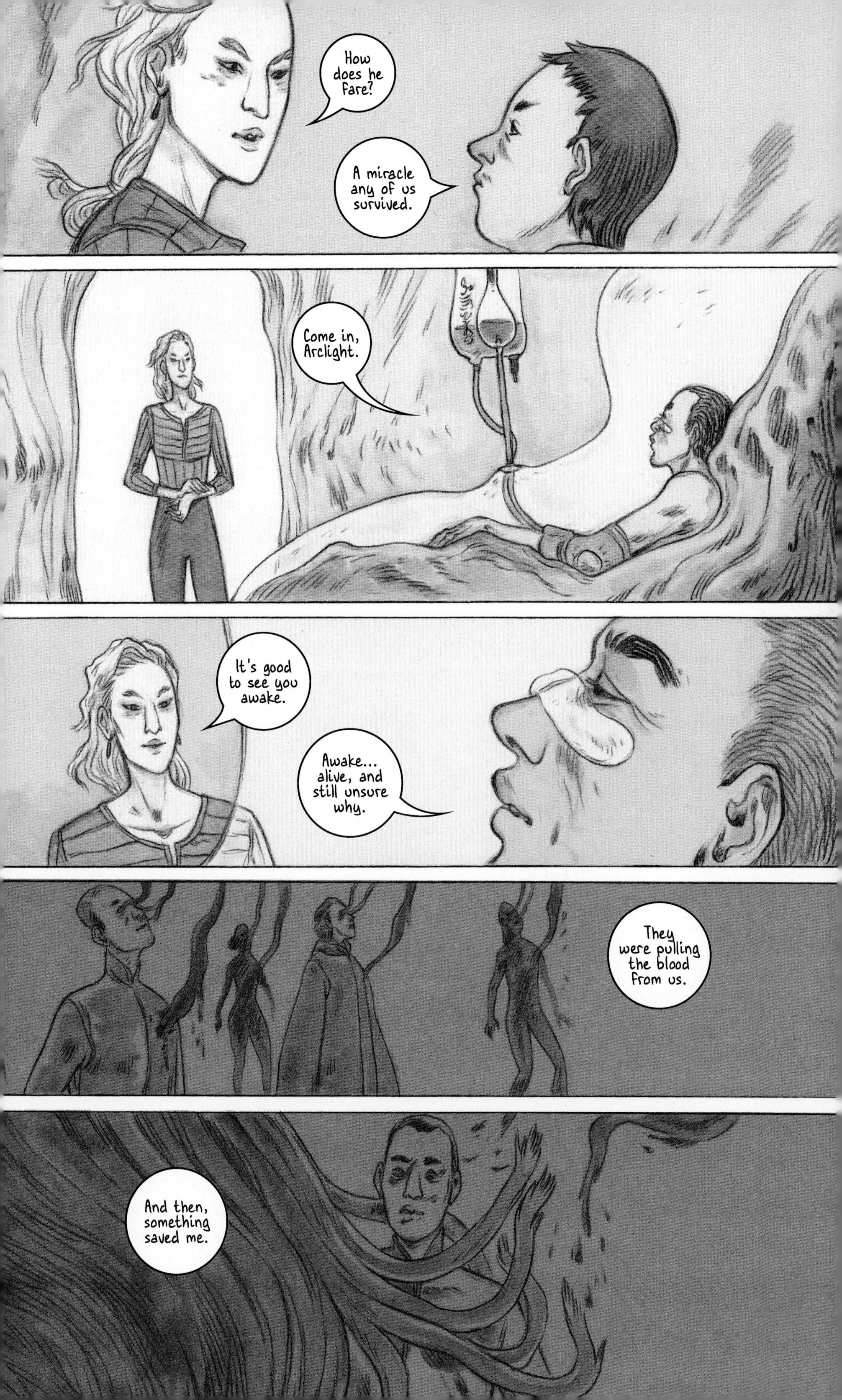
How does he fare?
A miracle any of us survived.
Come in, Arclight.
It's good to see you awake.
Awake... alive, and still unsure why.
They were pulling the blood from us.
And then, something saved me.

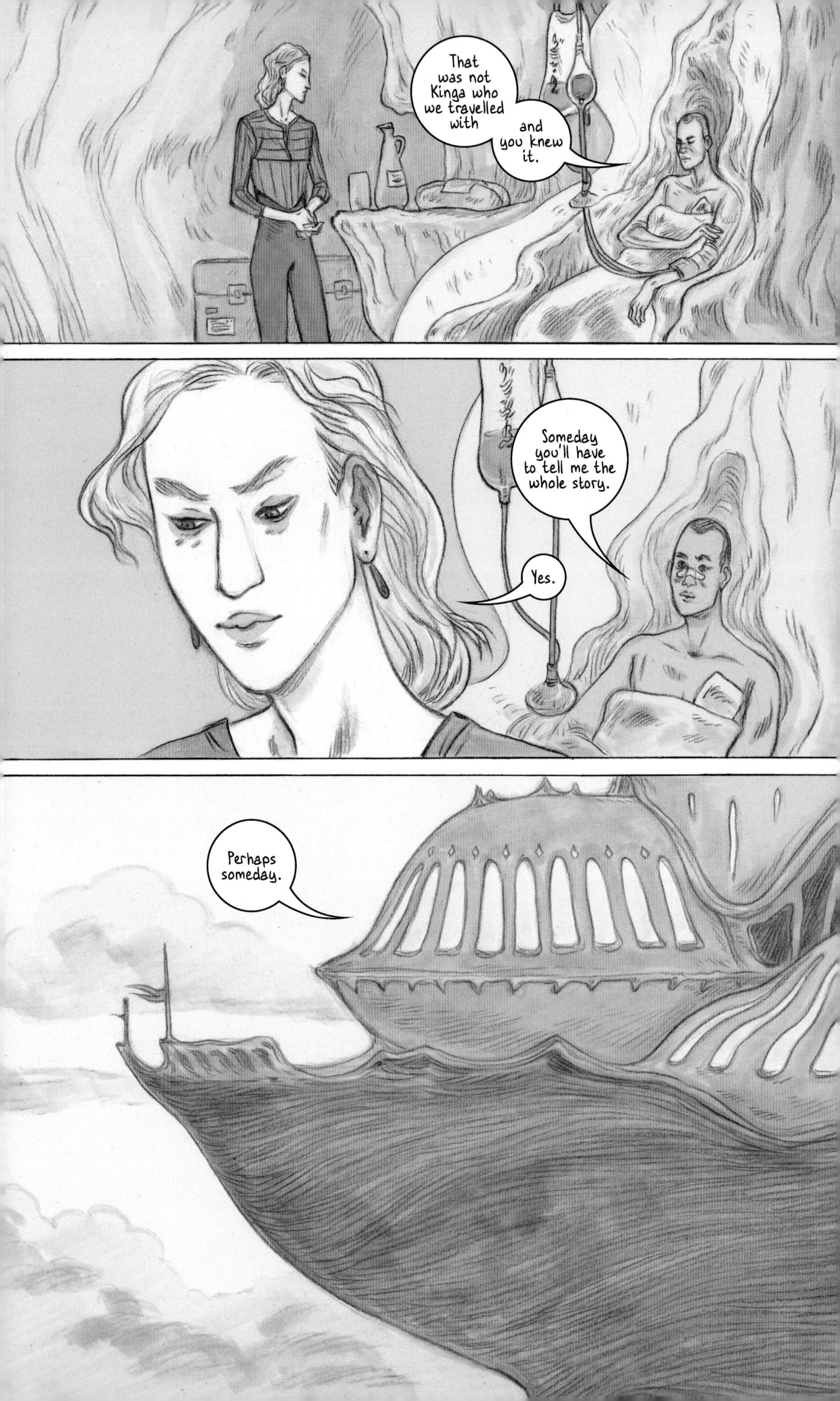
That was not Kinga who we travelled with
and you knew it.
Someday you'll have to tell me the whole story.
Yes.
Perhaps someday.

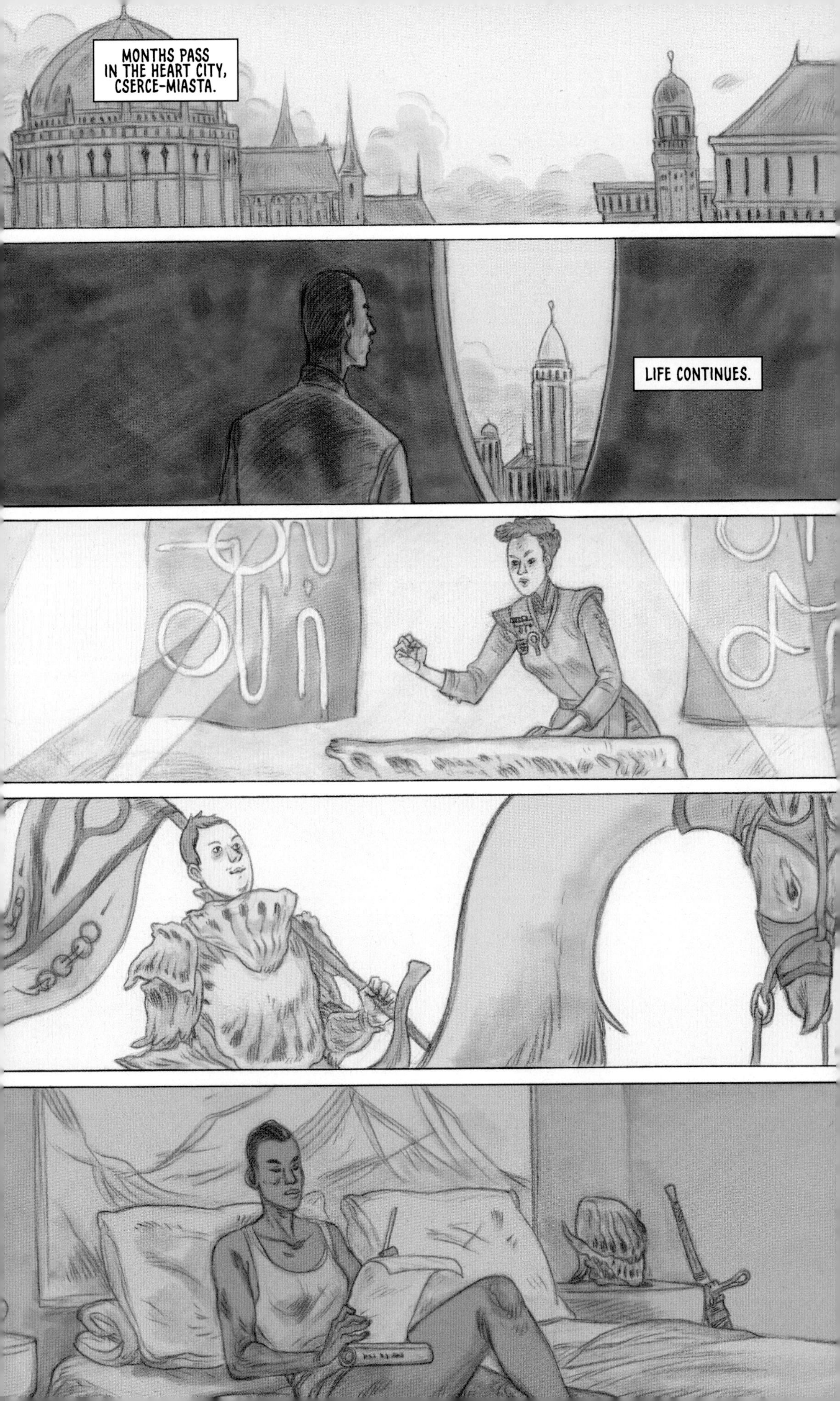
MONTHS PASS IN THE HEART CITY, CSERCE-MIASTA.
LIFE CONTINUES.

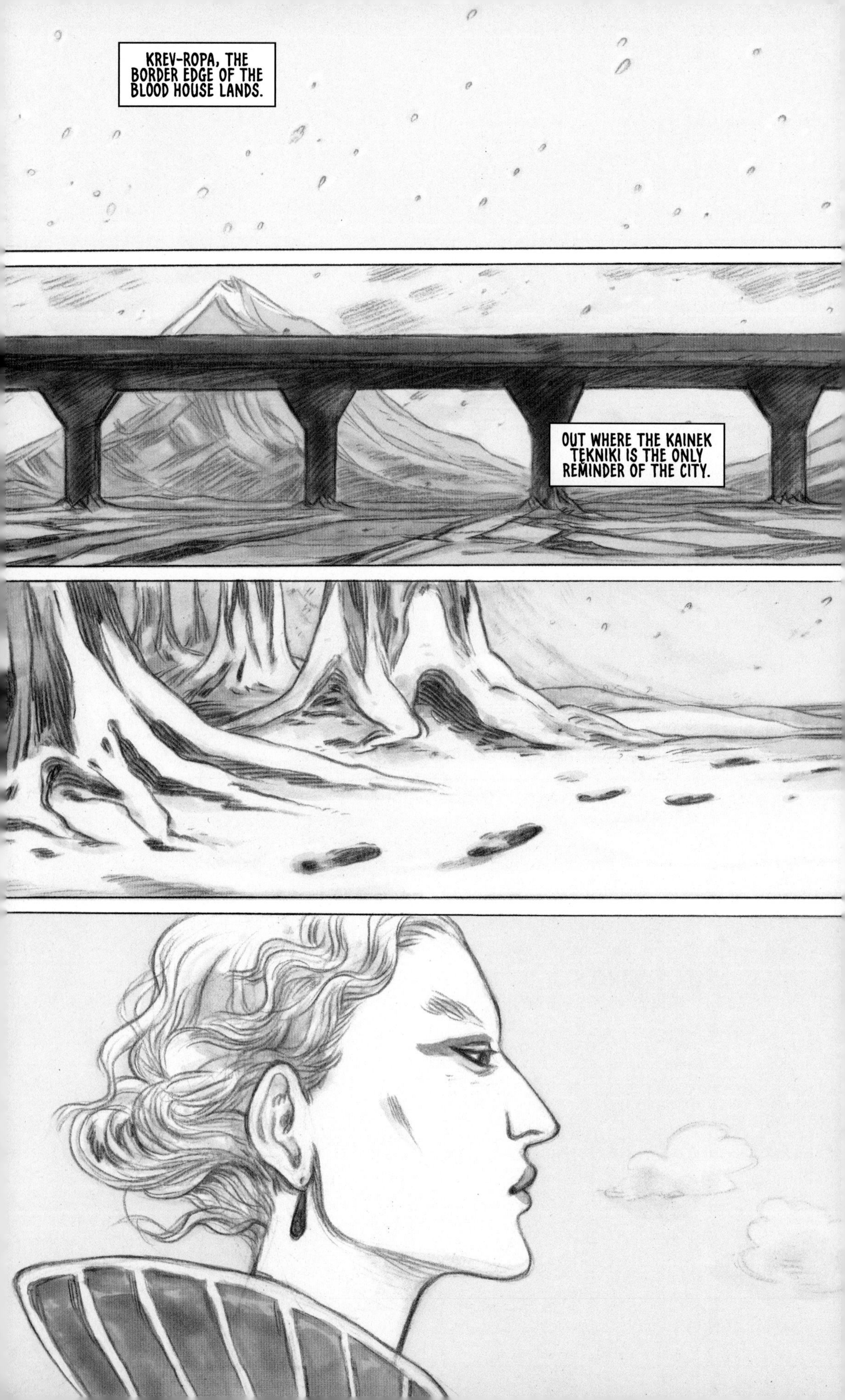
KREV-ROPA, THE BORDER EDGE OF THE BLOOD HOUSE LANDS.
OUT WHERE THE KAINEK TEKNIKI IS THE ONLY REMINDER OF THE CITY.

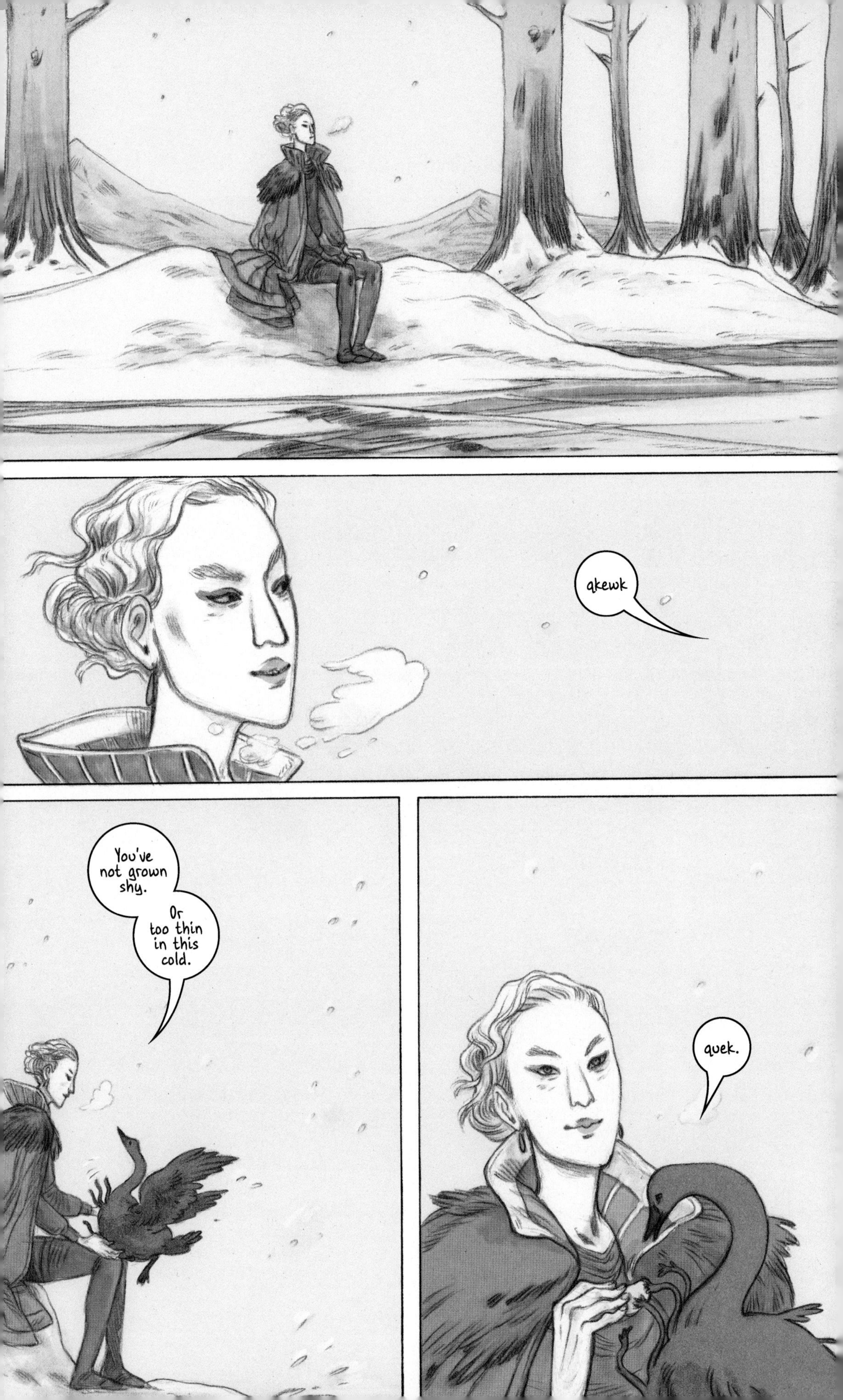
qkewk
You've not grown shy.
Or too thin in this cold.
quek.

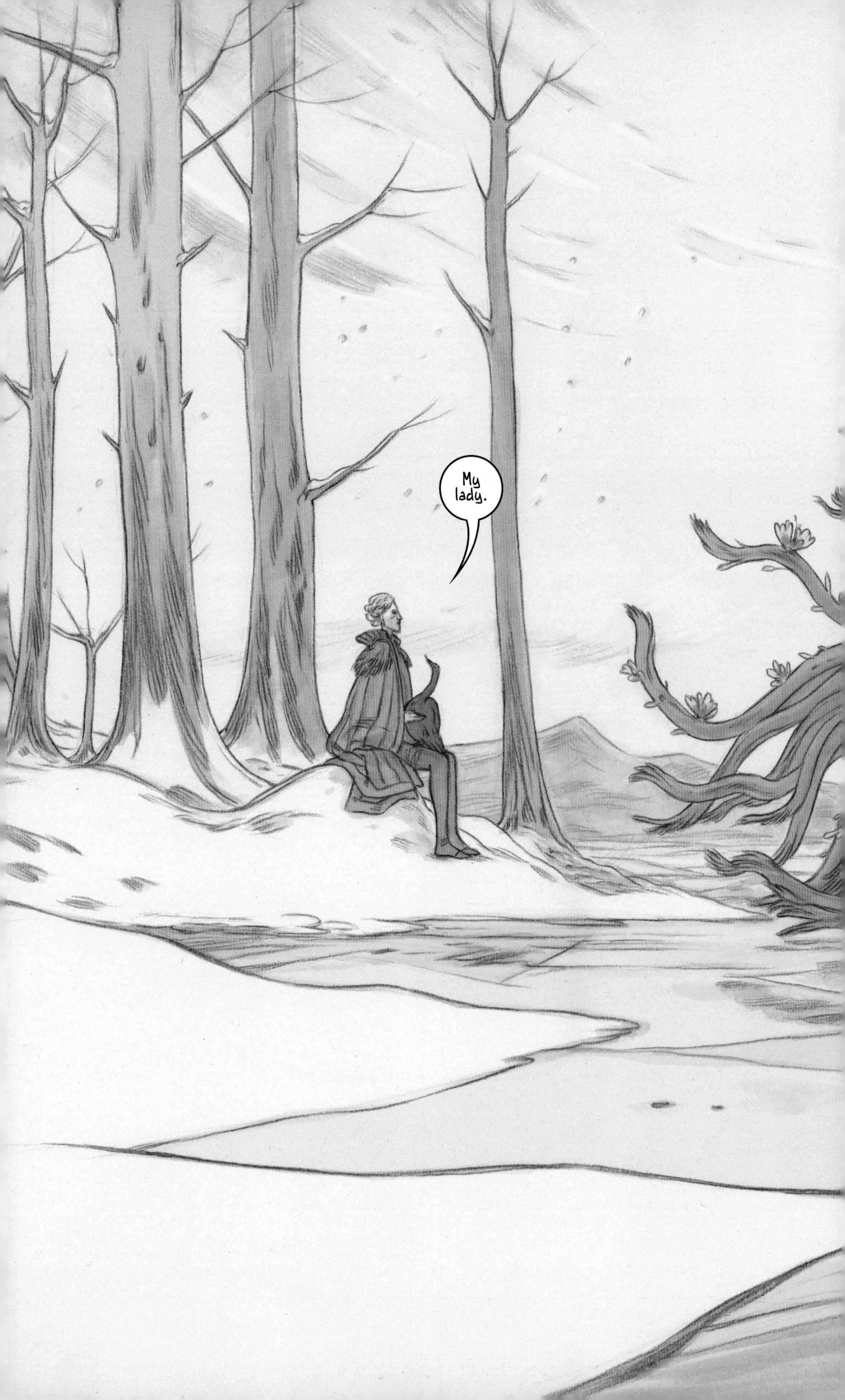
My lady.

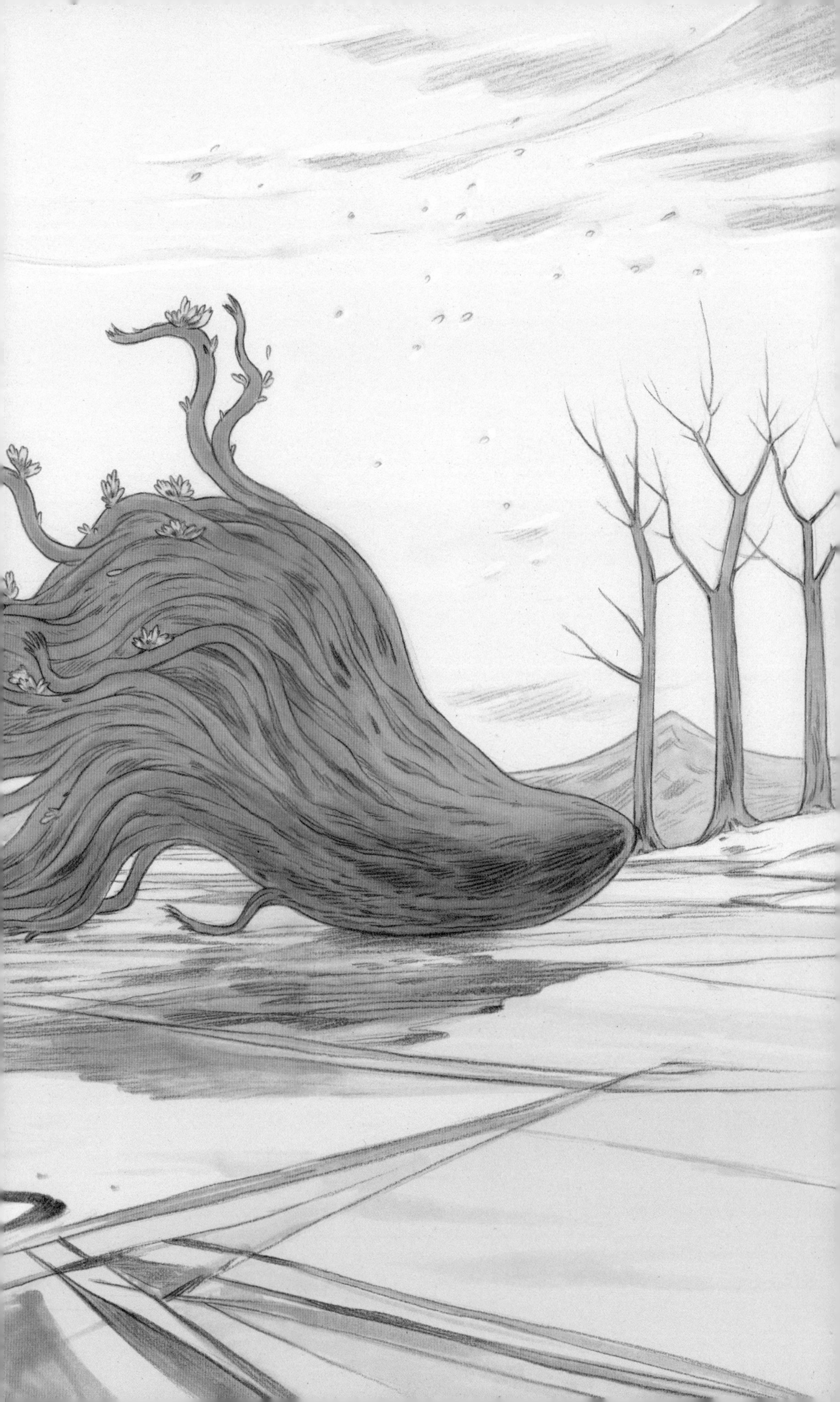

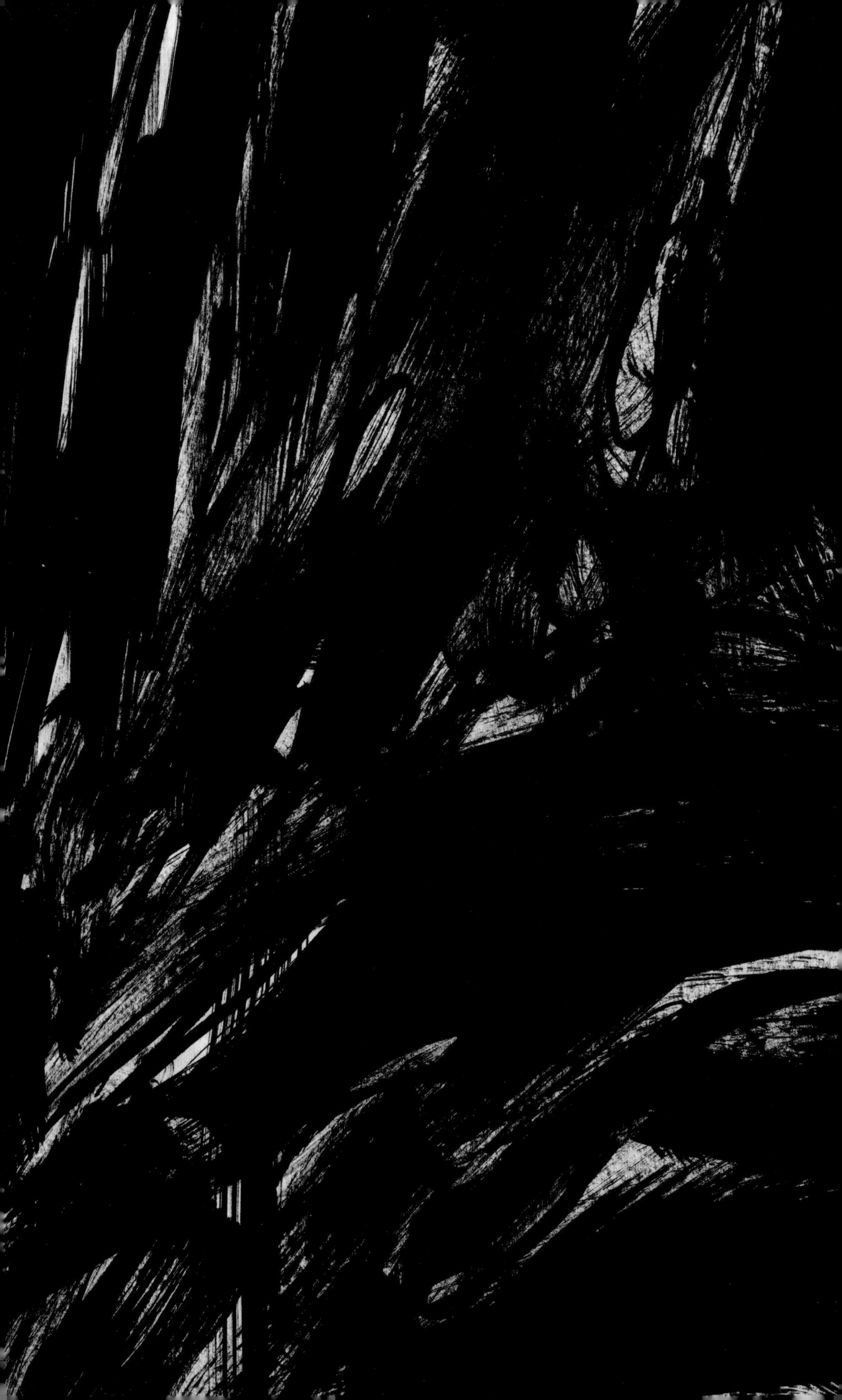

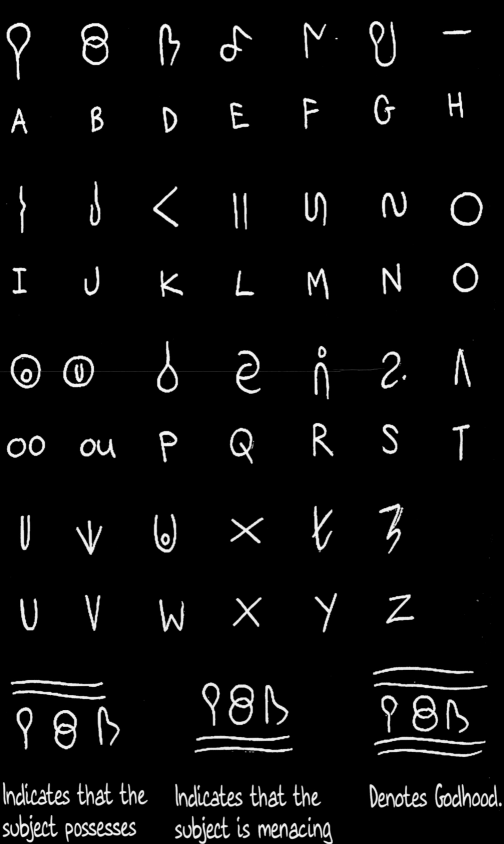

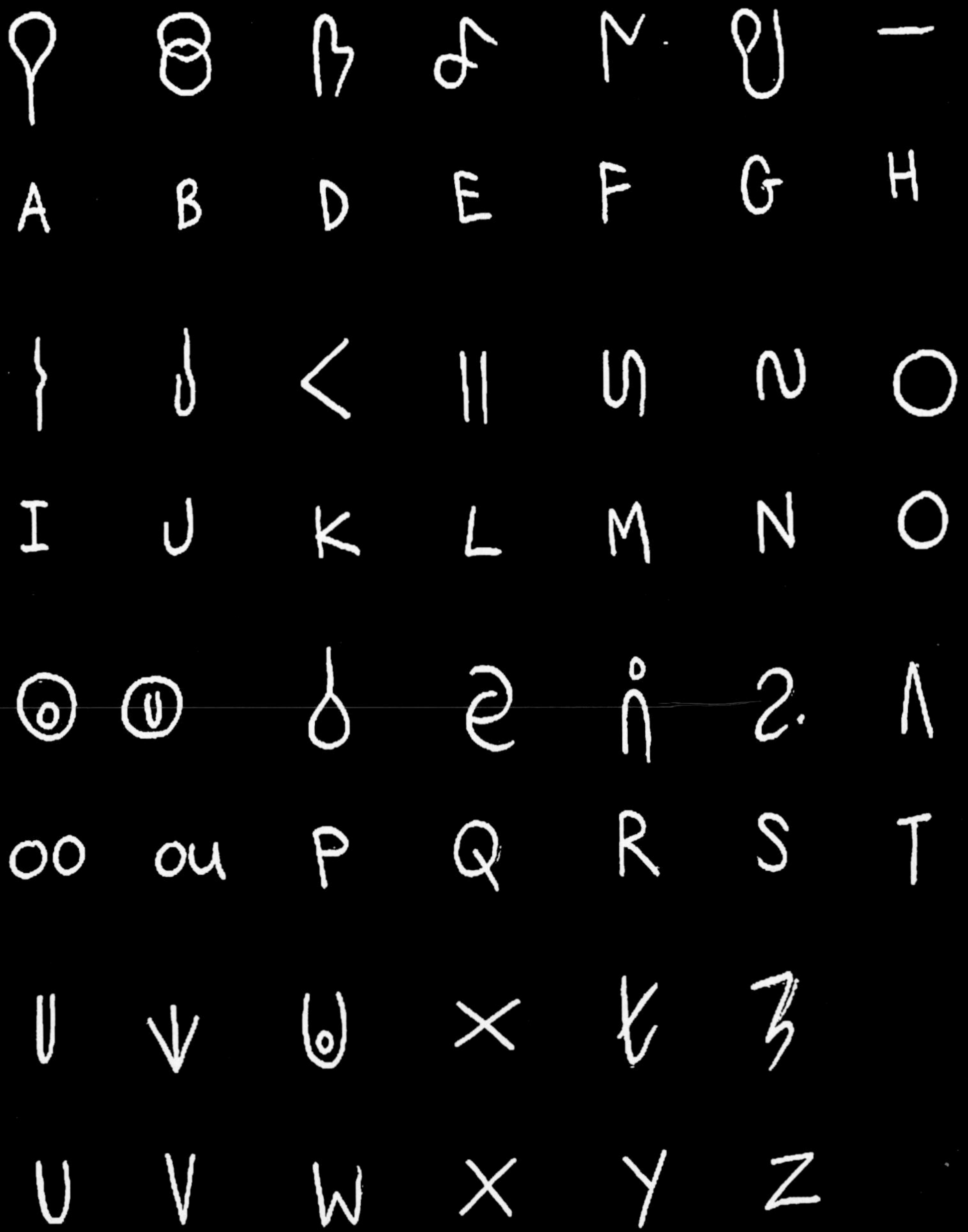
A B D E F G H
I J K L M N O
OO OU P Q R S T
U V W X Y Z

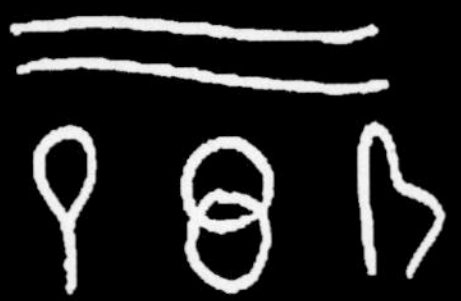

Indicates that the subject possesses authority or distinction.

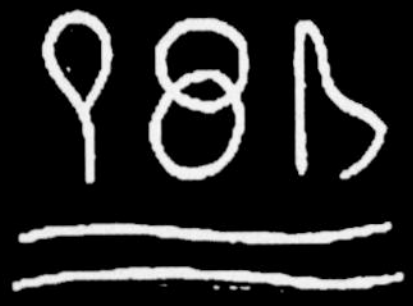

Indicates that the subject is menacing or threatening.

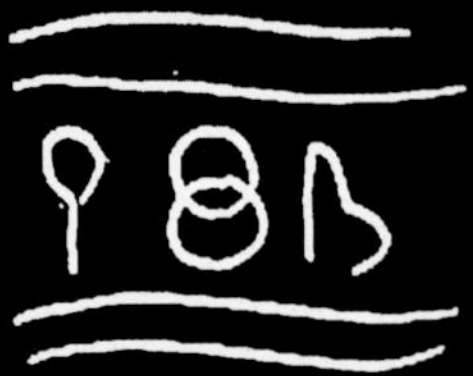

Denotes Godhood.

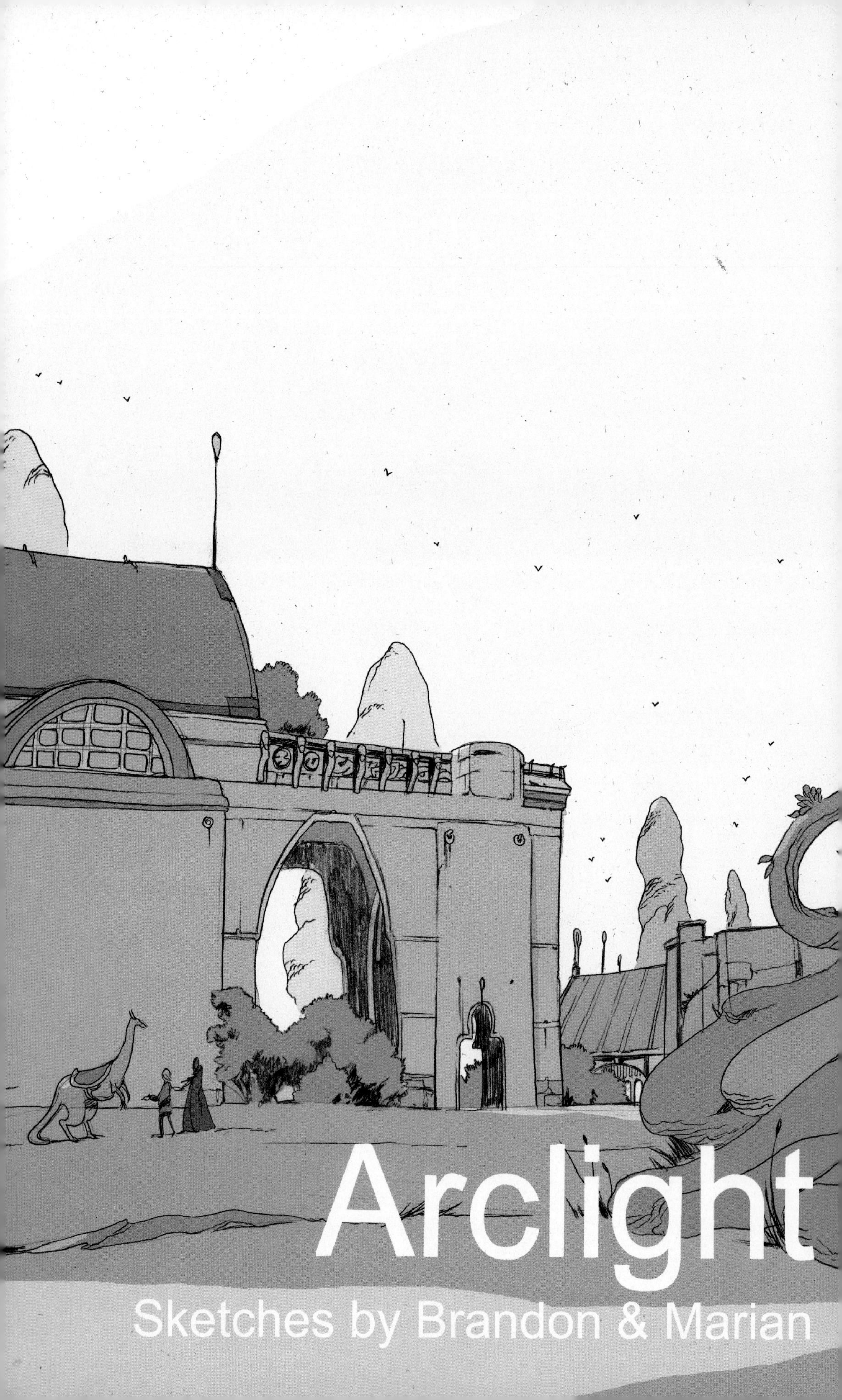

Arclight

Sketches by Brandon & Marian

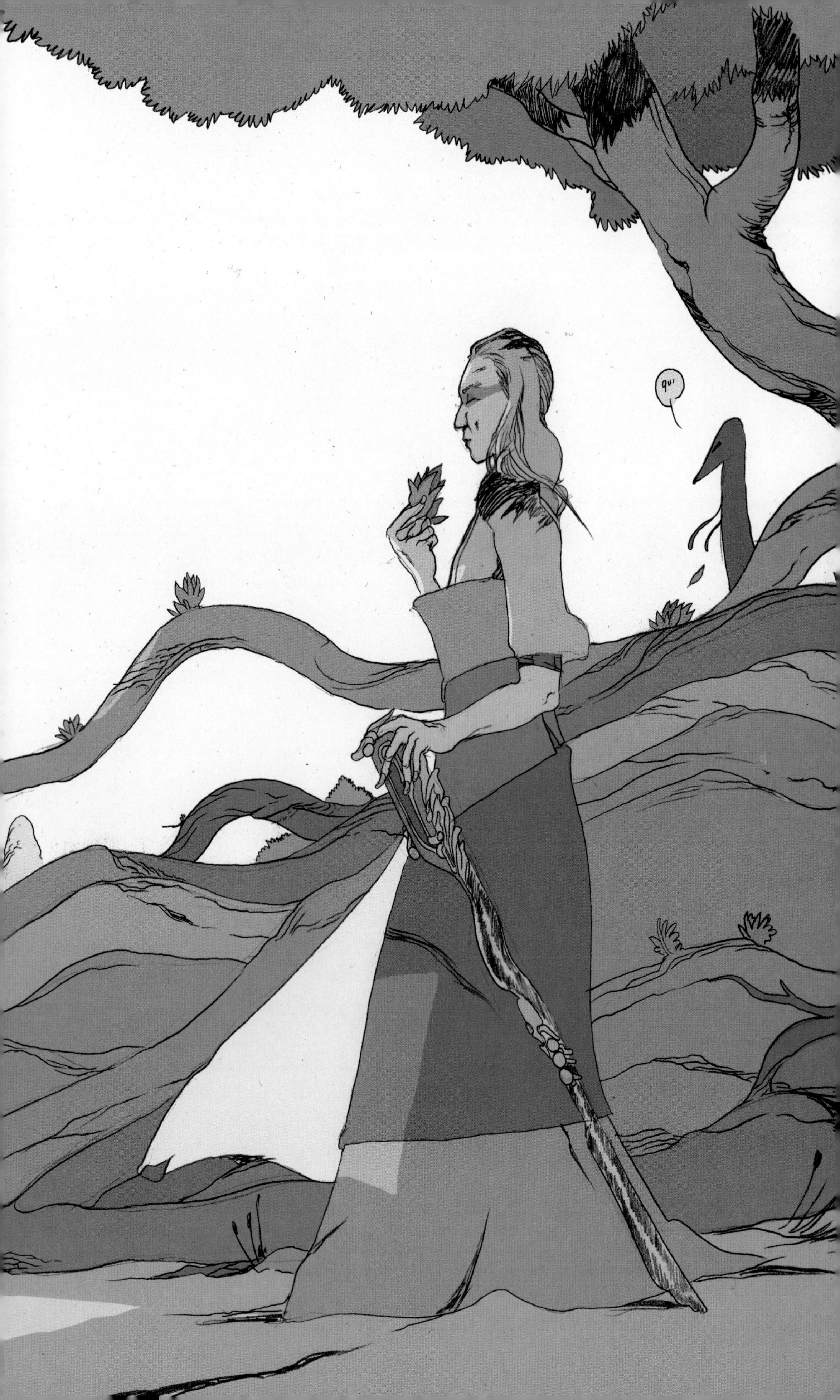
qui

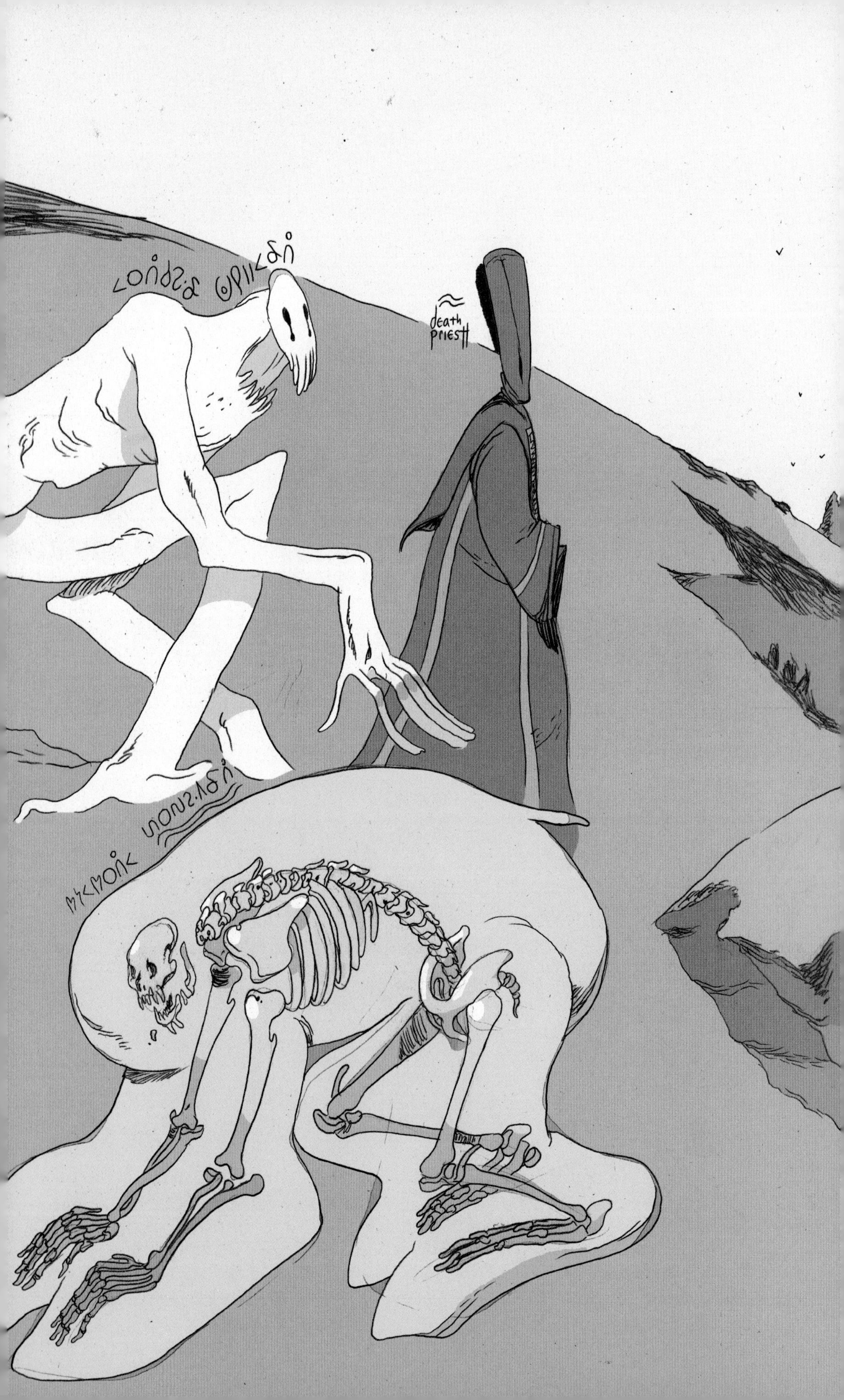
death priest

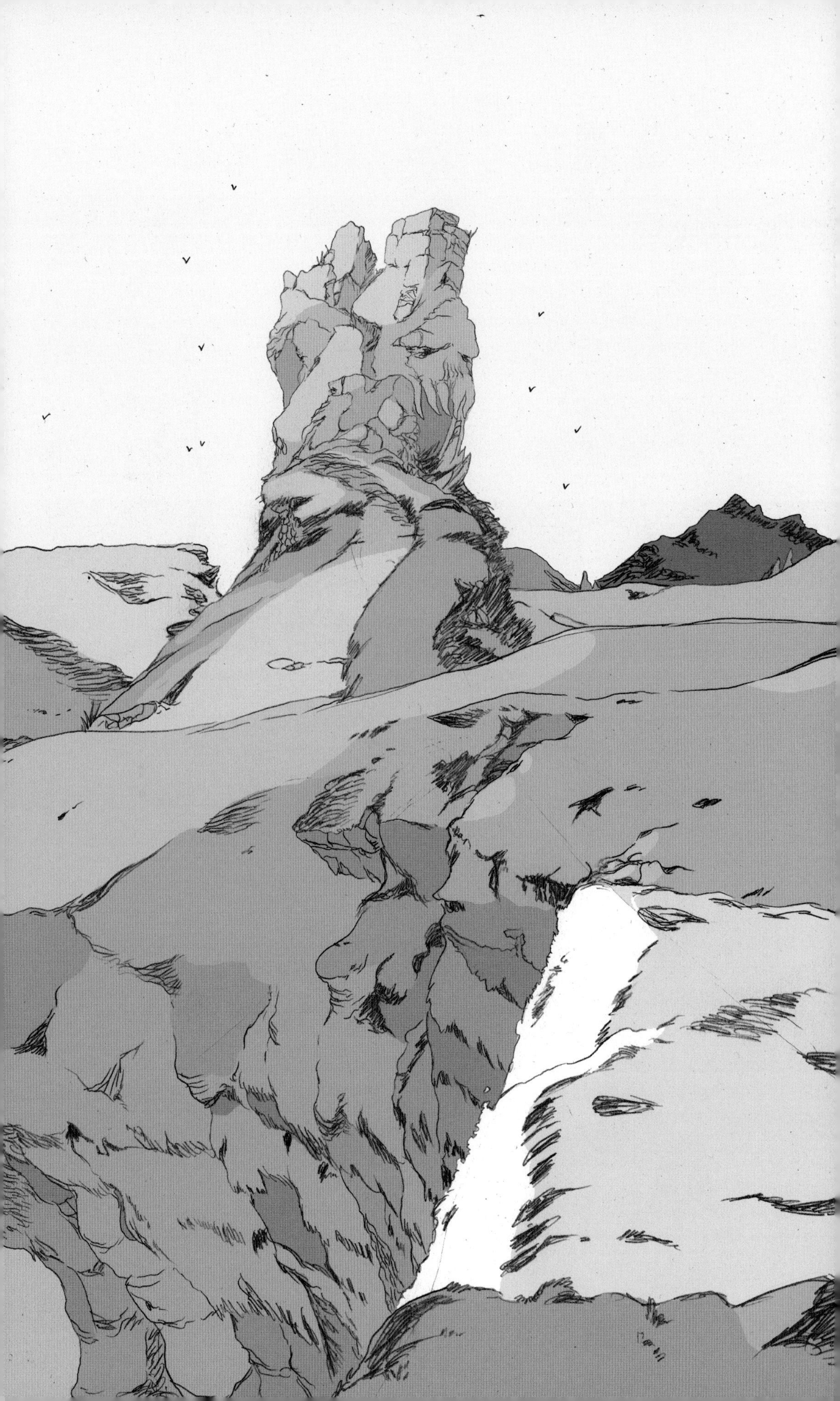

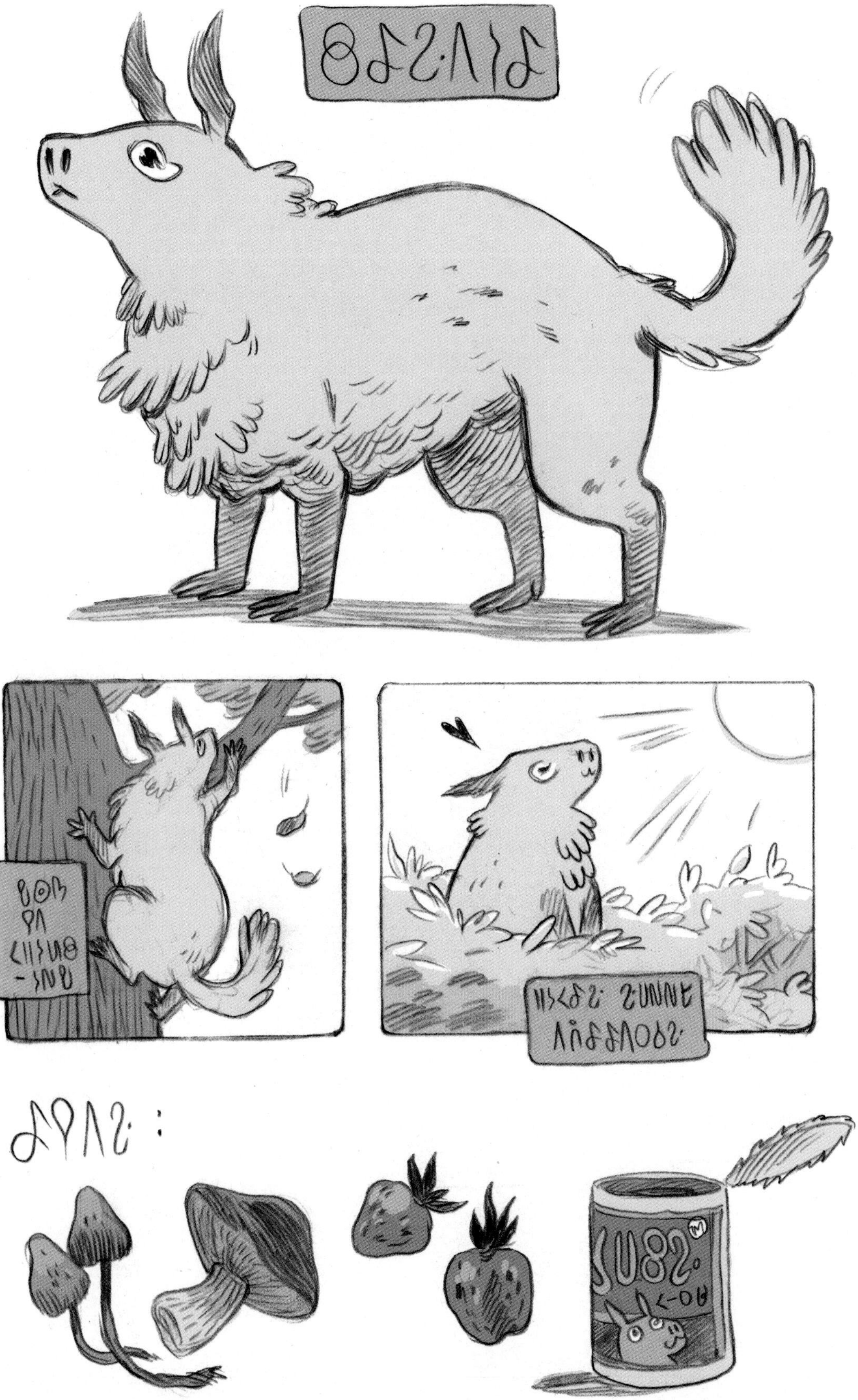

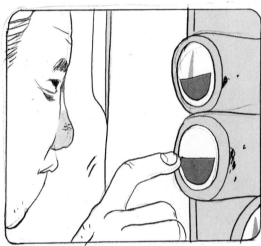

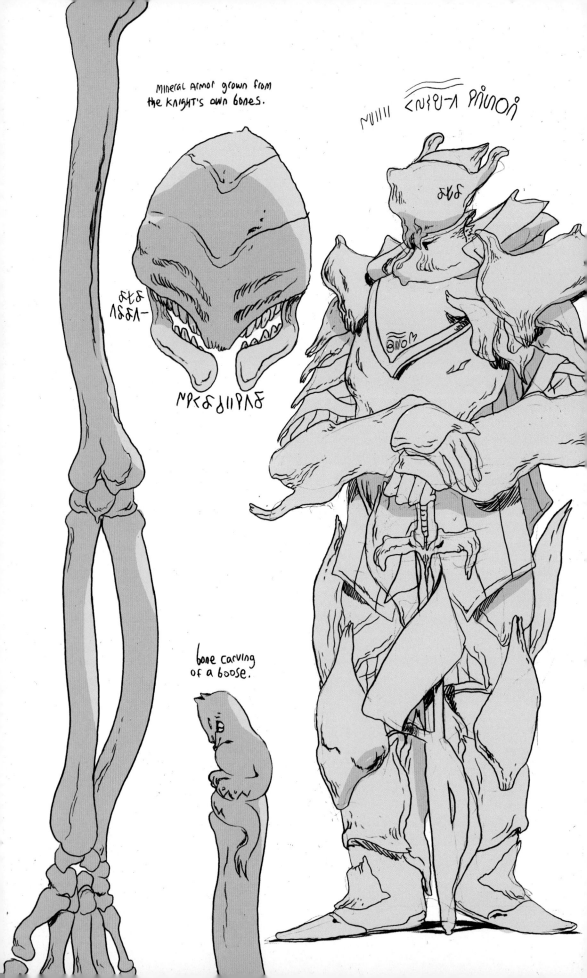

Mineral armor grown from the knight's own bones.

bone carving of a boose.

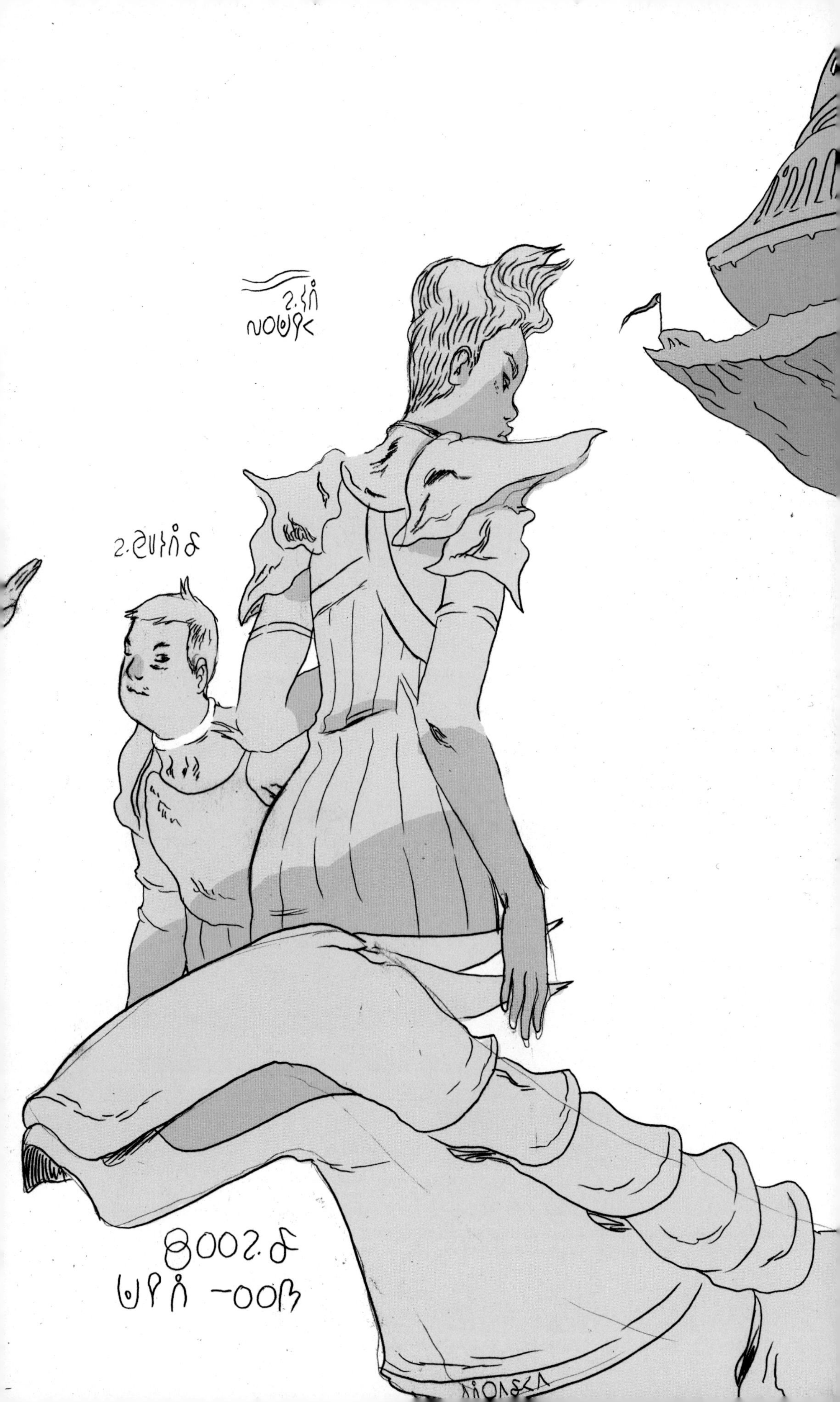

Bonded mounts of the Blood House, booses are selected and paired with their knights according to blood-type. Since they are genetically similar to humans, their blood can be used for life-saving transfusions, or to work magic.

Boose pups are given bone tattoos in order to bond them more closely to members of thei house.

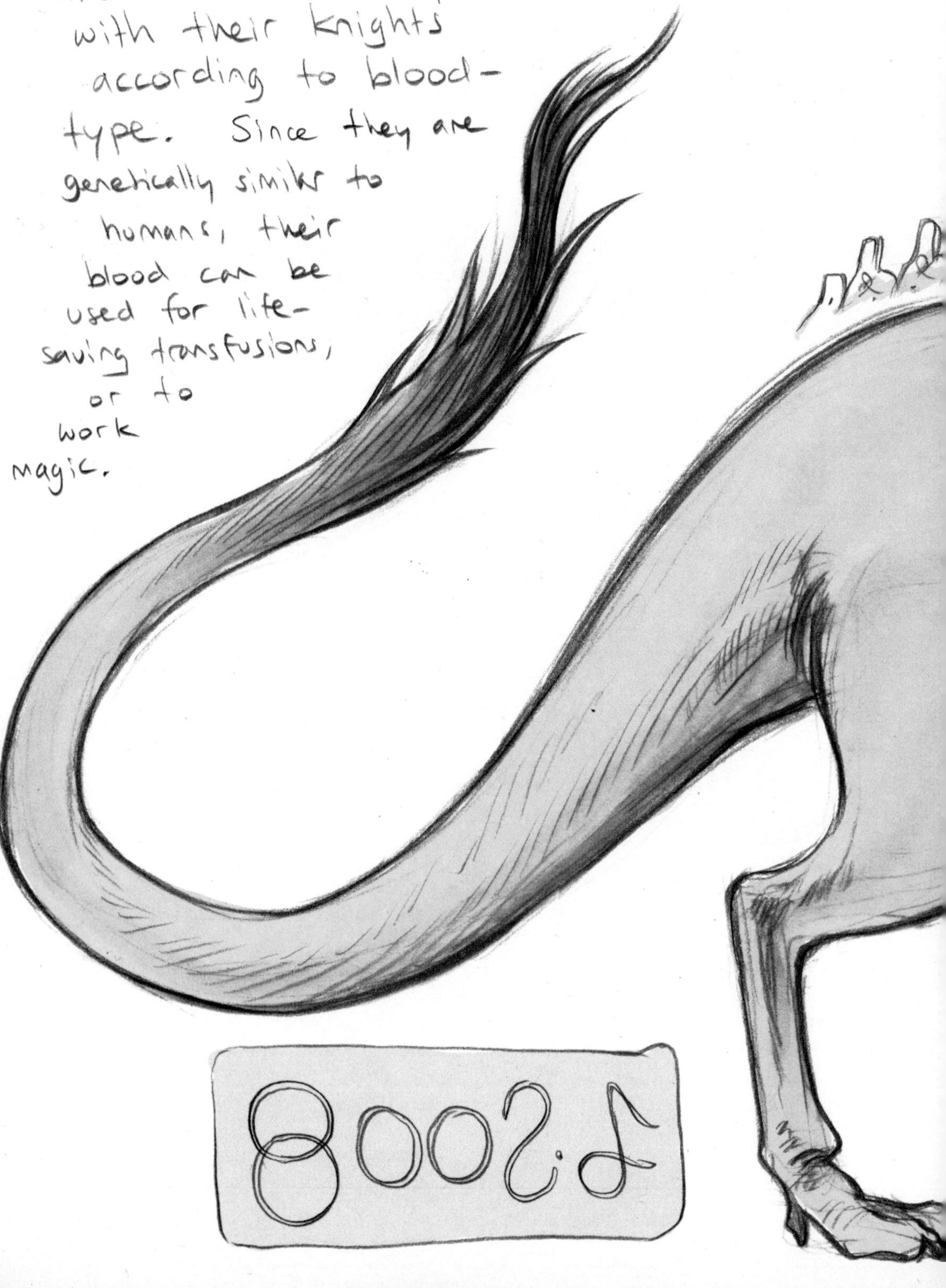

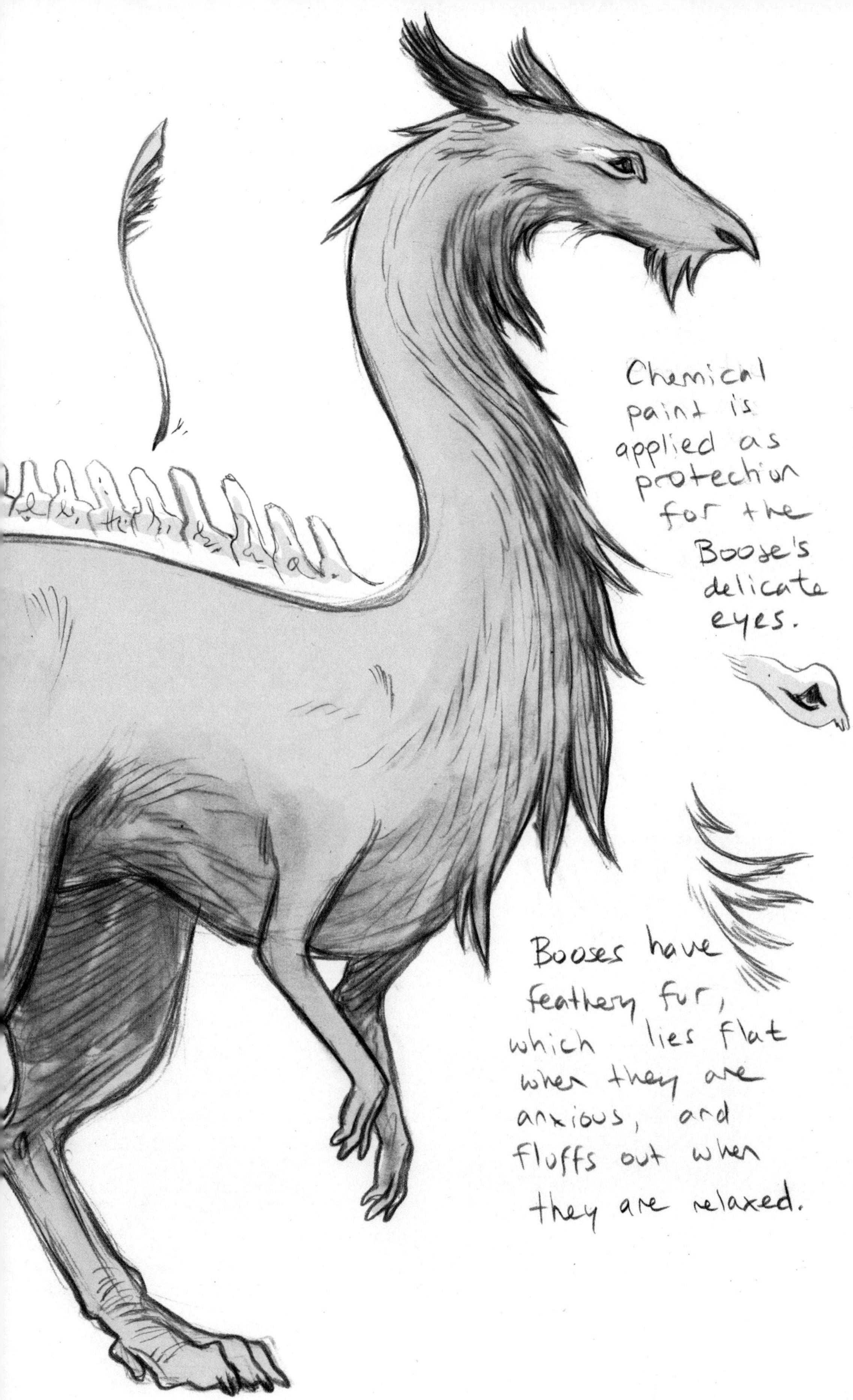
Chemical paint is applied as protection for the Boose's delicate eyes.
Booses have feathery fur, which lies flat when they are anxious, and fluffs out when they are relaxed.

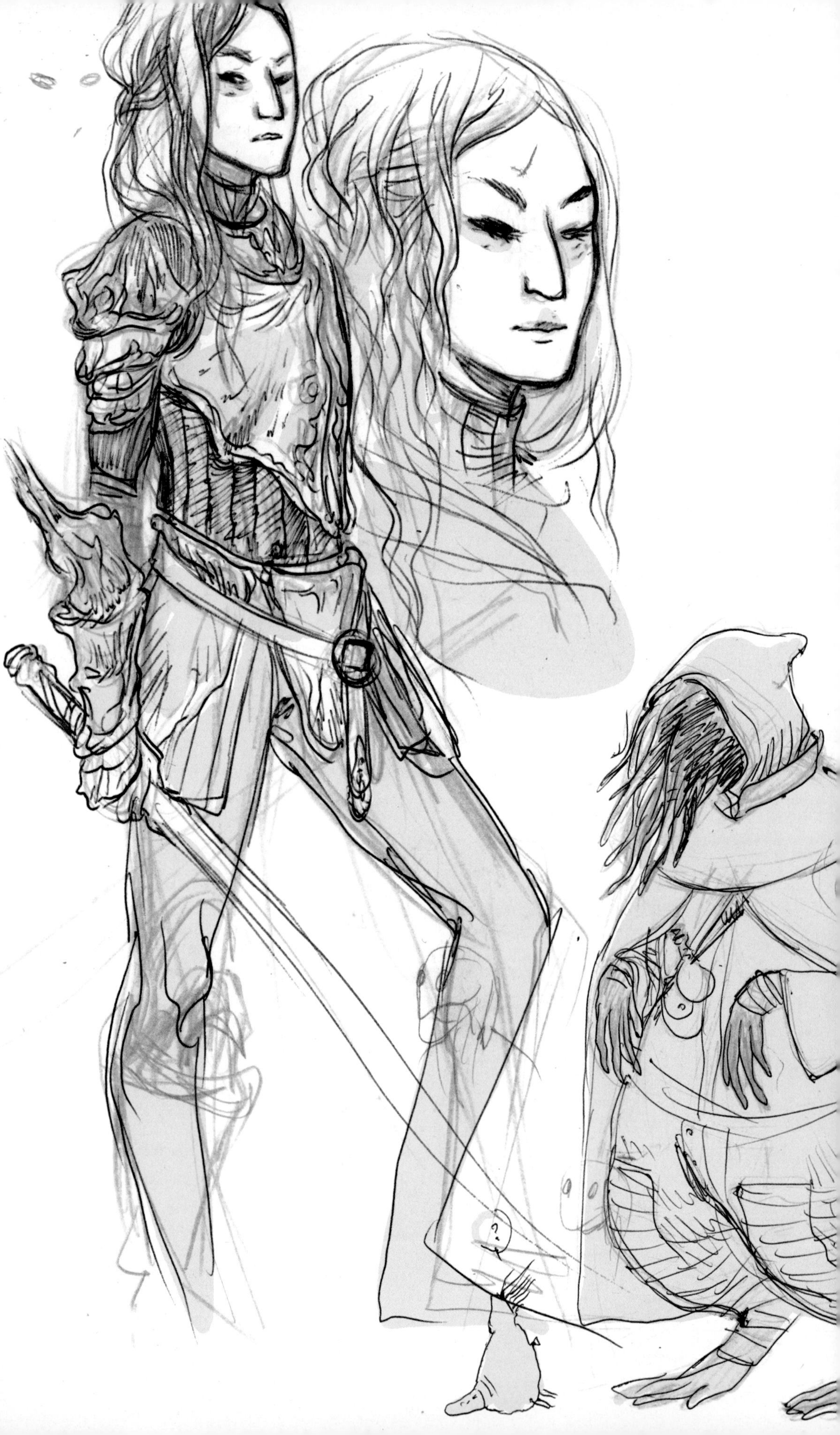

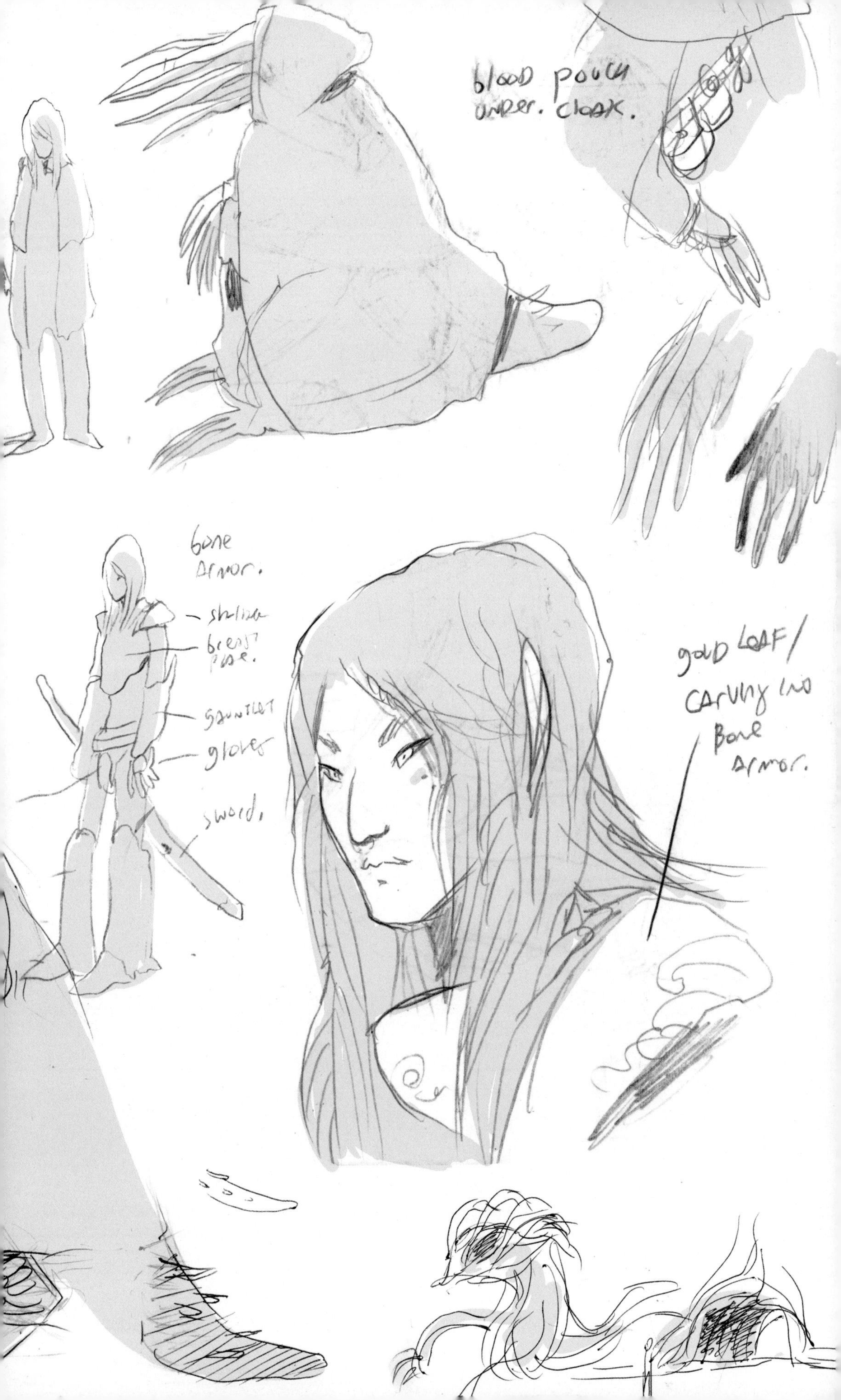
blood pouch
under. cloak.
bone
Armor.
breast
plate.
gauntlet
gloves
sword.
gold LEAF /
carving into
Bone
Armor.

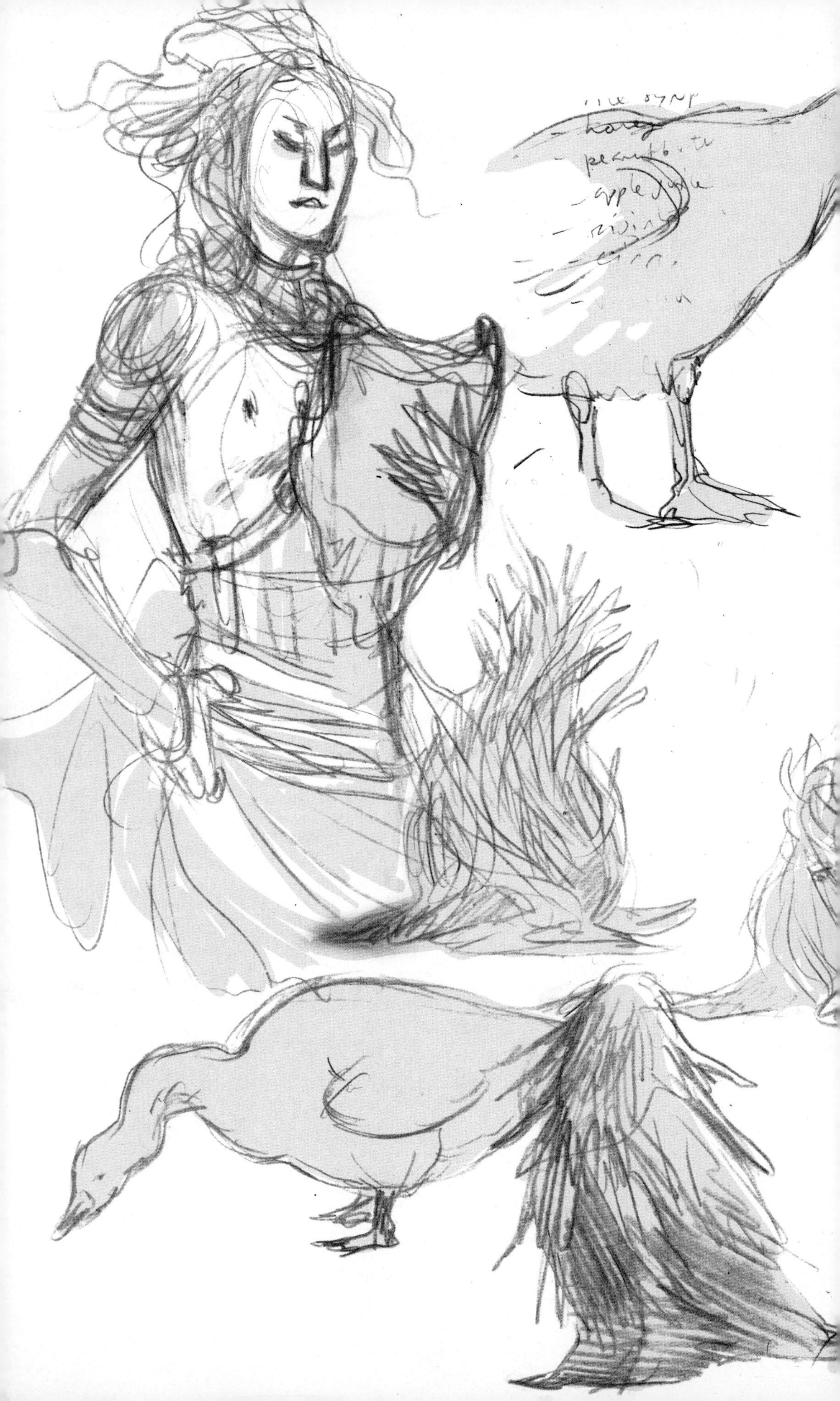

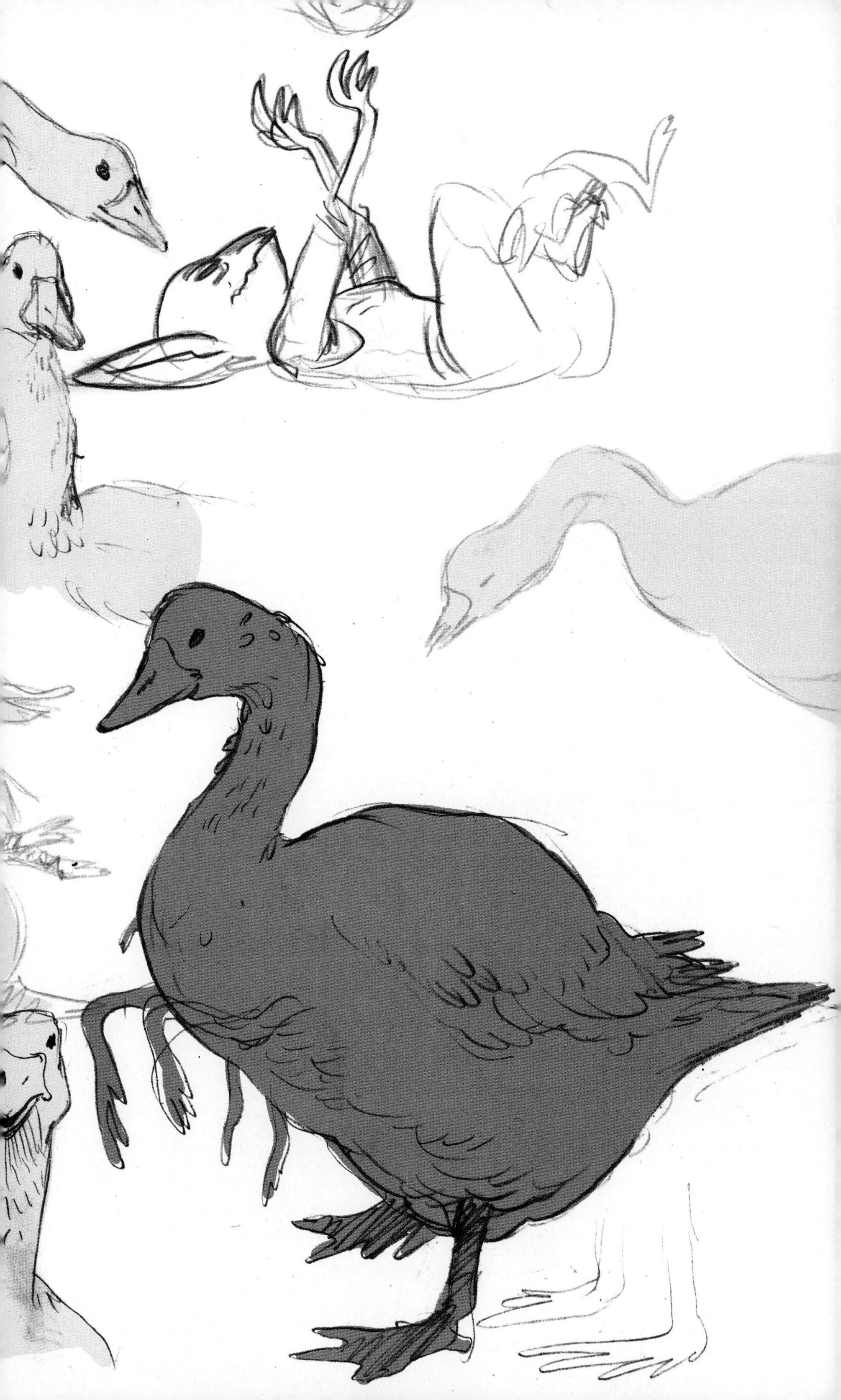

If you liked ARCLIGHT, try these...

PROPHET
1 REMISSION

PROPHET
2 BROTHERS

PROPHET
3 EMPIRE

PROPHET
4 JOINING

PROPHET
5 EARTH WAR

MULTIPLE WARHEADS

KING CITY

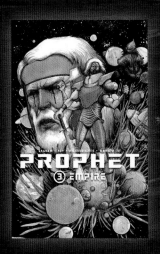

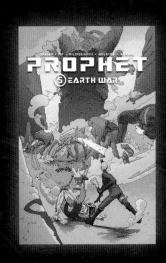

"[PROPHET is] *Conan* by way of Robert Heinlein and *Nausicaä of the Valley of the Wind.*"
—***Paste Magazine***

"His highly detailed, offbeat art ties everything together [in THE COMPLETE MULTIPLE WARHEADS]... Readers will want to savor the myriad details and silly puns."
—***Booklist***